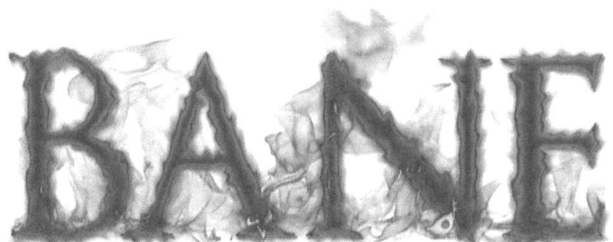

KRISTIN MAYER

Bane / Kristin Mayer – 1st ed.
Library of Congress Cataloging-in-Publication Data
ISBN-13: 978-1-942910-07-7

VISIT MY WEBSITE AT
http://www.authorkristinmayer.com

DEDICATION

For everyone who asked for
BANE's story from
THE TRUST SERIES . . . this is for you.

OTHER BOOKS BY KRISTIN MAYER

Available Now

The Trust Series
Trust Me
Love Me
Promise Me
Full-length novels in the TRUST series are also available in
audio from Tantor Media.

The Effect Series
Ripple Effect
Domino Effect

Stand Alone Novels
Dissipate

Joint Collaborations
Predestined Hearts

Coming Soon
Innocence

CHAPTER 1

BANE

Six Years Ago

I WAS DONE. Finished. Out.

For the past seven years, I belonged to a division of the government that wasn't on the books. I operated alone. There was a mission: I either failed or succeeded. If I failed, that meant I was dead.

After all the shit I'd seen, done, caused—I had survived. It was a fucking miracle.

I was the best at what I did, but there were times I saw my life flash before my eyes. But when you're the government's covert assassin, what else was there to expect. If I was captured, I didn't exist. If I died, I didn't exist. If I succeeded, I was assigned my next mission.

The plane wheels screeched as I touched down in Alaska.

Finally, I was where I wanted to be.

At times, I wasn't sure I knew who I was anymore. My identity was erased from the system long ago. For the last three months, I'd been working on getting released from the program. It was a slow process with how deep I was in with Black Division.

Those suits knew I wouldn't share anything I'd done. Hell, half the time I wanted to forget. After three months of debriefing, the government let me out. Of course, there was an underlying threat.

If we so much as suspect you've betrayed this country, consider yourself dead, Mr. Bradley.

Yeah, nothing else was new. I wasn't an idiot. I knew I'd be monitored for years to come, but they wouldn't find anything.

In all the dark bullshit that swirled around me, there was one person who kept me grounded over the last two years ... Jasmine. She saved my soul before it would have been lost completely to the animal beckoning to take over within me. Finally, I was going to spend the rest of my life with her.

The cabin of the plane dinged and the pilot came on to thank us for flying. Who the fuck cared? All the passengers wanted the same thing—to get off. The only thing I wanted was to see my girl.

Jasmine, the love of my life, waited for me at the front of the airport. I carried only a duffel bag. That was all I'd wanted from my previous life. Everything else I set fire to and tried to forget it. There was nothing good about my past besides her.

The last time I'd seen Jasmine had been a little over six months ago on my last furlough. I always flew her to different places to meet to maximize our time together, but the last time, I'd come here and fell in love with Alaska. Yeah, the winters were shitty, but it was isolated and away from the fuckedupness in the world. There was a true peace. Maybe I'd heal enough to be worthy of Jasmine.

Jasmine knew me as Bane Bradley. On the fly, I'd used it when we met at a local bar two years ago in New York. It stuck. And now, it would be my name for the rest of my life. I liked it.

The government hadn't even known about that name. All the names of my previous identities blended together, morphing into one. My mother called me *bastard* my entire childhood. That name was also fitting for the shit I'd done. Sometimes a person became a product of where they came from.

The cold air hit my face, and I debarked from the plane at the small airport. It was almost time to see my girl—Jasmine.

I was here. I was home. *Home.* The word lightened the load as I practically sprinted to the front of the airport. Over the phone yesterday, Jasmine said she had some news for me. Her voice shook minutely, which meant she was nervous. When I'd asked, *do you still want me to come?* The resounding *yes* was all I needed. We'd make it through anything else.

Until yesterday, when I'd been released, we hadn't talked since I'd last visited. But the moment I heard her sweet voice on the end of the line, I knew she still loved me. Jasmine knew I worked for a secret agency, although she thought about it more along the lines of James Bond type shit.

Nothing was further from the truth.

But, it kept her from asking questions and that was all that mattered, which, in turn kept Jasmine safe. As of that moment, all the other shit was in the past and didn't matter.

A secret smile formed as I thought what I had planned for us. Getting somewhere private was priority—another reason I insisted on Jasmine picking me up at the front versus coming in.

Outside the airport sat the love of my life in her old, tan four-wheel-drive SUV. Another bitter gust of wind hit me, but I made it to the vehicle in record time. As soon as I got in, her subtle vanilla scent greeted me. Oh how I missed that smell.

Jasmine leaned over. Our lips touched as she whispered against mine. "Hey, baby."

All the countless lie detector tests, questioning, and de-briefing were worth it in that moment. First, I had to taste her. As I cupped her face, her soft skin was a soothing balm against my callous palms.

Her lips formed to mine. My tongue sought entry in her mouth, and she opened to me, intensifying the kiss. That sweet little moan had my cock as hard as a rock. We needed to get out of here before I took her in the parking lot. As soon as we got somewhere, I was sinking deep within her—for hours on end.

A car honked behind us. Jasmine giggled and whispered against my lips, "Are you ready to go home?"

"Yeah, baby. Take me home."

Home. There was that word again.

I'd never had a home. Ever. There was no way the shithole I'd grown up in could be considered a home. As soon as I turned eighteen, I enlisted in the marines. Within two years, I was recruited to the Black Division. Life expectancy in the program was three years. I'd lasted seven fucking long years.

As Jasmine drove, I couldn't take my eyes off her honey-blonde hair and dark-chestnut eyes. She had a body made for worshiping that was hidden underneath her oversized thick coat. I was never going to have to let her go.

Glancing my way, she asked with a knowing smile,

"What are you looking at?"

"You. It's always you. I'm sorry it took me so fucking long to get home to you."

Her hand came out and held mine. "You made it. That's all that matters. And, you're here for good?"

"I am." A tinge of guilt raced through me. There had been several times through the last two years where I'd stood her up because I was on a mission in some hellhole. It was a miracle she'd stayed with me through it all.

While we were apart, I called as often as I could, but sometimes it was weeks before she heard from me. I craved to hear her voice like an addiction. Honestly, it was a miracle I got to date her. When you signed up to be an operative, there were no ties to the world. However, I'd disclosed our relationship as soon as it became one. After intensive monitoring and background checks, Black Division was satisfied and gave me the all clear to continue the relationship.

Driving to the small apartment complex in town, Jasmine parked. I'd only been here once, but with my photographic memory, I knew where we were. Jogging to Jasmine's side of the truck, I grabbed the keys out of the ignition and cradled her in my arms. The squeal of delight rang through me. I spun us around, earning peals of laughter. I had my girl in my arms, and I was going to spend the rest of my life cherishing her.

As we walked to the door, I kissed her slow. With my right hand, I managed to unlock the door while never taking my mouth from hers. I needed to know this was real and not a dream. Over the last year, I'd dreamed of being with Jasmine and having a child. Time would give me both.

I wanted it all—the white fence, the wife, the kids … everything. And for the first time in my life, I believed I deserved it.

The door closed with a loud thud as I kicked it. The atmosphere intensified as I plunged deeper into her mouth. A small moan of acceptance came from Jasmine as she held me firmly to her.

The next stop was the bedroom.

"Bane—"

Cutting her off, I murmured, "Later."

If she pushed me away, I'd stop. But right now, I needed her to know this wasn't a dream. Jasmine was here and pliant in my arms. It was tempting to fuck her hard in the living room, but the first time home, I was going to make love to her. Savor her. Adore her.

Sitting her down, I pushed the coat off her shoulders. Jasmine grabbed the hem of my shirt and together we took it off. A finger trailed down my abdomen eliciting a shiver.

"I missed this. I missed you." Jasmine's words fueled me as I reclaimed her mouth.

My cock ached to sink into that perfect pussy of hers. Going to her stomach to take off her shirt, I touched the soft skin. Jasmine's abdomen wasn't flat but had a bump to it. I took a step back. My eyes shot to hers.

Was she?

Both of her hands came up and caressed her stomach. "I wanted to talk to you first before we had sex. But then, we got in the moment." A beautiful flush crept on her cheeks. "Bane, I'm pregnant."

I nearly staggered back. Jasmine was pregnant. My girl was pregnant. With a baby. We hadn't been together for almost six months. Fuck, I wasn't sure how this worked. The baby had to be mine. Our baby.

She took a step closer. "Bane, it's yours. We're having a baby. I'm six months along. There was no way to contact you.

I wanted to tell you in person."

My hand shook as I touched her stomach. "We're having a baby."

The dream was becoming reality. A child. Jasmine as my wife. It was all real.

An unknowing feeling of love toward someone I'd never met flowed through me. I was connected to this little person already, and I'd known about her for less than a minute. It was a girl. I knew it.

Sinking to my knees, I kissed her stomach where *our* child grew. Instead of causing death, I'd helped create a life. If my soul was too damaged, I knew I'd never be given the responsibility to be a father. Maybe this was the world telling me I deserved to be happy.

Jasmine's hands came out and touched my shaved head. "Yes, the last time we saw each other. I found out about two and half months ago. It's a girl."

"We're having a baby girl." I swallowed hard as I remembered the little girl in pigtails on the swing from my dream. I couldn't stop giving little kisses to her stomach. My rough palms caressed as I whispered to our daughter, "I love you, little girl, with my whole heart. I will love you and protect you, little one. Always."

Glancing up to Jasmine, a tear came down her face.

What if she isn't ready to have a baby? What if she isn't happy about this?

Standing, I cupped her face. "Are you okay with this?"

She sniffled. "I love the thought of having your child. I was worried you would think I cheated on you. I've been so nervous."

"Never, baby. This is a miracle. Our miracle."

Bringing Jasmine to me, I felt her soft body meld to mine.

I smiled against her lips as the baby bump touched my stomach.

I was going to be a dad.

"I'm going to take you to bed and make love to the mother of my child."

"I want you, Bane." As she spoke her breathy reply, I walked her back to the mattress.

From this moment on, I'd never be the same.

CHAPTER

2

BANE

ON THE BED, I watched Jasmine sleep with her hair fanned out around her face. Peace. That was an odd feeling for me, but I had it. Finally. Through all the mayhem and destruction I caused in nearly every country of the world, I'd found a form of forgiveness through the child growing in Jasmine's stomach. I couldn't stop touching her.

Almost everyone I'd killed was a motherfucker. Knowing that was the only thing that kept me from completely losing myself to the darkness that tried to drown me.

In all the years I'd been part of the Black Division, I ended the life of five innocent people on accident. They were called casualties of war. I called it murder. That burden would be on me forever. The faces of the innocent haunted me when I closed my eyes. The motto of the agency—their deaths had

9

been a sacrifice to the greater good. Bullshit. Everyone deserved a chance at life.

Those innocents had been someone's child and the regret of what I'd done hit me harder than before.

I am so sorry. So very sorry for the sins of my past. I will spend every day for the rest of my life trying to make up for it.

Whoever I mentally spoke to, I hoped they heard my promise.

Thinking back to the night I'd met Jasmine, I'd been at a bar drowning my sins away with alcohol. I'd killed my fifth innocent person and was on leave. Who would have thought that night would change my life forever?

For the next three weeks, I was off until my next assignment for who-the-hell-knows how long to some forsaken shithole. All I planned to do was drink, fuck, and sleep. Simple.

The bartender approached and I slid my glass to him. "Another one."

Bourbon, of any kind, was my drink of choice. As long as it was amber and got me fucked up—I didn't care. Numb was numb and that's all that mattered.

New York was a good place to take a three-week hiatus. The city never slept and there was pussy galore. The stool next to me moved and I glanced that way. I always wanted to know everything that was going on around me. It was part of who I was now. Outside of the Black Division, I was a ghost.

A beautiful blonde that I could fuck into next week, if given the chance, sat alternating glances between her watch and the door to the bar.

She looked my way. "Excuse me. Is this the original Finnegan's everyone talks about? I'm meeting my girlfriend here and she's late."

For all that was holy, she had the voice of a goddess that would sound amazing screaming my name while I fucked her into oblivion.

The bartender sat my glass down and took an order from the girl. She liked girlie cocktails as she ordered a Cosmo. I brought my glass up in salute to the girl with the mile-long legs beside me. "The one and only original Finnegan's."

Fuck, I had no clue, but it sounded good if that meant she would stay.

"Oh, good." The gorgeous girl let her shoulders relax. "I'm from Alaska, so this big city is a bit intimating."

I took a small sip of the liquid heaven. "What brought you to New York?"

"I've always wanted to see the world. I've been saving up to come here for years. My friend from New Jersey is meeting me here to catch up while I'm in town."

Here was to hoping little Miss Alaska was at the wrong bar.

That first night we'd met there was no sex. Instead, I'd gotten her number and taken her on a proper date the following night. Shocked the hell out of me. I had to work five long days to get between her legs. The wait was worth it. The moment I sunk inside her for the first time, I was gone. Changed forever.

My life was perfect.

Sitting at the kitchen table, I sipped on my coffee while Jasmine finished eating the breakfast I'd cooked for her. I didn't care for breakfast. Maybe it was from all those years of waking up starving with my mom, only to be denied. I took another sip, letting the warmth of the liquid keep me from going to that dark, cold place called my childhood.

I loved seeing Jasmine's healthy appetite as she nourished our unborn child. Testing the waters, I threw a thought out there. "I thought we could look for a house today."

Watching her closely, she paused mid bite. "You want to buy a house together?"

It wasn't a no, and sounded hopeful. This was good. This was very good.

Not wanting to give her surprise away, I shrugged. "Yes. I figured it would be nice to have a place of our own, maybe get a dog."

Yeah, I was going for the whole fucking caboodle in this new life. I'd always wanted a dog. Jasmine's apartment was nice and felt homey, but I wanted us to have a home that stood by itself in its own yard. All my life I'd lived in apartments, hotels, or in some desolate place.

Thoughtfully, Jasmine rubbed her stomach. "You're not doing this because of the baby, are you?"

Scooting her chair out, I placed my hand on top of hers, touching her stomach while kneeling. She needed to hear and see my earnestness. "I promise. Baby or no baby, I wanted to get a house together. You'll see."

Quirking an eyebrow, I knew I slipped. Jasmine knew something was up, but I stood and gave her a quick kiss before taking my seat. To hide the slight curvature of my lips, I took another sip of coffee.

Biting her lower lip, she said, "I love the idea. It'll be nice to have a real home and family again."

Having Jasmine happy was all that matter. She'd lost her parents a few years back in a dog sledding accident. The dogs broke free when a bear came out of nowhere. The sled tumbled down the mountain with her parents still on it. They were found dead two days later. Up here in Alaska, it's beautiful but brutal. I knew how lonely she was, and it nearly killed her having to sell her parents' house. What was harder for Jasmine was seeing the new owners tear down the only place she thought of as home. Otherwise, I would have bought her parents' home for our place.

Taking her plate to the sink, Jasmine rinsed it and put it in the dishwasher. I couldn't take my eyes off her perfect body. I wanted her again and it hadn't been an hour. Fingers trailed along my shoulder. Jasmine leaned in and whispered, "I'm going to take a shower. I think there's room for two."

Seeing that ass sashay out of the room, I bounded out of my seat. Silently, I followed. My girl was as insatiable as I was. The shower curtain sounded as she got in. Quickly, I shucked my clothes and walked into the room as it steamed.

Pushing the shower curtain aside, Jasmine reached for the shampoo and glanced at me from over her shoulder, clearly pleased I'd followed her. "I thought you were going to stand me up."

I engulfed her in my arms. "I'll always be there for you."

After getting ready, we were in the car. Jasmine sat in the passenger seat, rubbing her stomach with her right hand while her left one settled on my leg. The early-afternoon sun was in the sky beginning its descent. Nights were long in Alaska during the winter months. The sign for *Fish Hook Road* was up ahead. I turned left and saw Jasmine look at me confused from the side. The driveway at the end of the street was where Jasmine's surprise awaited her.

"What are we doing here?" I didn't say a word as I parked in the driveway. Jasmine continued to talk. "Oh, Bane, I love this house. It's not for sale, though." There was longing in her voice as she looked at the two-story home. When I'd been here before I left Black Division, she showed me around town; Jasmine pointed out this house as one she'd always loved. There was no denying the dreamlike tone she'd spoken with.

Trying to stay nonchalant, I said, "I know, but thought we might look around to get some ideas."

"That's a good idea."

The snow crunched beneath our boots as we made our way up to the pale-yellow house. The smell of smoke filled the air from nearby fireplaces. Our breaths came out in little puffs. Jasmine danced about in front of me as she made her way to the front porch. I wanted to stop her, but figured being a crazed, overprotective guy this early was not smart. Jasmine had been fine for nearly six months. *Six months.* I'd missed over half of the pregnancy. When we had another kid, I vowed to be part of everything.

Touching one of the front poles, Jasmine said, "I saw them painting this a couple of months ago. I think it's my favorite shade of yellow."

I touched the door handle and turned the knob. "Bane, we can't trespass."

Opening the door anyway, I shrugged. "We're not going to harm anything. Let's take a look around."

Jasmine still protested, but I walked in. The living room was as I'd imagined it. Glancing back at the door, my girl stood at the threshold.

"Bane, it's wrong."

With a devilish grin on my face, I prowled toward her.

"Bane, no—" I ignored her and picked her up as she chortled. "You always get want you want, don't you?"

"Yes, because I got you." Jasmine gave me that soft look, filled with love, as her hand touched my cheek.

The builders followed the specs I provided perfectly. The

floor plan had been opened up. Bright colors were on the walls.

In my arms, Jasmine gasped when she looked from me to the sign on the wall.

WELCOME TO YOUR NEW HOME, JASMINE!

"Bane, this is ours?" Her voice was unbelieving. "You bought us my favorite house and had it redone?"

I could tell she was beginning to get excited as the reality sunk in.

"I did. For you, me, and now our little girl. Do you like it?"

Glossy eyes looked at me, on the verge of tears. "It's incredible." She kissed me. "I love you. I love you so much. We're going to be so happy together."

This was all I needed. Ever. "Let me show you what they did in the bedroom."

CHAPTER
3

BANE

LAST NIGHT, WE'D spent our first night in the new house since it was fully furnished. I had movers scheduled to meet us at her place in two days to pack whatever Jasmine wanted to bring. I think she felt the same as me—new life, new beginnings, new everything.

It was early in the morning. Sunrise was about forty minutes away. The timing had to be perfect for what I planned. For the hundredth time I mentally went over what I was going to say.

"So, where are you taking me?" Blindfolded, Jasmine curiously asked from the passenger seat.

I chuckled to myself. "It's a surprise. Be patient." My girl loved and hated surprises all at the same time.

Yesterday, we got a home together. Tomorrow, we would

go to the doctor where I'd be able to see the baby on the ultra sound. Today, well today, had its own surprise that would be memorable us.

While driving, I heard a sweet sigh. "I love the house, Bane. I've never been happier. I wish Mom and Dad were here to see it all."

That was the one thing I couldn't give her. Her parents. I knew how much she missed them. I'd do everything I could to be what she needed. "I know, baby."

"I believe they're with me still. I think loved ones always help guide those they've left behind to their right path. I almost didn't go to New York two years ago until I had a dream with my parents encouraging me to go."

I squeezed her hand that rested on my knee. Honestly, I wasn't sure what I believed when it came to life and death. "You coming to New York was the best decision. It changed my life."

"Our life, Bane."

How right she was. That night at the bar changed me … forever. I wasn't sure why I'd been chosen to cross paths with Jasmine. Jasmine brought me out of my thoughts. "Hey, were you serious last night when you mentioned me staying home to raise the baby?"

All the bullshit of the Black Division was worth being able to provide for her now. "Baby, I'd love nothing more. Jasmine, whatever you want … it's yours. We have more than enough to get by. It makes all the work I've done worth it, knowing that I can provide us a life."

Jasmine was an elementary school teacher. The children loved her and I knew she'd be a wonderful mother.

From the lights on the dashboard, I could see the delicate smile that graced her lips. "I want to try staying home for the first year. Take a leave of absence from the school."

I interlaced our fingers. "I want you home with us."

"That's what I want too, Bane. It's all I want." Jasmine fidgeted before speaking. "What do you think about the name, Faith?"

"Faith?"

"Yes, for the baby. It's through my faith that one day I'd find my happily ever after that I was able to open myself up to you for love."

A lump formed in my throat. I let go of her hand and caressed my child. I was rewarded with a small kick. My little girl was active when I spoke. Even after all the time I'd missed with the pregnancy, we were connected.

The more I thought about it, the more the name for our daughter fit. I cleared my throat. "Faith is perfect."

Jasmine placed her hand on her stomach. "Did you hear that, Faith? You have a name, my precious baby girl."

More little kicks pressed against my palm. "I think she likes it."

"I think she does." Life was abso-fucking-lutely fantastic. Over the last two days, the demons were lessoning their grip on my soul. It was Jasmine's presence—my light, my salvation, my everything. They say good things come to those who wait; well, it took twenty-eight years. *Better than twenty-nine, if I am going to start taking this positive approach shit.*

She snorted. "You know, I'm going to get all fat."

I couldn't wait for her stomach to get bigger. Could. Not. Wait. "You're going to be beautiful, not fat."

"And this is why I love you." Her thumb rubbed up and down mine. "Are we there yet? You woke me up at the crack of dawn."

I chuckled. It was true; I woke her up early to sink inside

her before we started on our way to this special place for us. Being inside her kept me from thinking all of this was a dream. "About ten more minutes. I promise it'll be worth it."

She gave a playful huff, but then resumed resting her hands on her stomach. Gasping, Jasmine said, "I love feeling her move."

I reached across and rested my hand on her stomach. There wasn't any movement. Faith was probably still sleeping. Then, a little kick happened, letting me know she was there.

"She loves your touch." Her hand came to rest on mine. We were a family. "I think we need a house full of little girls to give their daddy a run for his money."

The life she mentioned flashed before my eyes as I thought about chasing off every dick that came our daughter's way. No fucking way was she dating. No fucking way. She was never dating. Period.

A sweet laughter that always chipped away at my blackened soul filtered through the cab. "Bane, stop your thoughts right there. Our daughter will date."

"How'd you know what I was thinking?"

"Because I know you."

This would be a discussion for later since we arrived at our special spot. We still had five minutes before we needed to get out of the car. It was frigid outside at this time of day.

"We're here."

Jasmine perked up. "Can I take the blindfold off?"

I leaned across the seat and let my stubble scrape against her jawline. "Be patient."

Turning her head, she nipped my lip. "You're going to owe me some extra good orgasms when we get back to the house."

"I think I can handle that task, baby." We only had two

minutes until sunrise. "It's time. I'm going to come get you and carry you to the spot. I don't want you slipping."

Jasmine loved being taken care of, and I loved doing it. Stepping outside, I hoped to hell this turned out the way I wanted.

The light was barely peeking over the horizon. The ice on the lake sparkled in the early morning light. Opening the door, I grabbed the love of my life under her legs and securely held her against my chest. Even pregnant, she was still light. I was going to take her for a big hearty breakfast later ... giving us fuel for orgasms.

Cradled against my neck, Jasmine spoke. "You make my life complete."

I didn't say a word as I sat her down and the sun peeked over the horizon. Hell, I was nervous. Getting down on one knee, I said, "Take off the blind fold, baby."

She did as I asked and looked at me, a hand going to her mouth.

"Jasmine, until you, I was lost. You saved me in ways you'll never know. I love you with my whole heart. I thought I was lost forever until you found me. I brought you tour place the place where we first said *I love you* to each other when I was here the last time. It was through that last visit we conceived Faith. This is the same place where I want you to become part of my forever. Will you do me the honor of not only being the mother of our child, but my wife?"

This spot was special to us. On our last visit, she'd brought me here after we'd stayed up all night. It was the place she came to reflect on her life. No one knew about it.

Tears came down her cheek. "Yes! Yes! Yes!"

I stood and opened the ring box. She wouldn't be able to put it on with her gloves, but I wanted her to see it. "I bought this about nine months back, but wanted to wait until I was free."

Inside the black velvet box, a large diamond stood on a silver band. The jewelry guy called it a princess something or other. I knew from the price tag it had to be good, so I bought it.

Jumping into my arms, Jasmine kissed me hard. I'd never tire of her taste. It was like strawberries. She sniffled. "You had this planned before I became pregnant."

In between kisses, I tried to explain. "I planned on proposing all along. Being pregnant was an added bonus. Let's get home and consummate this engagement."

"I want nothing more. Bane, I never knew I could be this happy."

"Me either, baby."

I sat Jasmine down, looking at her face. Her glistening eyes could see into my soul. Because of her I was a better man. Even being able to see the bad and ugly, she still loved me. The darkness didn't matter. Jasmine was my light.

THUD.

On instinct, I ducked at the sickening sound and brought Jasmine with me. It had to be a hunter, but my gut told me something was up. I always trusted my gut. If it wasn't a hunter, a sniper was in the area. Were they looking for me? If so, what the fuck did they want with me? The first thing I needed to do was get us out of there.

If it was a sniper, I would hunt down the motherfucker and eliminate him. By the sound ricocheting through the area, he was a mile out, probably perched in a tree somewhere.

"Baby, I need to get us out of here."

I never dreamed this could happen. I'd taken every precaution I could think of. Up here, we were supposed to be safe from any danger.

I pulled Jasmine, but nothing happened. Dead weight. Turning back, I had a sickening feeling I wasn't willing to admit. Before my eyes, Jasmine slumped over as a red pool of blood spread from her head into the white snow.

Grabbing her shoulders, I brought her to me. "No! No! No! Baby, wake up!"

Jasmine laid before me. Lifeless. Dead.

Sobs erupted from me. "NOOOO!"

Everything worth living for was fading in that moment. I had to be there for my little girl as her movements faded. "Faith, I'm here! I'm here, Faith! Daddy is here!"

There was nothing I could do. Helpless. I prayed for a miracle as I begged, "Baby, don't leave me! Please don't leave me!"

In that moment, I lost all that I had. All that I was. Everything.

Visions of what could have been flashed before my eyes—putting a swing together, seeing Jasmine teach our daughter to read, eating as a family.

Cradling the love of my life's body, I rocked her. Rocked my baby with my hand on her stomach. My baby. My daughter. My Faith.

"I'm so sorry. I'm so sorry."

Life without Jasmine was no life at all. I screamed and my voice echoed through the open area. "KILL ME, MOTHERFUCKER! KILL ME! KILL ME NOW!"

Nothing happened.

Gone.

It was all gone.

The blackness took hold of my soul.

I let it.

Fire burned within my veins.
I welcomed it.
They should have killed me.
Now, I would hunt them down.
Every. Last. One. Of. Them.

CHAPTER 4

BANE

Present Day

I SAT UP, gasping for air, drenched in sweat. Different night. Same fucking dream—Jasmine's eyes looking at me right before she and our baby were murdered. The dream always left me hollow. It was the worst day of my existence that I lived over and over again—never able to escape. I deserved to be haunted for what happened in Alaska. If only the killer shot me instead, life would be better. The love of my life and child would be alive.

The clock read four in the morning. Two hours of sleep. I'd take it. Throwing on some jogging shorts, I hit the treadmill in my spare room. The speed of the belt propelled me forward while I pushed myself to the limit, which never seemed enough to do me in.

After the nightmare, most times, I ran while trying to burn away the rage that still loomed beneath the surface. I gritted my teeth as I thought about all I'd lost. My hands were balled into fists while I remembered.

I pushed myself hard, wanting to be numb.

I'd never be rid of it—that was for certain. All I could do was stifle the inner turmoil. There was nowhere left for it to go. I'd killed every motherfucker that had a part in Jasmine's death.

Every. Last. One. Of. Them.

To get my revenge, I'd enlisted with the Black Division under the condition I got to hunt down and kill those responsible. They welcomed me back with open arms, but with their own condition … that I took on six missions of their choice.

Yeah, I took the deal.

No matter the price, revenge was the only thing that mattered. I thought back to my last day when I left Black Division for good, after I'd killed the two people responsible for my loved ones' deaths … Enrique Consuelo and Eric Thornhill.

Sarge, my superior, walked up to me. The large scar on his face was from a knife fight in Afghanistan. "Are you sure we can't talk you in to staying?"

My six kills were completed, which was my deal in order to find the men responsible for Jasmine's death. The sorry son-of-a-bitch, Enrique, suffered. The memory of his screams were the only thing that brought me satisfaction. In hindsight, I would have made the pain last longer.

"I appreciate the offer, but it's time."

Sarge knowingly nodded. He'd been there through all of this. "I'll never forget all the help you and Hampton gave me in finding Enrique Consuelo."

I clenched my fists. Jasmine's death had been about re-

venge ... *for things I'd done. Eye for an eye. Except they took my entire reason for living, not my fucking eye. Enrique Consuelo was a Columbian drug lord. I'd killed his father, Rodrigo Consuelo—kill number sixty-two for me. Rodrigo liked to capture American girls and sell them on the black market for large amounts. The kill only made the world a better place.*

Sarge slapped my back. "Anytime. I'm sorry for what you had to go through. I wish I'd known about Eric. Sorry son of a bitch. You're welcome back anytime."

Eric fucking Thornhill, an operative within Black Division, was the insider help to Enrique Consuelo in exchange for a hefty sum. The trail of deceit ended with Eric—I was sure of it. I'd tortured Enrique for days and he stayed consistent that Eric was the only one involved. After how I nearly brought Enrique to the brink of death time and time again ... anyone would have broken if there had been more information.

I took a deep breath to calm myself and cracked my neck to the side. After going through all of Enrique's files while he was unconscious from all the pain, I'd found out Enrique had been keeping tabs on me through my last year of service at the Black Division. Pictures of Jasmine and me. The information regarding the house I'd bought. Miscellaneous identities I'd had. A picture of us declaring our love in our special spot. All of Jasmine's information. The intel he had astonished me. Enrique even had a copy of Jasmine's doctor reports. Fucking bastard knew she was pregnant.

"That motherfucker deserved what he got. I need to catch my plane to Atlanta. Thanks, Sarge."

Truth was I needed to escape before I lost it and fell to the craving to wreak more destruction on something ... anything.

"We're here anytime you need us."

"Thanks, man."

I grabbed my bag and headed to my car, knowing I'd never forgive myself for what I'd done—leading him straight to Jasmine and Faith without knowing he was even looking for me. Straight to my family. I deserved to have this nonexistent life after causing their deaths. Still, looking back, I knew I'd been careful. But I'd missed something somewhere. I'd re-traced my steps and memories numerous times and there was nothing out of place.

What had I missed?

The guilt would never leave me. Never. I had been wrong about deserving any happiness. The sins of my past were too great. As my mother mentioned time and time again, *I am a bastard that didn't deserve anything.* For two days I'd been completely happy and that was more than I deserved.

I pumped my legs harder as I increased the speed on the belt and I pushed myself to the limits in a punishing manner.

After Enrique and Eric were disposed of, I eliminated everyone related to the crime—no stone was left unturned, including the man who sold the sniper the gun.

True to my word, I left as soon as the six missions were done, which was almost a year exactly after Jasmine died. Oh, the Black Division tried to keep me—unsuccessfully. They threw all sorts of money my way, but I wanted nothing more to do with them. Death's door sometimes seemed like the better option. But I couldn't bring myself to end my life, and some-how I managed to always pull through. Not killing myself was the only piece of humanity I had left inside.

Sweat poured down my face as I worked on trying to calm myself from the dream.

The treadmill beeped as I upped the speed even more.

I'd kept my name, Bane Bradley. If there were any other motherfuckers left that wanted a fight, I wanted them to be able to find me. There was nothing left to lose in this world. The itch to let the animal inside me out was strong. I welcomed any bastard who wanted to rumble.

I hit the off button, jolting the belt to a stop.

"Fuck." My body was exhausted.

Making my way to the kitchen, I grabbed a bottle of water and chugged it. I lived in a scarcely decorated apartment in an upscale building for privacy reasons. Went in line with my motto—have nothing you couldn't walk away from in your life at any time.

Only a few people, all within Black Division, knew what happened to me in regards to Jasmine. I didn't want the pity stares from anyone else. Life dealt me a shitty hand … that was a fucking fact. As far as everyone was concerned, except my superiors, I'd missed the life when I came back to join.

My phone rang. It was Hampton. "Bane."

After the Black Division, I did odd intel jobs for him. He now owned Security Branch, but had been part of the covert operation.

"Hey, man. I figured you'd be up." The gruff voice from my old mentor brought back memories. He was the only one from the Black Division I'd stayed in touch with who knew about Jasmine. The only other two who knew were Sarge and Alex, Sarge's superior.

It was five in the morning now after my hour run. "Yeah, I'm up. Why are you up so early?"

"Client shit. Came into the office early. I wanted to talk to you about a case. You free today?"

I dragged a hand down my face. "Yeah, I'm free."

"How about the office? Does ten work?"

"I'll be there."

"Thanks, man."

I ended the phone call and finished chugging my water. Hampton hooked me up with one of my longest jobs with sports team owner billionaire, Damien Wales. The love of his life, Allison, was being threatened at the time I came on. Yeah, there was no way I would turn down helping a guy keep the woman he loved. He was a good man. I enjoyed working for him. The problem was I got too attached. Started caring. So, I quit a couple of years ago.

While I'd worked for the Wales, they'd welcomed me into their family. When they had their second child, a boy, I knew it was time to part ways when Allison let me hold him in the hospital. The last thing they deserved was to be hurt because of me. Everyone I cared about died. I would never bring my curse to someone else. Therefore, I refused to care about … anything.

If Damien ever needed something, I would be there. From time to time I'd see them, but nothing that would draw attention that they meant anything to me.

After I showered, I'd read today's current events before meeting Hampton in his downtown Atlanta office.

Parking the black Land Cruiser, I checked my surroundings. Nothing seemed out of place, but nothing did anymore. Why would it? Anyone who'd known my identity outside of the Black Division had been killed. I walked into the building. Hampton, like me, was one of the few who beat the survival odds at Black Division. Maybe that was a reason we kept in touch. Almost all the men I'd fought beside at one time or another were dead.

After Hampton left the Black Division, he'd become a private investigator and opened Security Branch. Since then, Security Branch expanded to include everything from security to protecting to investigating.

The pristine front office had a reception desk. Karen, an older lady who kept Hampton in line, greeted me. "Morning, Bane. It's been awhile. I would have made cookies if Hampton told me yesterday."

Karen was a sweet woman.

Tipping my head to her, I stopped for a second. "Hampton called early this morning. I may have to drop by this Thursday, say around nine, to get some double chocolate chip ones though."

I gave her a wink and she returned the gesture. Lowly, she whispered, "You got it. Don't tell Hampton. His wife has him on a strict diet."

The deep rumbles of my laugh echoed through the room. When I got the cookies, I was going to march in there and eat them in front of him on Thursday without saying anything. Teach that bastard a lesson for trying to set me up with someone a few months ago on a blind date. Just because I neared my mid-thirties did not mean I wanted anything to do with a family. That ship sailed six years ago.

"I won't say a word." Karen didn't need to know my alternate plan.

Hampton appeared in the hallway. Walking up to me, he patted me on my back. "Thanks for coming."

Running my hand on my smooth scalp, I responded, "Anytime. Where you want to do this?"

"Back in my office."

I followed Hampton who was athletic in build. Sitting behind the large, dark wood desk, the chair creaked as Hampton got comfortable. Following suit, I took a seat on a black leather chair. I studied Hampton as I brought my ankle up to my knee. He looked tired with his unruly white hair. From the way his desk looked, he'd been up for a while with the fifteen coffee cups sitting on his desk.

Something was off with Hampton, but I remained outwardly unaffected and relaxed. The dark circles under Hampton's eyes were more pronounced. I had a feeling this wasn't simply a business call. There was a brochure on the edge of the desk that was black with provocative red lettering that piqued my interest, but I didn't grab it. The way it laid, almost showcased, was obvious.

Hampton took a drink of coffee. "Listen, I need to ask a favor from you."

"Okay."

We were cutting right to the chase, which was the way I liked it. Until I knew the whole story, I never agreed to anything. It didn't matter who the person was.

Scrubbing a hand down his face, Hampton was weary and nervous. Strange combination. "Felicia is sick. I need to take her to the doctor. It's not looking good."

Felicia was Hampton's wife. She was a good woman— understanding, kind, and compassionate. I knew what it was like to have a woman like that. No one deserved to lose their soul mate. No one. "Fuck, man. I'm sorry. What do you need?"

Fidgeting, Hampton looked somberly down. At least that explained why he was out of sorts. "A potential account stopped by yesterday. The business is Discrete Encounters. It's a dating service. They're needing to make sure that they have the proper security in place."

Internally, I groaned. Baby-fucking-sitting jobs were the

worst.

Hampton watched me for a reaction, but I kept a neutral face. "I know you hate this kind of job, Bane. They could be a huge client. If this works out, they're going to hire me for the rest of their nationwide chains. It could be big for Security Branch."

Waiting to see if there was more, I rubbed the back of my neck. He had a team of his own employed … a damn good one. Why did he need me?

"I need to know the best is on it. My other guys are handling everything else. I don't want to worry about bringing on a new client. With you, I'll be able to focus completely on Felicia."

That was all I needed, which I knew made me a shitty friend for not blindly agreeing to it. "I'll do it."

Relief and gratitude flashed through his eyes. "Thanks, Bane. I owe you." Hampton stood and slid the black brochure with the red lettering toward me that had been on the corner of the desk. There was a manila folder underneath it. "Here's all the info. I'll be heading out of town tomorrow, but I'll keep my cell phone on if you need anything."

I took the folder and thumbed through it. Basic information was scrawled throughout. Before I went to Discrete Encounters, I'd need to do a complete background check on the place. Dating services could be seedy as shit. The last thing I wanted to do was be surprised at what they were doing. Hampton didn't seem like he was making rational decisions. If there was something else going on, I'd let him know and whether or not he chose to move forward with them was his choice.

"Did they request a date for the initial meeting?"

"Day after tomorrow."

Shit. That wasn't much time. Hampton had more important things to worry about. Closing the folder, I responded, "I'll get on it. Go take care of Felicia. That's all that matters."

"Thanks, man. You're one of a kind." Hampton looked torn.

Not wanting to get too caught up in all the feelings that were trying to surface about losing a loved one, I left. The fresh air felt good in my lungs as I quickly made it to the car. Winter in Atlanta was good. Not miserable, but tolerable.

It was time to investigate Discrete Encounters.

CHAPTER 5

BANE

FOR THE LAST hour, I'd been parked a block away as I watched the dating service, Discrete Encounters. The meeting to go over their expectations was in thirty minutes. The black building had the red rose insignia on it with the classy script underneath.

Behind the dating façade, I confirmed more went on behind the scenes. *Who the fuck pays for sex?* From experience, I knew there were plenty of women out there that didn't require a deposit put down to fuck. An average "overnight date" went for around three grand a night there. Some rates were cheaper and some were a hell of a lot more. Unless that pussy was plated in gold, I wasn't sure why the hell it cost that much.

Mainly men came and went from the building. I'd driven by the employee entrance around back, which had been primarily female. For now, I'd do the initial meeting while Hampton focused on his wife. I hated being put in these types of situations. Fuck.

As I was about to reach for the car door handle to head inside, a guy ushered a girl down the sidewalk. The deep blue scarf wrapped around her face made it hard to make out any features. The man looked like an arrogant asshole. That type always rubbed me the wrong way. They thought they owned women. They were all pricks.

Quickly getting out of my car, I headed to the front door. The black doors kept the outside world from looking in. Walking inside, the place was posh with all the deep colors and velvet furniture.

The man and woman who I'd seen earlier were in a heated discussion. She seemed defeated. The man's mouth snapped shut when he caught sight of me. I knew I was an intimidating motherfucker with my bald head and the tat that peeked out of the collar of my shirt. The muscles strained against my shirt as I stared him down. This guy was a class-A prick.

There were two people in front of him being helped by the receptionist. A subtle sweet smell swept over me, taking my focus off the asshole. It was understated but drew me in as I glanced to the woman who must have been in her late twenties beside the man. Our eyes locked and instantly I felt ensnared. The hazel eyes with green and blue flecks were breathtaking, even in their sad state—angelic like. I needed to break whatever spell I was under. Wanting to walk forward, I forced myself to remain in place.

What the fuck?

I tried to pull my eyes away from hers, but couldn't. Her tongue barely came out and wet her lips. Again, my legs wanted to take a step closer to the intoxicating woman, but I denied myself. An attraction this strong was trouble.

What the hell is wrong with me?

She wasn't able to look away either. Against my zipper, my dick stiffened as a small smile graced her lips. Hell, there was no denying it … she was beautiful.

"May I help you?" the front desk lady called, effectively breaking the spell as we shifted our attention.

The man, Frankie she'd called him, turned to speak to the receptionist. The mysterious brunette beauty locked eyes with me again and I felt trapped. The atmosphere charged between us becoming awkwardly uncomfortable, but I couldn't stop, like some sort of junkie.

The intensity increased as her expressive eyes watched me. I felt as if she penetrated my darkened soul. Only one person had ever been able to do that. The more she stared, the more I felt unnerved, but drawn to her. I needed to stop this shit in its tracks.

The bastard of a man she was with pulled her forward, breaking the connection again. Thank fuck. After they finished talking, the brunette beauty looked my way once before disappearing behind the door to the left. My gut instinct told me to run from here and not look back. But, I needed to help Hampton out. I could handle this. After all the shit I'd dealt with, this woman was not going to be an issue.

Wipe her from your brain.

If she was here, this woman was a hooker or turning into one. That was a situation I did not need to get involved with.

Do the job and get out.

"May I help you?" The receptionist with flame red hair clicked her fingernails as she waited for me.

I shook my head to clear the images of the woman from earlier. "Bane Bradley. I'm here for a meeting with Jewel Mason."

She efficiently typed something into the computer before responding, "Yes, you'll be meeting Jewel in the Onyx Room. It's down the hall and to the right."

Following the plush black carpet, I went down the hallway that the brunette had gone down. *Damn it, Bane. Stop this shit. She's a fucking prostitute.* Focusing on anything but the female, I stared at the red walls. Honestly, I didn't care what the wall color was, but if it kept me from seeing *her* again, I'd admire it.

There were two rooms beside each other with their doors ajar; Diamond and Onyx. Keeping my gaze on the walls, I glanced in the Diamond Room. Fuck me, the beauty from earlier sat at a table in the middle of the room, shoulders slumped, fingers knotted in her lap.

The last thing I needed was for her to look up and then be stuck in some fucking eye trance. Quickly, I entered the Onyx Room, took off my dark wool coat, and laid it on the back of the chair. I suddenly felt caged as I paced back and forth in front of the chrome table. The red walls only heightened my anxiety. She was next door … alone.

Taking one deep breath, I forced myself to stop and calmly take a seat.

"Bane?"

A woman with black hair and red tips walked in wearing a revealing outfit with a seductive gleam in her eyes. The last thing I needed at this point was another woman to deal with. At least this woman didn't have some sort of weird control over me.

"Yes, Jewel Mason?"

She had a raspy, sexy alluring voice, but it did nothing for me since the other woman was occupying my mind. "That's me. Thanks for coming. Hampton phoned me to tell me you were one of his best."

I ignored the compliment and got straight to business. The sooner I was done, the sooner I was out of there. "No problem. Hampton briefed me that you wanted me to check over all your security measures."

Jewel lithely sat in the chair in front of me and pushed her breasts out. No doubt this woman was used to using her body to try and get her way. I'm not sure why she was coming on to me. That shit was a complete turnoff.

"Yes, supposedly, we had a top-of-the-line system put in, but I want to make sure there are no gaps." She paused and raised an eyebrow. Lowering her voice, she continued. "We have a clientele that requires complete secrecy."

I acted like I wasn't aware of what really went on. "For dating?"

Giving me a knowing smile, Jewel didn't give much away. "Yes."

"Well, show me the system and I'll take a look."

She stood and I followed suit as she spoke. "Perfect. I'll need you to sign the appropriate disclosures."

"Of course."

Following Jewel out of the room, I wasn't able to resist looking in the Diamond Room. The mysterious woman was gone. I wasn't sure if I was relieved or disappointed. That thought bothered me.

***

Sitting at a desk, I made notes of all the gaps I'd found. This top-of-the-line security system Jewel installed was a joke.

A rookie hacker could get in without breaking a sweat. I needed more caffeine before I met with Jewel to disclose my findings. Within thirty minutes I'd be out of here. Heading to the break room I'd been shown earlier, I easily found the coffee machine. It was some fancy machine that gave a person all sorts of choices. Black coffee was the only kind there was in my opinion. I pushed the button on the machine and waited for the coffee to pour.

After today, I was done with this place and Hampton could decide if he wanted to get involved in an undercover prostitution business that catered to the rich. Before coming, I sent him the info but he asked for me to move forward with my analysis of the system.

A few girls giggled as they walked behind me. With my coffee in hand, I turned and nearly ran into the brunette beauty.

"Shit." I barely managed to keep my coffee from spilling as I cursed.

"Sorry, I didn't mean to sneak up on you like that. I'm Maren. I mean … I'm Candy." She glanced away shamefully. That voice. Those eyes. The creamy skin that lead to her tits had my dick hardening. And in an instant, the sensations I'd felt earlier returned in full force. Hell, I'd love to taste her.

Fuck.

We needed to stop running into each other. I was almost done with this job which meant I'd be done here. I took a sip of coffee and watched Maren—at least I assumed that was her real name. Candy seemed like something made up for hooking.

Taking a deep breath, Maren met my gaze again. Like many times, my silence prompted people to keep talking to fill the quietness. "Are you looking for a date? I saw you in the lobby earlier."

"Are you asking me on a date?" I quirked a brow. *What*

was I doing?

Maren flushed and stammered, "Umm—No, I'm not—I mean, I—wait."

It was evident I affected her like she did me. The only difference ... I was able to hide it. Taking a deep breath, she continued, seeming more confident. "I joined today. I wasn't meaning to overstep any bounds. When I saw you earlier, it surprised me that a guy like you was in a place like this."

This woman didn't seem to fit in here. I saw humiliation in the depths of her eyes. "I could say the same about you. Are you okay? I can help if you're not."

A slight downward motion in her lips was barely perceptible along with the dullness in her eyes. "Sometimes life deals you a shitty hand. I'm okay. I promise."

Truer words were never spoken. Without another word, Maren grabbed a Coke from the counter and left. There was a lot more to this woman's story. From the way she looked, I wasn't sure if she actually wanted to be on the backside of this business, but that she was being forced. I was intrigued and that was a bad-fucking-thing.

Glancing at my watch, I saw it was time to meet with Jewel. Maren wasn't anywhere to be found in the hallway that led to my desk. My mind only wanted to think about her and not this joke of a security system. *I am almost done with this job.*

As I rounded the corner, Jewel was at the desk, waiting. This felt awkward as she provocatively leaned against the wall. She was trying too hard and that felt off. "So, what do you think of the system?"

I took another sip of coffee as I watched Jewel's movements closely to see if I could pinpoint what was off. I looked at my notes on the black shiny desk. "I think you need to ask for your money back. It's substandard software. The firewall provides no real barrier and the encryption for all your secured files is not complicated. I'd suggest upgrading to actual secure software. It's top of the line."

She groaned and licked her lips. "I knew they were lying. How fast do you think you could get it installed?"

"I'll call his office and have a quote sent to you. If you agree, they'll put you on the schedule."

Jewel stepped closer to me and her tits brushed against my arm. "So, would you be installing it?"

I stepped back. There was no interest. No way was I going there with her. "I'm not part of the installation team. They're good. Hampton only hires the best."

Her tone turned more seductive. "Thank you, Bane. If you're ever looking for some company, I hope you keep Discrete Encounters in mind. I bet I could find you the perfect person."

Without thinking, I blurted the woman's name she'd told me in the break room. "Do you have a Candy on staff?"

Fuck. Where had that come from? I never spoke before thinking.

"The new girl?" Jewel quirked her eyebrow as she watched me. I'd already messed up. Might as well see where it goes. Hated feeling like my balls were in a vice when I exposed my thoughts.

I stayed straight-faced and took another sip. "Yes, I want to book an evening with her."

"When?" Jewel look affronted.

"When is she available?"

Business mode took over as she looked at her phone, before speaking. "Tomorrow. You'll have to pass the initial screenings. There is an extra fee for expediting."

I wanted to see Maren again. Plus, I'd get to make sure she wasn't being forced into something she didn't' want to do. "That's fine. If I pass, I'll take tomorrow. I want to reserve the rest of the month too, in case tomorrow works out."

What the hell? The whole month.

Jewel's expression became shocked as she cocked her head. "There's a fifty percent non-refundable deposit. Candy's rate is three-thousand a night. Nothing is guaranteed. It's up to the girl. And all this is assuming you meet our requirements."

Pulling out my credit card, I handed it over. "That's fine."

"We'll also need the place you plan to meet her for our approval."

I had no idea where I was going to meet her. First, I needed to think about everything I'd done before I committed to anything else. "I'll send over the location later."

Taking my credit card, a pleased smile came across her face like something had been won. Maybe the awkward behavior was about enticing a new client. I said, "I'll send over the particulars in an hour."

"Okay. Come with me and we'll start the paperwork."

Something with Maren wasn't adding up, and I wanted to figure her out. What the fuck had I gotten myself into?

CHAPTER 6

MAREN

COMING OUT OF the lush five-star hotel's bathroom, I tried to create a safe haven in my mind. I was about to become someone's whore. What was I doing? Abruptly, I changed my direction from the bed to the door, wanting to leave … escape. Then, I stopped in my tracks, remembering why I was here in the first place.

Frankie, my older brother, was the reason.

"Gah!" I screamed and went back to the bed, sitting in a huff.

There was still five minutes until I met some pervert that couldn't get a girl on his own but had to pay for it. I wanted to cry, but I couldn't let Frankie down. He'd raised me and been there for me my entire life.

Every part of this situation was messed up.

When I turned eighteen, something switched. The responsible brother who'd raised me got mixed up with the wrong crowd. He was a shadow of the loving brother he used to be, but I couldn't leave him. Mom died giving birth to me. Dad died in a car accident when I was thirteen. If it hadn't been for Frankie, I would have been absorbed into the system. But at eighteen, Frankie took on the responsibility of raising me and sacrificed a lot. He'd gone to work full-time and gave up his football scholarship.

Then, when I became a legal adult, Frankie digressed to being a juvenile. Now, I took care of him. In fact, I'd been taking care of him for the last nine years. My twenties being nearly squandered away as I was nearing twenty-eight.

I had three jobs to try and keep up with Frankie's gambling addiction. But, two months ago, Frankie got into some serious debt with a different loan shark. Apparently, he felt lucky that night and knew it was his time to shine. He'd been wrong, so wrong, and lost everything. Since then, I'd sold my car and all my possessions of any value. It wasn't enough to cover the fifty thousand Frankie needed by the end of the month to keep him alive.

If we paid back the fifty, he still owed two-hundred thousand more. I wasn't sure how we'd come up with rest.

How could Frankie do this to us? To me?

Becoming one of Discrete Encounters' harlots was the only way to save his life. Of course, it was one of his ideas that Frankie heard from one of his gambling buddies. The job provided a means to earn large amounts of money quickly, since I earned fifty percent of what I made. We were twenty grand short of meeting the fifty and if I could stay booked, we'd exceed it. A shudder ran through my body at the thought of what I had to do to accomplish getting the money.

Sweaty strange hands would touch me. I would become cheap. A whore. Nothing more than a shell of who I'd been. The untold damage would never leave me, haunting me forever. Any innocence that remained would be gone—forever. I wasn't a whore. But if I went through with this … I would become one.

Frankie sacrificed for me for five years and I couldn't let him die. After this time though, I was done bailing him out. Hopefully, after all this, enough of my soul remained intact to gain some semblance of life back.

I was wrecked inside. Torn. Not knowing if I would follow the path of self-preservation or sacrifice.

Click.

My head shot toward the door and I drew the robe tighter around me. The modest lingerie felt like I wore nothing. The door opened and I knew I couldn't do this. My heart went to my throat and I wanted to throw up. There was no way I could do this. I'd have to figure out another way to get the money. There had to be another way.

Standing, I wrapped my arms around myself. Whoever came through those doors, I would let them know I changed my mind.

I couldn't do this.

To my surprise, the gorgeous man from Discrete Encounters walked in. An involuntary shudder ran through my body like before. On a molecular level, my body was driven toward him, but I remained in place. He was gorgeous with the bad boy edge, his bald head and muscular body.

With the same dark and brooding attitude, the nameless man locked his dark eyes on me and a shiver ran up my spine, which was the same reaction I had yesterday. We'd been so close in the break room and I couldn't help the flirty side that came out, never thinking he'd be the one paying for sex with me.

The man took a step farther in the room, letting the door shut behind him. Knots laid heavy in my stomach as I took a step back, intimidation filling me. What did this man want with me?

There was no doubt he could have his pick of women if he wanted, yet he used basically a prostitution business in disguise. Regardless, I still needed to leave. I couldn't be paid for sex. If only we'd met outside of Discrete Encounters.

"Maren." That deep voice had so much authority laced within it.

I took another step back, fighting my response to get closer. "There's been a misunderstanding. I can't perform the service you paid for. I'm sorry I wasted your time."

"Talking?"

What? Talking? Is he serious?

I was stunned into silence. Under his intense gaze, I felt urged to begin speaking. "I-I-I thought you wanted sex?"

Taking a seat, he watched my every move. He gave a slight shake of his head. "I don't pay for my fucks. If you want to leave you can."

Was he serious? All he wanted to do was talk. Hesitantly, I sat on the green bedspread that was adjacent to the cream-colored couch.

"You only want to talk?"

"Yes."

I watched him closely to see if there was any hint of a lie. There didn't seem to be. Talking for money. For some reason, that still made me feel cheap. Maybe if I was dressed more appropriately, I'd feel less vulnerable. "Can I change first?"

"Yes."

I nodded and silently went to the bathroom. This was the strangest situation I'd ever found myself in. What was wrong with him if he paid girls to simply talk to him? My heart hammered in my chest like a freight train. That voice. It was deep and vibrated something on the molecular level within me. Attraction was not an issue, but trepidation overtook my thoughts. Changing out the silk lingerie, I put on my jeans and pale-yellow sweater.

Creaking the door open, the man still sat on the couch. His gaze trained on me. I smoothed my hands down the front of my jeans.

Taking a seat on the edge of the bed, the man kept staring at me. He was a man of few words and gave me the urge to fill the silence. "I don't think I know your name."

"Bane Bradley."

If I was going to stay, I needed more. "Why did you pay to talk to me?"

He shrugged while running his hand over his bald head, dark eyes watching me. "I'm not sure. Jewel, the owner, asked if I wanted some company and I said your name."

"Why?"

"I find you intriguing. I wasn't busy. So, I figured why the hell not."

I shook my head. "You don't give much away, Bane."

"I could say the same about you." A smirk appeared as I crinkled my brow. There was no way I wanted to delve into my issues. Trust me, I knew how it looked with helping Frankie and I loathed myself for feeling like I had to. Needing a subject change, I asked, "Would you like a drink?"

Rubbing the back of his neck, Bane seemed tense as he responded, "Bourbon."

This would give me something to do while I kept trying to

process everything. Standing up, I took in an imperceptible steady breath as I made my way to the black granite bar across the room. The ice bucket was filled. Quickly, I made the drink and grabbed myself a bottle of water from the mini bar.

My fingers flexed before I grabbed Bane's drink, trying to squelch the nerves. Bane's gaze never faltered off me as I came back to him. The way he appreciatively took me in, I had the impression he was as attracted to me as I was him—at least for some reason I hoped that was the case. But, I was probably reading everything wrong. The situation was confusing. After handing him the drink, I took a seat on the far end of the couch.

He tipped the glass to me. "Thank you. Have you decided if you're leaving or staying? Regardless, you'll be paid."

"Staying. I'm staying. No sex."

"No sex."

I believed him, but it didn't keep the thoughts of what it would feel like if he touched me. Nervously, I rubbed my hands together while I cleared my mind of all the thoughts my mind conjured of what Bane looked like without clothes.

This was crazy.

I am crazy.

More silence resumed. Bane took appreciative sips of his bourbon. Unscrewing and re-screwing the lid on the bottled water, I watched him, hoping to piece this together. Bane was in complete control of his emotions and actions. Every move seemed calculated.

I decided to keep talking since he was paying me to do so. Taking his money felt wrong, but I wasn't ready for our time together to be over. "What do you do for a living?"

"I'm in security. It's why I was at Discrete Encounters. What do you do?" His eyes went wide. "I mean. I meant. Fuck,

I didn't mean to ask that."

Sarcastically, I chuckled. "What don't I do? Through the week, I work mornings at a dentist office, afternoons at a vet clinic walking dogs, and weekends I wait tables."

"And an escort?" Calling her a hooker didn't feel right.

An awkward silence filled the room. Bane thought I was a hooker. Who could blame him? I responded, "I think we know my escorting days are over after this talk. I'm not cut out to be a prostitute."

For the first time, I saw humor in Bane's eyes versus the emotional dark depths. "What made you sign up?"

Even with Bane's forbearing presence, I wanted him to know the truth. It was important, for a reason I didn't want to explore, that Bane knew I wasn't a hussy. "My brother. He's in trouble and needs the money."

Leaning forward slightly, Bane laid his drink on the coffee table. "How much trouble?"

"Enough that the three current jobs I have won't cover the trouble." I squirmed. This conversation was getting a little deeper than I wanted to go. Not being strong enough to stand up to my brother was shameful. Maybe taking the offensive in the question asking would help steer the conversation. "What do you do for fun?"

"Run." A gruesome look passed over my face and Bane chuckled. "It's relaxing."

"If you say so. I tried that once and thought my lungs were going to burst from lack of oxygen. Running and I aren't a mix." I folded my legs underneath me to get more comfortable.

Bane mimicked my relaxed posture. "It takes some training."

It was hard to concentrate as the outline of his defined abs became more defined through his snug shirt. *Stay on track, Maren. Talk. He's paying you to talk.* "Okay, what's your favorite junk food?"

"What's yours?"

Ugh, he had a way of out-maneuvering any personal question asked. I wondered if that was a defense mechanism. "Without a doubt, cheesecake. I could live without everything else in my life … except that."

Unexpected laughter came from Bane, which made me smile. He had a deep laugh and the matching smile enhanced his handsome features. From the stiffness of his posture at Discrete Encounters when we first met, Bane didn't seem like the type who laughed much. Me being able to make him laugh pleased me more than it should.

I gave a slight playful pout. "Your turn."

"My junk food of choice would be Cheetos."

Bane's phone rung before I had a chance to comment. Answering, he said, "Yes. Okay." There was a long lingering silence. "Give me an hour. No problem. Thanks."

Hanging up the phone, I knew our time was over and I was disappointed. "I need to leave. I've booked you for the next month if you're up for more talking."

I had no idea that my month was filled. Jewel only mentioned I had a date tonight, and I wondered why that large detail was left out. First, I needed to understand what Bane wanted from me. This was not normal. "Why?"

I wrung my hands in front of me as Bane watched me closely—caressing me with one sweep of my body.

"Because you have no expectations. I enjoy it and I haven't let myself enjoy anything in a long time."

Whoa.

Biting my lip, I tried to determine what I should do. Bane

stood. "Maren, there's no strings. No pressure. We can meet here again if you want to keep up the illusion until you figure out how you want to handle things with your brother."

Bane figured so much out about me in the short time span of talking. "What are you expecting from me?"

Another long pause, but the way Bane's eyes burned through me had my body temperature rising. "Nothing. Absolutely nothing."

I wasn't sure what to say. "Thanks. I'll think about it."

For a split second, his brow furrowed, but the blank mask quickly went back into place. "Sounds good. I guess tomorrow we'll see."

Without another word, he left the room. I sat there, figuring out what in the world Bane wanted and if I thought he told the truth. Earning the money couldn't be as simple as it seemed. Nothing was that easy in life.

CHAPTER

7

BANE

SHIT. ALL I thought about was Maren since I'd left the hotel room yesterday. I knew I was distracted and that was a bad thing. Jeremy, friend and head of security for my former employer, Damien Wales, needed an in depth review of a man wanting to meet with Damien for a new business venture.

All had come back clear.

From time to time, I helped Jeremy out when things got busier for the Wales. Football season was always stressful. So many people to watch and control. And of course, Damien wanted his family with him as much as possible when he was at the games. They had a private suite at the stadium, which helped. At some point, I needed to stop by and see them again. It'd been awhile.

Tossing my keys to the valet, I gave him my name.

"Bradley. Room 2314."

"Yes, sir."

As I approached the elevator, I pushed an excited energy away and ignored it. The feeling felt foreign, nearly unrecognizable. There was no doubt, Maren was a fresh breath of air. A nice change. Someone I wanted more time with. But … that's where it ended. Money wasn't an issue, but eventually I'd have to break this habit so as not to endanger her. I never wanted anyone to think there was anything I couldn't live without. If they found out … that person would have a death sentence, like Jasmine and Faith. I reminded myself of those final moments.

The best thing I could do was turn around and leave, but I couldn't. And that scared me. Maybe if I indulged the craving, it would vanish. If not, I'd force myself to stop.

As I hit the button for the twenty-third floor, I wondered if Maren would come today. She was hard to read, which I guess would be the pot calling the kettle black. In the Discrete Encounters kitchen, Maren had been flirting, and yesterday she was a different girl completely. As I thought about her junk food question, a slight smile crept on my face.

There were a million different things I figured she'd ask before that. I'd been expecting something more personal. That alone made me want to get to know her some. For now, she wasn't giving me that moony-eyed giggly shit that girls do when they wanted something more. In fact, Maren had been pretty adamant about no sex. Though my dick wouldn't mind some relief if she changed her mind. As long as whatever this became over the next month didn't become complicated. I didn't do complicated when it came to people.

The door to the elevator dinged and I stepped out, eyes trained on the door down the hall. A fellow guest passed me and gave me a courtesy nod. I returned the gesture.

For now, I booked this room for the month so I wouldn't have to continue checking in each day. Why I was doing all this ... there was no answer—at least not one I would entertain. I wasn't sure what was going on with her brother, but I planned on getting more information to investigate. This whole situation was like a clusterfuck of questions. I mashed my teeth together at the thought of her own flesh and blood pimping Maren out. She was a good person. Even with my darkened soul, I could still see the goodness in others.

Slipping the keycard in, I opened the door, holding my breath, wondering if the angelic brunette beauty would be here again. Much to my delight, Maren sat on the cream fabric couch, at the end, with a bottle of water. Today she was in some sort of dress that emphasized her tits. My dick pressed against my zipper, having a mind of its own around her.

Calm the fuck down. This isn't puberty.

It wanted inside Maren. Badly. I wondered what her tight pussy would feel like as it clenched around me as I brought her pleasure beyond her wildest dreams. Fuck, why was I torturing myself with all this talking?

"Hey, stranger." Her cheery voice was similar to how she'd been in the kitchen at Discrete Encounters.

I took the same place on the couch, but slightly turned Maren's way. "Hey. Seems like you decided to come back."

Her genuine smile created an involuntary one on my face as well. This was the most odd and fucked up way to meet someone, but it did give us anonymity to escape ... for a bit. At least that was what I wanted. Freedom from the past. Maybe I'd be able to flee from the nightmares even though I deserved each one.

"It would seem so. I wasn't sure if I would come back."

There was a small part of me that thought she wouldn't, but hearing her voice the words created a desire within me to want to know more. Her leaving now would be the best for us. But, I had to know where her head was. "Why's that?"

She casted her eyes down. "Let's say that I wasn't prepared for the grilling I got."

"What kind of grilling?" Anger boiled under the surface, assuming her brother gave her a hard time.

She gave a tired sigh and twisted the lid of her water bottle on and off. A nervous habit. "Jewel told my brother yesterday that you booked me for the entire month. He asked what I did to make you want me like that. He wanted me to do things."

"Things?"

"Things to make you want me more, to pay more. This is so messed up. I wanted to come, but I don't want to drag you into anything with my brother."

Fucking bastard. I bet the self-entitled prick didn't even have a job while he mooched off his sister who had four, if you counted the escorting. "What's his name?"

Alarm shot through her eyes as they met mine. There was good reason for her to feel that way. "Why?"

Stay calm. There was information I needed. "I'm curious. He obviously has my name now. Don't you think it's only fair we're on equal footing?"

I'd rather have the information from Maren. But, I'd get it regardless. I still had access to Discrete Encounters' mainframe while the security team updated the system. From the front desk run-in at the dating service, I knew his first name was Frankie, but that could be a nickname. It'd take me longer, but I'd still find out who he was.

Leaning forward slightly, to look me straight in the eyes,

the dress moved slightly revealing the side of her breast. And damn it, I wanted to run my fingers against the soft plumpness.

"You promise you aren't going to do anything?"

Countering with a question generally distracted anyone and kept me from commitment to anything. "Why would I?"

Maren shifted toward me and that intoxicating perfume came over me. "Because I think you can be dangerous if you want to be."

"Then why did you come back?"

We leaned into each other, only a few inches separating us. "I don't know."

Maren's chest heaved as her breath quickened, eyes darting to my mouth. Hell, this was dangerous. Abruptly, I stood and made my way to the bar, pouring myself a glass of bourbon.

Hesitantly, Maren approached as her hazel eyes watched me. "Did I say something wrong?"

"No." I took a big sip and allowed the burn to cover my throat.

"Our last name is Kincaid. He's Frank Kincaid."

I nodded. Maren made her way around the bar and came within a few inches of me. "Listen, I'm sorry for whatever I did."

"Why are you dressed like that?"

She looked down before looking back into my eyes. Her wrap-around dress needed to come off her body. "I had an interview after my shift at the vet clinic and changed there. I forgot more clothes and didn't have time to run home. The bus route would have put me getting here an hour late and I didn't want to miss seeing you again.

I nodded as my thumb went to her cheek, slowly dragging its way down her neck. Her skin was as soft as I'd believed while jacking off in the shower this morning to the thought of Maren. I'm not sure what's going on between us.

Lust clouded her eyes as she watched me intently. Continuing to draw the line down the center in between her breasts, leaving a wake of goose bumps, I murmured, "You're beautiful."

The fabric moved easily as my fingers descended.

Shit! This woman made me lose all of my composure. She blushed, but didn't back away as we stared at each other while my finger stopped level with the bottom of her breasts. "Thank you."

That same stare trance started, and I felt Maren lean in to my touch. She wanted this as badly as I did.

Maren broke the silence. "I'm not taking your money. I'm going to call Jewel and tell her. It's not right. You're a good guy, Bane. I can sense it."

How wrong she was.

"Why do you stay with your brother?"

My words ended our moment as Maren took a step back, breaking the connection. Her nipples were beady points against the fabric. To keep from closing the gap, I took another large gulp of bourbon.

Giving a tired sigh, Maren explained, "Because when Dad died, Frankie kept me from getting absorbed into foster care. He took care of me. When I turned eighteen, he changed. I took his youth. I owe him."

Like fuck she did. At this point, if he planned on pimping her, the odds would have been better with foster care. "What about your mom?"

"She died giving birth to me. Frankie helped my dad raise me. I'm helping him out of this last bind and then I'm done. I've paid my debt to him. I realize he's out of control with him willing to whore me out. It'll only get worse from here. I've been a pushover for a while. It's time I found myself again—the person my father raised. It took a big wake-up call for me to realize it."

This woman confused me. *Did she have an alternative agenda?* Watching her closely, she seemed innocent and sweet. Not someone out to fuck people over.

Giving me a sweet smile, she said, "It was nice meeting you, Bane. It's been awhile since anyone has been kind to me." She touched my hand and warmth emanated from her. "Thank you."

She turned and walked toward the door. Propelled into motion by the thought of not seeing her again, I caught up to her and placed my hand on her back. "Wait."

A gasp of air escaped Maren. "Bane."

"Hear me out."

If she chose to leave, I would let her go, which would be best for us. When she turned, we were but a breath apart. The movement of her tongue touching her lips filled me with a need to taste them. I knew it'd be even better than feeling her soft skin.

Patiently, Maren waited for me. What the hell was I doing? Why the hell was I even contemplating? I wasn't even sure why I was drawn to this woman. "Stay. Let's spend the month together."

Maren raised an eyebrow. "And what would we do?"

"Whatever the hell we want to do. I'll pay for your time to keep your brother off your ass. Use this month to recharge. Stay here at the hotel."

"Bane, I'm not a whore."

Her words infuriated me and I raised my voice. "Have I treated you like a whore?"

"No." She took a step back.

I knew I needed to calm down. "I won't touch you unless you want me to."

Maren massaged her temples and took another step back. "And what am I going to tell my brother we're doing? What are we doing? I'm confused by all this."

A headache loomed at the base of my head. "Tell your brother we fuck like animals." She gasped. "I don't care what you tell him, Maren. Quite frankly, it's none of his damned business."

"I can't accept money."

"Then, accept a gift."

The breaths expelled from her body became quicker. Swallowing hard, she took a step back. "I can't become a paid prostitute."

"You won't. If we fuck, it will be because we want to. Not because I'm paying you." I could feel Maren's walls breaking down and I was happier than I should be about the fact that she was going to agree.

"But—" Maren looked torn as she chewed on her lip, contemplating.

I held my hands out to the side. "There are no *but's;* I'll leave and not come again. However, take this month and recharge. Tell your brother and Jewel whatever you want." Rooted in place, I tried to decipher what Maren thought. "If you want me to leave I'll go, Maren. No questions."

She took a step forward and a little tension eased out of her shoulders. "I don't understand; why are you doing this?"

"I don't have a damn clue as to why, but I want to spend the next month away from all the nonsense of the outside world." This was either going to be the best or one of the worst ideas I'd had.

The familiar charge built around us as she asked, "Will we have sex?"

I stayed in place. If Maren wanted me to touch her again, she'd have to make the first move. "If we want."

"Do you want?"

Hell yes, I wanted this. "I'm a man, not a saint, Maren."

A small chuckle escaped her. "And if I don't want to?"

"Then, we don't. It's as simple as that."

Maren headed to the bar and took a sip of my bourbon, coughing as the amber liquid made its way down. "What happens at the end of the month?"

This woman made my head spin.

"We go our separate ways." I took a few steps in her direction, but stopped a foot away.

Maren took another sip of my drink. "What about staying friends?"

It was best to get it all there up front. I would leave after the month. There was no way I would break my motto. "Maren, I don't do relationships. I don't do friends. I lead a solitary life with no connections."

A frown appeared. "That sounds lonely."

"It's my life." That was all I would say.

She took a step toward me. "Okay. I can respect that. After the month, I'll leave and never contact you again."

I believed her and that's what made this perfect. She took another step toward me, now only inches from me. "I'll see you tomorrow evening."

"Tomorrow."

Maren reached up on her tiptoes and kissed my lips. I thought she would pull back, but she pressed against my body.

That was my cue.

Things turned in an instant when we tasted each other. My arms surged around her as I sought entry into her mouth. Legs wrapped around my waist and I pushed my dick against her core, eliciting a moan. She tasted of sweet cherries. Hell, I wanted all the way in her.

I sat her on the bar, putting her heat at the perfect fucking height. Reaching for the tie of her dress, I pulled it open. Blindly, my hands sought her nipples. As I rolled them between my fingers, she threw her head back, arching her tits into my hands. Sliding my hands down her stomach, I wanted to rip off her cotton panties. She breathed heavily as she watched my hand.

Nearing the lips of her pussy, a knock came from the door.

"Fuck!" Maren gave a frustrated sound. "I'll be right back."

Whoever the hell was outside that door had a death wish. I wrenched the door open.

"Housekeeping. Would you like the turn down service?"

"No."

She nodded and turned. A turn down service cock-blocked me? Coming back in the room, ready to pick up where we'd left off, I found Maren dressed again.

She wasn't ready.

"Why don't you go home and pack? I'll meet you back here tomorrow night."

My statement obviously threw Maren. She'd probably expected me to seduce her into having sex with me.

"Okay. Thank you." I needed to get out of here so I did the right thing. Starting for the door, she called, "Bane?"

I turned my head back to her, but kept facing forward, fighting the urge to taste her again. "Yes."

"Can we keep this a secret? What we're doing."

What the hell were we doing? "Absolutely."

CHAPTER

8

MAREN

ZIPPING UP MY suitcase, I prepared for the month ahead and what was to come after. The kiss from last night played in my head for the millionth time. Bane captivated me in a way I never thought possible. The moment he took control, I let go. When the knock interrupted us, I was grateful and disappointed at the same time. With those warring emotions, I knew I needed to leave.

I wanted Bane, but I needed to make sure that I knew the score before sleeping with him. There was no doubt he had been one-hundred percent honest with me last night. Frequently, girls thought they could change someone, but I knew that wasn't the case. People were who they were and change only came from within.

Bane had a dark painful past.

He was the type of man I could lose myself in feeling more than I should if I wasn't careful. That was something I refused to let myself do. After thinking all night and compartmentalizing everything, I was ready to have fun and let loose for a month. I welcomed it.

Nearly done, I glanced at the clock. I'd finished at the vet clinic two hours ago. The bus would be here in forty-five minutes. There were a couple of dishes I needed to clean before I left. Heading to the sink, I turned on the water.

It was hard to believe for the next month where I'd be staying—somewhere clean and safe. Honestly, anything would be better than this rat hole I lived in that could barely be classified as suitable living conditions. The bug traps were changed out daily. It was a necessary expense to be able to sleep at night and not feel insect legs from time to time. I lived by myself in the one-bedroom apartment where the heat worked … some of the time. Frankie stayed elsewhere. I didn't ask nor want to know.

Washing the cup in the rusty sink, I screamed when a roach scampered across the floor in front of my feet. "Damn it!" I threw the plastic cup down and stepped back.

All I wanted to do was cry at how my life had been reduced to this. After this month, I was getting out. No one deserved to live like this. Working my ass off and condoning Frankie's behavior was only making him become more reckless. This wasn't a way to live. I would take this month, recharge, and plot my escape.

A lone tear fell down my face. Wiping away the tear, the handle of the door rattled. All it took was a slight shake of the door knob to open the door, making the lock useless. It was probably Frankie, but I grabbed the bat in case. I was completely exposed here. That's why I normally scooted the dresser along the wall in front of the door when I was home. Being distracted, I'd forgotten today.

How had I let myself sink this low?

"Hey, sunshine. How's it going with lover boy?" I cringed at the childhood nickname Frankie used. It was what my father called me as a kid. Now instead of endearing, it felt tainted.

Frankie was coming off a gambling high as he strode in with a swagger. I could always tell by the way he wore his fedora crooked to the side—his *lucky* gambling hat. Luck was the last thing that *hat* brought him … I wished he could get a refund.

All I wanted to do was leave for the hotel. Bane, an almost complete stranger, felt safer than my flesh and blood. Before Frankie suggested pimping out my body, I never would have imagined those thoughts. All this nearly caused me to see red. Frankie didn't care about me. The truth hurt.

Taking a deep breath, I tried to evenly respond. "Hey, Frankie."

Eyeing my suitcase, Frankie narrowed his eyes. "You going somewhere? I thought I could count on you to get Tommy Tricks off my back?"

Tommy Tricks was the loan shark Frankie had taken the ginormous loan from.

"I am. I've always been there, Frankie. The man wants me to stay at the hotel." The fact that my brother couldn't see all I'd given up only affirmed my feelings.

Pulling out his phone, Frankie spat, "He better be fuckin' paying for your time. I'm contacting Jewel."

"Frankie, please let me handle it. I'm the employee of Discrete Encounters." Gently, I put my hand on top of his to stop the dialing. I'd be horrified if they contacted Bane for more money. It was hard enough being okay with sleeping with him while I knew money exchanged hands.

He gave me a non-committal smile. "What does he talk to you about? Why is he so hung up on you?"

Good question. I wasn't sure why Bane picked me. Answering, I followed a version of Bane's advice. "We don't talk. He doesn't say much."

"So, all you do is fuck?"

I shrugged. "Frankie, I'm trying to get through this, okay?"

Cocking his head to the side he watched me, I tried to remain passive. Even if Bane affected me on a fundamental level, I didn't want Frankie to know.

"Okay, sis. No more questions. Just do your thing and get us out of this mess. I'll keep working my luck to help anyway I can." Coming to kiss me on the forehead, I wanted to cry. Our days of seeing each other were numbered. When I disappeared, I was vanishing so as not to be sucked back in. Regardless of what he'd done, I loved him. And I knew he'd end up in this situation all over again.

Frankie strolled toward the door. Laying a hundred-dollar bill on the window sill, he called, "Buy something nice to keep him interested. He may pay off my debt for me … and more. I got a feeling."

There was always a feeling. A feeling that ended up with me working more hours. Not saying a word, I stared at the hundred dollars. It took me so long to earn that kind of money and Frankie was casually throwing it around. He should be the one stressed about paying Tommy Tricks back. This was on him, but he knew I'd do whatever I could out of the false sense of debt I felt.

"Keep smiling, sunshine." Cringing again at the nickname, I gave a weak smile.

Finally, I was alone. Everything I owned was in my two suitcases. Anything I left would be ruined or stolen. Still, I left the place as clean as it could be as I rolled my functioning suitcase while carrying the broken one. It was only a few blocks to the bus stop.

An hour and a half later, I walked up the drive to the five-star hotel. The water fountain in the middle gave a magical ambiance to the white palatial hotel with gold trim. It was a place you only read about with how elegant it was.

A black shiny SUV drove past me. My fingers were cold having been exposed while carrying my luggage for the six blocks I'd walked from the bus stop. Resting, I flexed my fingers to get the blood flowing again and turned toward the street for a second. The sun set and the glow of the city street lights turned on as people milled about. Dusk was my favorite time of night. It meant the end of a day and the hope for a new one tomorrow.

"Maren, the bellboy's going to take your bags to our room. Let's get you inside."

Startled by the voice, I turned to face Bane. A bellboy with a cart was not far behind. Bane looked good in his black turtleneck and jeans. Mouthwatering good. My hormones were in overdrive as my senses came alive around him.

"Thank you, Bane, but I don't mind taking them to my room." The offer was sweet.

He shook his head minutely. "No, they'll handle it. Let's get some food. Are you hungry?"

My stomach growled at the mention of food. I was hungry almost all of the time, but I always made sure to have two meals a day. So far today, I'd only managed one with everything going on. "Food sounds good. Thank you." The hundred dollars would help feed me while I was here. I knew how to eat cheap and save.

Placing his hand along the lower part of my back, Bane guided me in to the hotel. Instead of going to the elevators, we made a left for the elegant restaurant. A faint rose smell permeated the hotel air, adding to the luxury feeling. As we approached the large mahogany doors, I remembered underneath my coat I wore jeans and a sweater. For this restaurant, I knew I was underdressed as women approached wearing their elegant dresses bordering on evening wear.

A sneer from another one stopped me. "Bane, I'm not dressed properly." Though it shouldn't bother me what people thought, I wouldn't be able to eat with everyone staring, wondering why I was in a place that nice.

Assessing, Bane watched me for a second. "What are you hungry for?"

"A salad is fine." That was always a cheap option on the menu that I knew I could afford. More people in dressy clothes walked by as they engaged in polite conversation.

Adding pressure to my back, Bane got my attention. "What else would you like besides a salad? Do you like steak? They're known for their steaks. My treat."

Another woman walked by and couldn't keep her eyes off Bane, while his eyes never left me. Ignoring her, I protested, "Bane—"

"Maren, it's a steak. Let me treat you."

I nodded and gave an appreciative smile. "Steak sounds great."

"Okay, give me a second."

Confidently, Bane strode to the hostess and spoke to her. Being underdressed didn't seem to bother Bane. I was afraid they'd think I was a hooker and with the current arrangements, I didn't want to deal with any of it. This was still the oddest situation—one I wasn't able to classify.

He knew how to read people and I was grateful for not pushing me to go into the restaurant. With Bane, a complete stranger, I felt like I had choices opposed to my life with Frankie, my own family.

On his return, Bane repositioned his hand on my lower back. That sexual, excited feeling that I hadn't felt in ages until I saw him at Discrete Encounters broke its way to the surface. Bane pushed the button for the elevators and the doors opened without delay.

The doors closed, encapsulating us into a world of our own. "I ordered us dinner. It'll be delivered within thirty minutes."

"Thank you, I appreciate it. But I honestly don't expect you to take care of me."

Bane gave me a gentle expression as the elevators ascended. Electrical charges danced across my skin causing me to momentarily close my eyes. This man began to be in almost all my thoughts.

"I know. Just let me. It's not a big deal, and you're not demeaning yourself." His voice brought me back from my temporary refuge. The manly smell encompassing all around me was nearing unbearable.

"You look beautiful today, Maren."

Needing to lighten the sexual tension, I lightly responded, "Thank you. You look dashing yourself." Really, sexy as hell was a better description.

Rewarded with a chuckle, the elevator opened. *Thank goodness for fresh air.* Nervous flutters returned as we made our way to the hotel room. Behind those doors we would be, as Bane put it, *fucking.*

The lock clicked. Opening the door, Bane let me enter first. I let out a breath. I'd be safe here.

The suitcases I brought sat on two luggage racks along the wall that lead to the bathroom. Compared to the lavish surroundings, my bags were out of place—filthy rags in comparison.

"Everything okay?" Bane asked.

All of the sudden I needed to get a few things straight or rather re-clarified. "So, you expect nothing in return for me being here?"

"No, I don't."

Bane appeared in front of me and his finger ran down my cheek, leaving a warm trail in its wake. "Maren, there are no expectations. This isn't a trick. Let's be two people escaping for the next month. Whatever happens … happens. There are no rules to how this works. If either of us wants to stop, you stay here for the month and I'll leave you alone. It's as simple as that."

"Okay. Two people. No expectations."

Bane made his way to the bar for a drink. Idly, I wondered if he hid behind the glass to keep from showing any emotion.

Taking off my coat, I hung it in the hall closet, busying myself with the nervous energy that also showed itself when Bane was around me.

In the main area, Bane sat at the table, feet crossed at his ankles, taking sips of his bourbon. I cleared my throat. "Do you mind if I take a shower before dinner arrives? I didn't have time after I got off work at the vet's office?"

"Not at all." The simple sentence Bane generally responded with elicited want within me, escalating the need to an all-time high.

Maybe a hot shower would help relax me. Unzipping the bag, I got the essentials and a change of clothes before making my way to the bathroom. Lavish, sleek tiles covered the walls as I ran my hands along them. Placing my clothes on the marble counter, I looked at myself in the mirror. This was happening.

Compared to a year ago, I looked worn down and tired with the dark circles under my eyes. Life had taken its toll, but I was getting my life back. I was a survivor.

All I wanted was to work and live comfortably. The lavishness wasn't necessary for me to be happy. Growing up, we'd been middle class but our home had been filled with love. How times change. After turning on the shower knob, I waited for the water to heat up. Multiple showerheads created a cascade of water.

Stepping in, the hot water enveloped me, easing my sore muscles. At the clinic today, a large Great Dane nearly jerked my arm out of its socket as I walked him. A rabbit peeked up underneath a fence. The huge dog charged, and I was barely able to hold on.

The complementary shampoo smelled of floral, and the soap felt like rose petals caressing my skin in the clean shower. Compared to my apartment with the rusty shower, this was a nice change. It had been a while since I'd had a hot shower. Lukewarm or cold was the norm for me.

Drying off, the plush white towels were soft. They smelled heavenly. I wanted to pinch myself to make sure I wasn't dreaming.

A knock proceeded Bane's voice. "Dinner is here."

"Okay, I'll be right out." The steam from the shower clung to me. There were terry cloth robes hanging on the wall. Grabbing one, I cinched it tight around my waist while messily throwing my hair on top of my head. I hated getting dressed while my body was damp.

The main area smelled of food that had my mouth salivating. Standing to the side of the table, Bane took off the silver domes covering the plates, revealing a dinner fit for a king. Holy hell was I hungry.

Opening the wine, he asked, "Did you have a good shower?"

"Yes. There was a dog about my size that gave me a run for my money today."

Bane's brow furrowed. I remembered I picked up something for Bane and now was the perfect time to give it to him. Grabbing my purse, I brought it to the table. As always, Bane intently watched me.

"I brought you something."

"You did?" Surprise laced his voice.

I fished out the bright-orange bag of Cheetos and proudly handed them to him. "I figured after how crazy all this has been, you needed a hit of your favorite junk food. Cheetos a la carte."

A deep rumbled laugh erupted as he grabbed the bag. The dinner was now complete with the orange interrupting the elegance. It was perfect. A secret knowing smile came upon his face. "This will go great with the steak."

"I think so too."

Taking a bite, my mouth watered at the tenderness of the steak. It was hard to suppress the moan wanting to escape. I couldn't remember the last time I'd eaten something as delicious as this. This month of recharging and whatever other pleasures it would bring would be nice.

Bane poured two glasses of wine and slid one across the slate table to me. It was delicious as the crispness coated my throat. Through dinner we made small talk such as the weather. Mainly I talked. There wasn't anything revealing, but I could sense Bane relaxing around me. It had to be exhausting being on guard like he constantly was.

Maybe this month was as much a break for him as it was for me.

CHAPTER 9

BANE

DINNER HAD BEEN pleasant. Maren ate with gusto, which I liked seeing. It had probably been forever since she had eaten a good steak from the way her life sounded. I was amazed at how she didn't complain, but kept pushing forward. Maren filled the silence with meaningless talk, but at times she let the quiet linger. She was getting more relaxed around me.

My mind drifted to the e-mail from Hampton. I'd resent him my brief with more details on Discrete Encounters and their involvement in prostitution. He'd simply responded back, *Thanks, Bane. I'll get this handled.* By his short-clipped response, I knew he was stressed. Normally, he'd call me and we'd hash it out.

The clanking of the fork brought my focus back to the now. Maren looked replete which helped chip away at my charred soul. At least she'd learn through this month what it felt like to be away from that asshole brother of hers. If she left him, I'd do whatever I could to help her relocate.

Standing, I held out my hand to the woman who sat clad in a terry cloth robe. It had been hard to concentrate through dinner wondering if she was naked underneath. Without hesitation, Maren grabbed my hand as I said, "Let's sit on the couch and finish our wine."

"Sounds good."

There was a surprise for Maren on the table. When I saw the desserts I knew I had to get Maren her favorite junk food. Seemed we were on the same page tonight. I hoped we were on the same page for another activity, but time would tell. Maren watched me with rapt attention as I removed the dish. A cheesecake drizzled in caramel sauce was on the plate.

She smiled and stood on her tiptoes as she gave my cheek a quick kiss. I was tempted to possess her, but maintained control. Maren was in charge on how far this went.

Seductively she spoke. "Seems we were thinking the same thing tonight."

"So it seems." I refused to look at this as anything more than a coincidence.

Taking the plate, Maren folded her legs under her on the couch and took an appreciative bite. "This is amazing. Thank you."

I'd have cheesecake sent up here every night to see the look of contentment on her face. There was no telling how rough she had it. I planned on looking into it more tomorrow. Today, I'd gotten her address and located her brother. Fucking bastard, living in a hotel while his sister barely made ends meet.

We needed to get something else out of the way. I knew

Maren wasn't going to like it, but hopefully my logic was persuasive enough. "What time do you have to be at work tomorrow?"

"Eight. There's a bus leaving at six thirty that connects with two other buses. I'll get there in time."

Here was to hoping this happened smoothly. "How far away is your work by car?"

She thought for a moment. "Probably like thirty minutes with the morning traffic."

"I'd like to have a car take you. You could leave around seven-twenty." Maren protested, so I quickly continued on. "You'll get a lot more time to sleep. It's not a handout. It's simply a nice gesture. Just think about it."

She nodded while she ate. I wasn't able to tell what she thought. As she took the last bite, she laid the plate on the coffee table. "I'll take the car. Thank you."

As Maren sat back on the sofa, her robe became loose, leaving a direct line of sight to her tits. It had been hard as hell not taking her the moment I saw her on the sidewalk outside the hotel.

Glancing down, Maren saw where I stared. Not moving to close the robe, she grabbed my hand. "I want this, Bane. But, I don't want to feel cheap."

That was my cue.

I quickly moved Maren and positioned her straddling my lap. That flowery fragrance bewitched me. Undoing her sash, I spread the robe open. Hell, she was bare and my dick wanted out to conquer her. Splaying my fingers along her flat abdomen, I said, "I won't ever treat you like you're cheap, Maren. We are two consenting adults, agreeing to give each other pleasure. The hotel is only a means to give us privacy."

"Then, take me."

My right hand roamed up her thigh while my left hand went to her waist to start its upward ascent to those luscious nipples I'd already felt, but needed to again. The inner muscles of her legs squeezed mine as anticipation took over her, beckoning to touch her.

She was about to get fucked.

Hard.

As my fingers grazed the lips of her pussy, Maren's hands rested on my legs behind her, granting me better access. I loved a bare shaven woman. The position arched her breasts closer to my face. Maren's body bucked as I touched her clit, massaging it enough to have her begging for more.

"Bane, please. It's been so long."

Hearing her ask me for something changed everything. I'd planned on having her mewling while she waited to orgasm, but I knew Maren never asked for anything. I wouldn't deny her. With my left hand I rolled her beaded tip as I pulled it to the point of pleasure on the verge of pain. She loved it as she ground down on my right hand.

"Bane …"

"It's coming, angel."

Her slippery folds sucked my middle finger within her pussy while my thumb kept up the assault on her clit. Fuck, she was tight and greedy for me. It had been awhile since she'd slept with anyone. I massaged her walls and began a more vigorous pace as she loosened up.

"Yes, Bane! Yes!"

Leaning her head back and putting more weight on her arms, Maren rode my hand. She was close … so close.

I switched nipples and Maren stiffened as her heat clenched down on me, her orgasm taking over her body.

"Don't stop!"

Not stopping, I massaged every last ounce of pleasure out of her body. Maren slumped against me, her breathing fast and erratic. My dick wanted to get inside her.

Pulling my finger out, Maren straightened up with a satisfied, lazy grin on her face. Watching me intently, I brought my fingers to my lips, tasting her. Holy hell, she was sweet. "Pure-fucking-honey, angel."

She snickered. In one movement I stood, holding her ass and kissing her hard, capturing a gasp.

Against my lips, she murmured, "I taste myself. I like it."

That only spurred my need for her as I devoured her mouth, moaning. The animal was about to become unleashed. It had been awhile for me too. I tossed her on the bed and her robe fell to the side. This afternoon, I'd been by to drop off a box of condoms in case things escalated. I opened the night stand drawer.

Teasing, Maren looked at me as she propped up on her elbows and saw the large quantity on the box. "Someone thought they were going to get extremely lucky. Many times."

"Hoped."

Another giggle escaped. "I think you're about to get lucky."

Enough talking. I unzipped my pants and put on a condom. There wasn't enough time for me to get naked. Throbbing, my dick sought her as I pushed against her entrance.

"Are you ready, angel?"

On a breathy exhale, she responded, "Yes! I need this."

By the way her body heaved in anticipation, Maren needed this rough ... like me. We needed to escape the nightmare of life we were trapped in for different reasons. Her body was the welcome distraction I was looking for. I plunged in, balls deep.

"Shit!" I murmured.

"Bane, don't stop!"

With her legs locked around my waist, I pulled out and relentlessly pushed back in. That sweet smell of desire permeated the room, further driving my maddening pace. Maren clutched the sheets, thrashing her head. Her walls were quickened against me. She was close. I was close. We were going to explode together.

Every muscle tightened within me as my balls drew up. I twisted my hips slightly. Maren arched her back as she yelled while her pleasure engulfed her while she tightened around my dick. My own release sent that orgasm all through my body as I relinquished the built-up sexual tension from the last few days.

I'd fucked her.

Made her mine—for the month.

Maren collapsed as her eyes fluttered shut. Pulling out, I discarded the condom and zipped myself up. On the bed, Maren's beautiful body laid exposed and thoroughly well-fucked. She looked beautiful and I wanted to touch her more.

Fuck.

It was time for me to go.

Removing the robe from her body, Maren only muttered incoherent contented words.

"What time do you need to get up, angel?" Nicknames were trouble, but this was temporary. Once I'd said that in the heat of the moment, I knew there was no going back. She was an angel.

She muttered, "I need thirty minutes."

Covering her with the bedspread, Maren snuggled deeper into the pillow.

Fighting my body's request to be near her again, I left. I'd get her wakeup call and breakfast settled at the front desk. Hopefully things stayed as they were.

Excellent fucking.

CHAPTER 10

MAREN

THE DOGS BARKED like mad as I placed the Doberman back into his kennel. Work was over. The car service not only took me to the dentist office, but picked me up and delivered me to the vet, allowing time for a quick bite to eat. My conscience continued to try and nibble away at me, telling me that at the end of the day I was a hooker, but I ignored it. Bane didn't make me feel like one. I knew the truth and that was all that mattered. I hadn't spoken to Jewel since she'd told me about my first appointment.

The sex. My word, the sex had been amazing last night. Bane took care of my needs while he brought me to orgasm—twice. I'd never been able to orgasm back to back, but I wanted ed to again. Last night I'd slept soundly for the first time in who knows how long.

Bane was complex. He made no pretenses about this con-tinuing, but did sweet things like the car service, the wakeup call, and the breakfast. It was nice being taken care of, but I frequently reminded myself that this was only going to last twenty-eight more days. That was it. No more. However, I knew Bane was someone that I could easily fall for.

Clocking out at the computer, I waved bye to Lisa who was the front desk receptionist. Everyone here was kind to me, but I always declined their invitations to go out. That was money I didn't have. When I started over without my brother, I made a vow to become more social and do things that I en-joyed.

The black town car from the hotel waited out front. Cold gusts of wind blew around me as I dashed to the car. The driv-er, Jake, opened the back door. He was quiet and barely spoke unless spoken to. The only reason I knew his name was from the name badge.

"Thank you, Jake. Do you mind taking me back to the ho-tel?"

He tipped his head. "Not a problem, Miss Kincaid."

"Thank you."

The car drove through the city and I watched outside as we made our way back to the hotel … to Bane.

Getting out of my scrubs, I hopped in the shower. The last thing I wanted was to smell like a wet dog when Bane arrived. I'd given the dogs baths before walking them. Which meant I'd gotten bathed too as they shook the water off their fur coats.

Toweling off, I blow dried my hair before putting on jeans and a light-weight green cardigan. Makeup was always kept to a minimum.

My heart nearly stopped for a second when I saw someone perched on the edge of the bed, waiting for my brain to catch up.

Frankie. I stopped in place as I registered the hate emanating from him. Something wasn't right.

Keeping it light, I asked, "What are you doing here, Frankie?"

Standing, Frankie shook his head exasperated, and my heart rate quickened. "I talked to Jewel this morning. She had no idea about your new arrangement. In fact, she hasn't heard from you since you received your first assignment. What are you doing to me, MAREN?" His voice only got louder as he spoke.

"What am I doing to you?" He had some nerve, but I needed to stay rational. If this was the last time we saw each other, I didn't want it to be fighting. Placating, I held up my hands. "I'm not doing anything. I'm spending the month with the guy for you. You're getting all the money from this."

Cocking his head, Frankie looked at me—coldly. "Liar. Are you trying to cut me out? I need that money."

At the hateful tone, I needed distance and backed up against the wall. Things were not as they should be. Frankie had never been this aggressive. "No. I didn't know I was supposed to call in. I promise."

"Cut the fucking crap, Maren! You're trying to cut me out!"

Frankie grabbed my arm viciously, wrenching me from the wall. "Ouch! Frankie, you're hurting me!"

The sneer on my brother's face sent a thrill of fear through me. I'd never been afraid of him, but I'd always done as he asked. But this was a misunderstanding. Hopefully, he'd see the reason and the truth behind my words.

Before I had a chance to calmly talk to my brother while my arm felt like it was about to snap in half, the door opened and Bane strode in.

"What the fuck are you doing here?" The deathless stare Bane gave Frankie caused chills to run down my spine. Bane stood with one leg slightly in front of the other while his eyes glanced to me. Bane's hand crept to the back of his pants. *Please don't let there be a gun. No guns.* My brother may have used me for the last few years, but I loved him and didn't want him hurt.

The two men were measuring each other up. I feared for Frankie. Bane definitely knew how to handle himself.

Frankie choose that moment to squeeze my arm harder, forcing a wince and yelp out of me. "Let her go, Frank." The tone brokered no argument.

"She's my sister, asshole." Frankie squeezed harder and I squeezed my eyes shut. Speaking would spur Frankie, thinking I'd sided with Bane.

"I don't give a shit. Let. Her. Go." Bane rolled his shoulders and his muscles drew tight. Formidable, he took a step forward.

Frankie shoved me onto the couch and my arm got a rush of blood through it. The pain caused tears to prick behind my eyes. What was wrong with Frankie? Why was he acting like this? Bane moved toward me, concern etching his face while he glanced toward Frankie, then back to me. "You okay?"

"Yeah, I'll be okay."

A fist came and hit Bane from the side, knocking him down. I cringed and screamed, drawing my body up tight. Lithely Bane popped back up to his feet in one movement without using his arms. Only in the movies could someone move like that. Who was he?

"You got one free shot, motherfucker. That's it." Bane cracked his neck to the side moving to the other side of the room away from me.

Frankie wasn't a fighter. It was obvious with how his fists were raised up. "Bring it. What's wrong with you that you have to pay for sex from whores?"

Tears streamed down my face at the hurtful words. "I'm not a whore!"

Without a word, Bane stalked Frankie and clocked him once. Twice. Three times. The punches were fast and Frankie dropped like a rock.

"Frankie!" I scurried off the couch to Frankie's side. His eyes were rolled back in his head. Was he dead? He couldn't be dead. No! He can't be. "Frankie! Can you hear me?"

A shadow loomed over me. "He'll be fine, Maren. He's knocked out. We need to go."

"Go?"

I glanced to Bane. His expression softened as he talked to me, losing the aggressive hostile edge, "He's pissed off. He hurt you. I'm not leaving you here with him. Grab a few things and we'll get this sorted. If he wakes up, he's going to be mad as hell. I'm not letting him hurt you again."

Standing, I looked down at Frankie's limp body. Bruises were already forming on his cheek. "Okay. You promise he's going to be okay?"

Bane put his hand on my waist. "He'll have a hell of a headache, but your brother will be fine, which is more than he deserves."

Knowing Bane was right, I decided to leave with him. Before I left, I'd try to smooth things over with Frankie. Grabbing the black backpack I'd put in my suitcase, I quickly put some clothes in and the essentials. Frankie didn't move.

Bane went to the bathroom. Not knowing how long Frankie would be out, I placed a pillow under his head and covered him with a blanket. At the last minute, I remembered putting my birth control in the nightstand. Opening the drawer, the condoms were next to my pill pack. A blush crept up on my face as I grabbed both. My brother laid, not five feet from me on the floor out cold and I prepared for safe sex.

Frankie stirred.

"Let's go, Maren, before he wakes up." Bane's booming voice caused me to jump as he passed me.

Behind Bane's footsteps, I followed without a word. There was a lot to process. In essence I chose Bane over my brother. What had gotten into him? Where did this leave everything? I wasn't sure. One thing I knew, I wasn't safe with Frankie.

My brother was mentally manipulative, not physically abusive. At least not until today. Numbly, I went on autopilot while we got in to the car and drove off. Things would be forever changed between Frankie and me. A heartache blossomed in my chest as I digested the thoughts. If only we could go back to before I was eighteen when I thought we were happy.

I stared out into traffic.

"Maren, are you okay?"

Looking to Bane, I answered, "I will be. He's never been physically abusive before."

Taking out his phone, Bane dialed a number. "Jewel, please." He paused. What was he going to say to her? A slight bruise appeared on Bane's chin from the hit. I reached out to touch where Frankie sucker punched him. Bane looked at me, giving me a small smile before he spoke again, "Jewel. Bane. Why was Frank Kincaid in my hotel room today?" He listened. "Okay. Yes. Not a problem. Bye."

Quietly, I sat in the car after Bane hung up. That had been more civil than I'd imagined after the scene up in the room.

Bane looked deep in thought as he squinted at the road. After a few minutes, he asked, "Did you know Frank called Jewel?"

"No. Frank came by my old apartment as I packed. He said he wanted to call Jewel. I told him I would take care of it. I never planned to tell her I'd moved into the hotel."

Bane was still, too still, as he drove. No doubt he assessed everything including me. "Why?"

"Because you shouldn't even be paying anything to them. You've done more for me than anyone else has. And quite frankly, Jewel doesn't own me. I wanted to quit, but didn't to give us uninterrupted time to escape. Now that Frankie's ruined that, I'm quitting."

"What about the money he owes?"

"I'll figure something out."

"What about the month?"

"That's up to you."

"Maren, what do you want?"

This conversation moved quick, not giving me much time to think. The only thing I could do was think with my heart, which was dangerous considering our agreement. "To spend the month together like we planned, then go our separate ways."

Parking the car, Bane nodded to the building where Security Branch was in large white letters. "You said old apartment. What did you mean by that?"

I felt like this was an interrogation, but I wanted to be truthful with him. "After I help Frankie out this last time, I'm leaving. Escaping. Getting away from this life. I want to live."

"I need to pick up something here. I'll be back."

That was a rapid change to the pace we were talking. At times, Bane was his own island state. I noticed I wasn't given the option to come with him. "Okay, I'll stay in the car."

Bane nodded while grabbing his sunglasses from the middle compartment. Checking the rearview mirror first, he got out of the vehicle, locked me in, and jogged toward the door while checking his surroundings. My eyes couldn't leave his ass. Last night I hadn't been able to see him naked, but I wanted to.

Stop thinking about sex, Maren. There were issues I needed to deal with. Distracting myself with sex was not healthy.

To the core, I was shocked at everything that went down. I watched the traffic come and go to distance my mind. I was with a semi-stranger who I was sleeping with. My brother took it too far. I still had to come up with a large sum of money. What the hell happened over the last few days?

A few minutes later, Bane came out of the black shiny glass doors with a leather backpack slung over his shoulders. Mirrored Aviators were in place on his face. Bane seemed tenser as he got in the vehicle.

"Everything okay?"

"I called the hotel. Frankie left. I figured we'd get all your stuff and check in somewhere else that no one knows about. How does that sound?" There was something Bane wasn't telling me as he reversed out of the parking lot.

Shifting in my seat, I looked out the window. "That's fine. Bane, I want you to know there's no pressure to continue this thing. I'll be fine."

"I want to."

My head snapped back to Bane at his simple sentence that rang true to my ears. The thought of Bane wanting to spend more time together had the familiar ache returning. A giggle escaped as I thought about the condoms. Was this what it was like to be sex crazed? After one time together?

Amused, Bane glanced my way. "What's funny?"

"When you told me to pack a few things, I saw the condoms next to my birth control and grabbed the condoms too." I laughed harder. "I guess I wanted to make sure we were prepared if we didn't come back." Tears. I had tears from laughter.

Bane's hand came to my chin as he brought my eyes to meet his, a devilish grin on his face. "We'll be fucking soon. It's all I've thought about since last night. But, it's good to know we're on the same page."

"I am." That was the one thing I was absolutely sure about in all this.

Bane returned his focus to driving and moved his left hand to settle on my leg. I liked the contact and what it did to my insides—slowly turning them into a wanting mess. The hotel came into view as we pulled up the drive. The valet came to the driver side as another one opened my door.

As I got out of the vehicle, I heard Bane say, "Don't park it. I'll be back in a few minutes."

"Yes, sir."

Bane's hand took position on the small of my back, guiding me inside. Looking down after a slight pressure on my shoe, I noticed I'd nearly tripped on my lace. "Oh wait, my shoe is undone."

Stopping, I kneeled down while Bane faced the entrance patiently waiting for me. The hotel was quiet and I felt like people were staring. As I stood, Bane put his hand at my elbow. "I forgot my cell phone. I need to grab it. Do you mind hopping in the passenger side while I make a quick phone call? Then, we'll get everything sorted."

The edge to Bane was different, like he was preparing for something.

"Of course, not a problem."

The cool air greeted us as we came back outside. The valet was in the driver's seat. I thought Bane asked him to leave it. The hairs on the back of my neck prickled in apprehension. Bane casually raised his hand, halting the valet's movement. "I need to get my cell phone before you move it."

The valet looked behind him nervously then nodded quickly—too quickly. "Yes, sir."

Following Bane's advice, I got in the passenger side. Casually, Bane got in and his aviator glasses were still in place. The car was off. As Bane glanced around the area, I noticed his other hand pushed something on the underside of the steering column. The SUV roared to life. Without missing a beat, he shifted the car into gear, shooting out of the drive as his tires squealed.

"Buckle up, Maren."

The steely command had adrenaline pulsating through me. A larger truck came out of the drive at the same speed.

"What's going on?" The car shifted hard to the right, avoiding a stoplight.

Bane's voice became hard. "Buckle up, Maren! I need you to listen to everything I say and do it."

Fumbling with the buckle, I managed to get it fastened. The vehicle sped faster. The truck behind us followed Bane's every move. Out of fear, I grabbed the door handle. The car darted in and out traffic at an alarming rate. Bane shot to the left causing my right shoulder to hit the door.

Frozen in fear, I prayed I survived this.

CHAPTER
11

BANE

MOTHERFUCKER.

The first thing I needed was to get us somewhere safe. I wasn't sure who, but somehow either Maren or I had a target on our back. And I assumed the target was on the latter. Shit! This was why I should have never entertained anything with Maren. The hotel implied Maren meant more than my normal occasional fucks.

I had to keep Maren safe. History repeating itself wasn't an option.

The unmarked truck I'd noticed as we pulled into the hotel kept up and anticipated my next maneuver. The familiar charge I always had when entering combat rolled through me as I became acutely aware of all my surroundings, seeing if anything in my environment could be of use to take this bastard out.

Whoever followed us had training. Glancing to Maren, I knew she was terrified as she white-knuckle clutched the door frame. Once I got us somewhere, I'd explain what I could. She didn't know it, but life as she knew it was over. What the fuck had I been thinking? A month escape. Of course, that would be when the enemy would strike.

Keeping Maren safe was my objective.

After years of training, my heart rate stayed even. An opportunity presented itself that would keep this asshole away for a bit. Up ahead a trailer rig was about to block the entire road. I pressed the accelerator more, revving the engine and speeding up to a dangerous rate. It would be tight, but we'd squeeze through. Normal human reaction would cause the rig driver to automatically stop.

Maren screamed. "Bane, the truck!"

Not responding, I needed my full concentration as men for the crew were waving at me wildly to stop. I didn't. Positioning my car, I pushed the gas harder. The space was tighter than I'd assumed and the maximum momentum would be needed to clear the area. Otherwise, we'd be stuck—sitting ducks. Bracing myself, I held the steering wheel on course and pushed the vehicle to the max.

Metal scraping, as if someone screamed, sounded along the length of the vehicle, taking the side mirrors off. Our speed decelerated and I hoped we could push through. The teeth-clenching protest ended as we cleared the area and I let out all of the air I had been holding in.

Thank fuck.

In the rearview mirror, the unknown vehicle screeched to a halt not able to clear the opening. I jerked the wheel right to take a side road. With the vehicle badly damaged, we'd become easily recognizable. Backroads were the best option as I made our way to a safe house I had in the city. No one knew about it. It'd buy us some time while I figured out what happened.

Then, I'd hunt every motherfucker down who was involved. The familiar fire within me burned. To be safe, tomorrow we'd relocate somewhere else. I didn't want to be too far away from the fight unless I had to be. There was a more remote location in Colorado I owned that would buy us however much time we needed.

Seeing Maren huddled in the passenger seat, shaking, I felt like an asshole for not communicating to her. But, this was war and I knew what it took to survive. "Maren, I'm taking us somewhere safe. I won't let anything happen to you."

Eyes wide, Maren nodded. "O-o-kay."

There were no signs of pursuit which told me that this afternoon hadn't been planned. Something happened to make them jump the gun. *Frankie.* He was the only answer I could think of. Ten minutes later, I pressed the door opener to the garage in the alley filled with garbage.

From the outside, the place looked like a dump. Inside though was our refuge and supplies. "Bane, where are we?"

Maren leaned up looking through the window while she took in the practical industrial-like space. "In my safe house. We'll need supplies. We can stay here for the night."

Parking the car, I shut the garage door. First, I needed to secure the perimeter and see what else I could find as I got out of the vehicle. The control pad to the left of the garage illuminated as I punched in the code and the heavy locks engaged, echoing through the room as the security system went online.

Turning, Maren stood in front of me. She shook and tears formed in the corners of her eyes. I was an asshole for getting involved with her.

"Bane, please tell me what's going on. Why do you need a safe house?"

I grabbed her hand. "I need to check some things and then we'll talk. I have a limited window to get some answers."

The people after us were probably scrambling to find us which meant their attention was divided. I needed to take advantage of that distraction.

Along the wall, a computer with several monitors sat. Maren held my hand as we walked to the desk. As I hit switches along the panel, the fifteen screens came to life. Cameras were around the building and I was remotely plugged into my house.

Maren pointed to one of the screens seeming to calm some. There was no doubt she was a fighter—a survivor. "Is that your house?"

I sat in the chair and opened my arms for Maren to come. Her presence was a soothing balm. But, I knew I wanted to touch her to keep her calm—or that's what I told myself. There was only a slight hesitation as she came to me. Fuck! I deserved that, but I didn't want Maren to be scared of me.

"Yes, that's my place in town." The screens rotated through the different rooms in my house.

Studying the screen, Maren asked, "How long have you lived there?"

"About four years."

"Oh." I knew she thought the place was sparse with only the essentials.

Rigid, Maren barely sat on my knee. "Bane, why would you need a safe house? Are you a spy?"

Pausing, I rubbed my hand over my scalp deciding how much I wanted to tell Maren about my past. The answer—not much. "Long ago, I worked for a branch of the government. It's been six years since I left when I finished my term."

She relaxed. We were making progress. "What happened today? It started with Jewel's phone call, didn't it? And Frankie's visit?"

My angel was perceptive. How much did I share of what happened today? There was a fine line. Too much information only made Maren a larger asset if she was caught. When someone knew too much, they were eliminated or used to get results. But when someone was tied to me, they were already in too deep. I wanted Maren to know what she was involved with, hoping it would keep her listening to me and … safe.

Confirming, I asked, "Yes, are you sure you want to know?"

Taking her eyes off of the screen, she searched mine, imploring. "Bane, I don't like secrets. My brother has been keeping them from me all these years. I want to know. I can handle it. I promise."

Maren shifted farther in my lap, letting me know that we were getting back to where we were. "I confirmed something was going on when I called Jewel. When I initially asked for you, they gave me a rule book I read. Frankie showing up wasn't protocol for Discrete Encounters. If someone goes missing, the dating service comes first to the location with their personal security. It keeps the anonymity of the client who is their main concern. When I called Jewel, she stuttered to get her story straight. I think Frankie's visit was unexpected. If someone heard us, I didn't want them alerted. I simply agreed and ended the conversation. That's why I went to Security Branch."

Giving Maren some time to digest the story, I paused, letting her lead the inquiry. "Where were we going to go beforehand?"

My hand caressed her hip and she scooted further back into me. The speed of her pulse reduced as I inconspicuously watched the vein in her neck. "Before I talked to Jewel, I'd planned on us going out to eat. I figured we'd go to dinner, check into another hotel room. Tomorrow while you were at work, I was going to change hotels."

Maren didn't comment on my last comment, but refocused the conversation. I wanted her to at least acknowledge it. "What happened when you got to Security Branch?"

"Since they're redoing Discrete Encounters security system, I used one of the tech's computers who was gone to log on. I was lucky he wasn't there. Our records were deleted from the mainframe, effectively eliminating a paper trail. As I was about to leave, an alert came through on my phone telling me someone cut the security-specific power to my house, which would have left me unknowing. A few months back, I'd installed a backup. No one came in, but I logged in remotely and wiped all my computers in case he did manage to get through the security."

Maren's hand absentmindedly drifted to my hand on her hip as she rubbed soothing circles. Hell I wanted inside her, but I needed to get a handle on things first. Then, we'd fuck. "What was in the backpack you came back out with from Security Branch?"

"A laptop, a gun, some ammo, money, and a few other devices. If we weren't able to get away, I needed some essentials." Maren slightly stiffened at the word gun.

I wasn't sure what Maren's limit was at this point, so I would let her keep prompting the conversation. "What happened at the hotel? Why'd we go back?"

Gathering my thoughts, I responded, "I needed to make

sure I was right before I disappeared with you. I hoped to draw them out to see who we were dealing with. I knew they wouldn't make a scene in the hotel lobby. Too many cameras, too many witnesses, too many variables. As long as you and I appeared normal, they would have no reason to take us ahead of time until we were somewhere less open."

Maren flexed her feet as she thought for a second and introspectively said, "My shoe coming untied wasn't an accident."

"No, I did that. While you were tying your shoe, I caught a man in the reflection of the sign ducking behind it. I gave them no reason to think I was on to them as I asked to get my cell phone from my car."

Maren grew quiet as she watched the screens. I needed to be researching, but having her collected and not panicked would help me keep her safe. A slight hum filled the silence from the computers. Any moment now, I expected whoever was after me would be going back to my place to do a more thorough search.

"How long before we leave here?"

"We'll leave tomorrow after we get some sleep. In the next garage over, I have another car we'll use. Before we make our next move, I want to see if we can get any leads." The fact was, people got themselves killed by reacting and not assessing. If we instantly went somewhere else without any intel, we could be going straight into the lion's den. I avoided rash decisions whenever possible.

"What about my brother?" That was one of the many questions going through my mind as well.

I scooted us closer to the console and laid my cell on the desk. "I'm not sure. Let's see what happened when he left the hotel."

Maren leaned back against my chest. "How?"

Turning my head, her neck was opened to me and I needed to taste her. I gave it a kiss and watched her reaction. A shy smile came over her face as she turned to me. We were but a breath apart as I answered her question and gave her a quick kiss. "By hacking into their system."

"Oh."

I wasn't sure what she thought as we stared into each other's eyes, the gold flecks in the irises sparkling under the light.

She broke the connection, which I needed. When around Maren, I seemed to get lost. Cuing up the mainframe for the hotel, I typed several commands and finally was rewarded with access. If the person after us watched the hotel security, they'd figure out I was in the system. I had less than five minutes to find the file and get out before they tried to trace me.

Maren watched the screens intently. Bringing up the front door hotel footage I found, the time Frank would have been potentially leaving the hotel. Maren's and my departure flitted across the screen as I fast forwarded the feed. Ten minutes later, Frank strolled through the lobby, head down. He had to be sporting one hell of a bruise with how I clocked him. At the thought of him holding Maren roughly, my teeth mashed together. Fucker. She rubbed my leg as she felt me tense.

I slowed the feed, watching all the surrounding feeds. The same black unmarked truck pulled up to the front lobby. Maren gasped. I saw red. The asshole sold out his sister. Frank's visit had been planned all along. But, why?

Maren sat forward within inches of the screen. "Bane, why is Frankie getting into that vehicle?"

"I don't know, angel."

Someone popped out of the backseat. I froze the screen and downloaded the image to my computer. Pressing play, the man was pissed. He wrenched the door open and then slammed it after Frank was shoved into the front seat. The truck took off.

Looking at the time, I had approximately two minutes before I needed to logoff.

I put the feed on high speed again to see what happened after. Two men walked in five minutes later. They had earpieces in as they headed to the elevator. I froze and saved their faces as well. They exited on our floor and went to our hotel room. Changing screens, I kept monitoring the front camera. The truck pulled back in not twenty minutes later and parked off to the side. No doubt waiting for my return. They planned to take us up in the room.

Time was running out as the timer showed less than ten seconds left. I closed the connection.

Maren remained quiet on my lap as I mentally sorted through everything. Grabbing a secure line from the desk, I dialed the hotel I knew Frank Kincaid resided in from my research. He deserved worse after I'd seen the conditions his sister lived in.

After two rings, the hotel picked up. "Hotel Dumont. This is Claire."

"Frank Kincaid, please." Maren quirked a brow at my request. I nodded and mouthed, *I'll tell you in a minute.* My phone vibrated letting me know someone entered the house. I brought the house feed up on the monitors while I was on hold. It was hard not to go and face those fuckers head on, but I had Maren to think about.

Three masked men entered and went straight for the different cameras in my house, disconnecting them with efficiency. Somehow they'd gotten a plan of my security system. Maren pushed further into me. I held on to her tightly. This was fucked up ten ways to Sunday.

Clicking sounded from the other end before Claire came back on the line. "I'm sorry, sir. Mr. Kincaid checked out this afternoon."

"No problem. Thank you."

The line disconnected. Frank knew the unidentified truck and now he was checked out. There was no doubt Frank Kincaid was involved, but was probably a pawn being used to get to me through Maren. He wasn't operative material.

Why? Was the man Frank owed money to involved? Did they get to Frank after I'd booked Maren? To have him on the front side seemed unlikely. The lobby meeting was by chance and Maren wasn't the type I normally went for. None of the facts were fitting together.

All the feeds from my house were gone, except one—a camera I'd installed within the last two months in my office. It ran independently off another battery source. Those assholes were well-informed.

Barely above a whisper, Maren said, "Do you know who these people are?"

"No."

I studied the masked man as he entered my office. He sat at my desk and pulled up the computer. Only blank screens greeted him. He pounded the desk and slipped off his mask, but his back was to the camera.

Turn around, motherfucker.

The chair spun around and my heart stopped at the face pensively taking in my place.

Holy fucking shit.

Eric Thornhill, the Black Division assassin responsible for giving intel to the cartel, was alive.

CHAPTER

12

MAREN

BANE STIFFENED AGAINST me at the sight of the man looking into the camera. His breathing barely audible. Something was wrong. Well, worse than it already was. I felt nauseous and anxious all at the same time. Somehow Frankie was involved. The taste of betrayal left a bitter taste in my mouth. Trying to stay positive, I hoped that was the reason why Frankie acted so terrible to me at the hotel room.

Had he been trying to get Bane to get me out of there? I wasn't sure.

The guy that had Bane nearly becoming mute stood and walked around looking in various cabinets and folders.

"What's going on, Bane?"

He was frozen as he stared at the screen. As if on autopilot, he responded robotically, "Frank checked out of the hotel he lived in this afternoon. And that man is Eric Thornhill."

"You know him?"

Bane's mouth set as his eyes narrowed in hatred. "Yes, he's a traitor to the country. He's supposed to be dead."

"It looks like he escaped somehow." People covered up death all the time, or at least in the movies they did, which was the closest thing I had to relate to this mess.

"I saw him get a bullet to the head."

I had nothing to respond with. Seeing someone shot … in the head … did put a finality to it. The hairs on my arms stood as I stared at the man who was supposed to be dead. This brought things to a new level of scary. "Oh."

"Yeah, oh. What the fuck is going on?" Bane typed furiously on the keyboard as a million different screens flitted across the screen. He sat back. "None of this makes sense. None of it." Bane stood and gently sat me back in the chair as he paced with his hand rubbing his neck. Ten steps to the left, turn, ten steps to the right, turn, repeat.

Stopping on a dime in the middle of his paces to the right, Bane jogged to the beat-up Land Cruiser. The sides were crunched in with the paint missing. It brought home the fact how we narrowly escaped. Taking my backpack and purse out of the car, Bane walked over to another counter across the room. He held a black wand thing over my bag. Nothing happened. Then he held it over my purse and a squealing noise occurred. I sat back in my chair, further fearing what that meant. Dumping out the contents, nothing else squealed except the purse.

Quickly Bane went back to the car, retrieving the bag he'd brought out of Security Branch. His bag was silent. Grabbing another stick, he pressed a button while holding it over my purse and I wasn't sure what happened. Only silence followed. My heart hammered in my chest as I waited to see what this meant. Putting all of his belongings and mine in the two backpacks, Bane came over to me where he unplugged a computer and smashed his cell phone. I jumped as the pieces splintered in every direction.

From a drawer he grabbed a filled duffel bag.

"We need to go. Now! I'll explain."

I stood, without question, on high alert. Bane may be dangerous, but I trusted him. If he wanted to do something to me, he would've left me to those crazy people or hurt me himself. All I wanted to do was escape somewhere to have a few minutes to process everything.

Carrying both backpacks and the duffel bag, Bane grabbed my hand and pulled me along. I had to run to keep up with him as we made our way past the metal bed and metal shelves. Bane stopped, released my hand and grabbed a larger duffel bag.

"Keep up with me, Maren. We need to get out of here now."

The fear from earlier returned, but I pushed myself to stay next to him. Whispering in case someone could hear us, I said, "I thought this place was safe."

"It's not."

Bane jogged through a door at the far end that led to a larger garage. Another black SUV that looked like it was hyped up on steroids sat shining.

"Get in."

Without hesitation, I got in the car, feeling like I was going to be sick at any moment. I fumbled nervously with the buckle as Bane cranked the car after throwing the bags in the back seat. The garage came open and we rapidly left. Casually, Bane drove, but scanned the area. I felt cold as I kept glancing out the window, waiting for someone to chase us again. Two blocks turned into five, which turned into eight. I wanted Bane to drive fast, but he kept with the speed limit. I hugged myself to keep from shaking.

Glancing back in the rearview mirror, Bane thundered, "Fuck!"

I jumped at the tone of his voice, feeling ice flood my veins. Daring a glance back to see what type of scene unfolded, the building was surrounded in black vehicles as men got out wearing what looked like bullet-proof vests. We'd been traced through my purse. The mysterious black truck pulled up. I glanced to Bane, whose knuckles were gripping the steering wheel to the point where one or the other was going to snap.

"Will you get my new cell out of the bag I grabbed from the desk?"

"Yes."

We were going within the speed limit. Leaning over the console I unzipped the bag with shaky fingers. It was hard controlling the fear. Bane obviously had years of practice with his overall ability to internalize his feelings. Within the bag, electronics and money were neatly stored. I took the cell and came upright into my seat.

I handed him the black phone. "Here you go."

Bane took it. "Thanks." With one hand, he hit a few buttons.

Re-fastening my seatbelt, I was ready to be somewhere safe. "What are you doing?"

"Burning the place down." Those ominous words spoken, without an ounce of emotion, were dreadful. I sunk back into my chair.

Knowing death and destruction were bound to happen at

some point, I still hated the fact of anyone losing a loved one. "Do you think there were any men in there?"

He shrugged. "Maren, this isn't a negotiation with them. If they found us, I'd be dead and who knows what the hell they would have done to you. I'm not letting anything happen to you. If that makes me a sadistic bastard for not caring about if someone died back there, so be it. They knew what they were coming against when they came on the mission to get me."

Merging onto the interstate, Bane sped up to the limit. "What made you think to check my purse?"

The blinker sounded as he maneuvered around a vehicle going under the limit. "Things were timed too perfectly when we arrived back at the hotel. They had to have a tracker on us. It would be too risky to put one on me. If I took you with me anywhere, your purse would be the one thing you'd grab."

All of this made my head hurt. It was like conspiracy theory times one-hundred. The constant calculating, planning, plotting was exhausting. "Where are we going?"

"To the train station. I'll book us tickets after a bit. We'll be able to get you on without showing an ID since I haven't had time to make you a false identity. They'll be monitoring all ticket purchases made within the first two hours. The first initial reaction for anyone is to flee."

I massaged the temples at my head. The one thing I knew was that I was safest with Bane. "Won't whoever is after us think the same thing?"

"They may. I'm not leaving from a station. We're going to North Carolina. Plus, running isn't my normal mode of operation."

"What is?"

"Bringing the fight to them." The sun set as the orange rays cast magnificently across the sky. I turned on the seat heater to chase away the chill that resided bone deep. Bane touched my leg. "Maren, I'm sorry I got you involved in whatever this is. I will keep you safe."

There was no mistaking the vow in his words. "I know. I feel safe with you."

I looked back out as the day turned into night. Weariness invaded my body and I let it take me under.

The lights from a parking garage woke me. Groggily, I tried to figure out where we were. Then, I remembered … Frankie … the chase … the people who were after us and I shot up in my seat erect.

Bane touched the side of my face and I leaned into him. "It's okay, Maren. We're in North Carolina at a parking garage outside of town. A cab is meeting us out front."

The soothing voice helped ground me, but I still felt out of sorts. The terror was ready to take seize of me if I let it. However, I knew that wouldn't help matters. All I wanted to do was forget temporarily. Sleeping in the car gave me that. I got out of the car and stretched, then became leery if someone was here watching me and leaned against the vehicle.

Bane came over to me, invading my space. "We're safe. If I thought there was a chance anyone would be here, we'd keep going. I made sure we weren't followed and there aren't any more bugs." Tears pricked my eyes, but I held back from losing it. "Let's get to the station, angel."

Leaning into Bane, we walked through the dimly lit parking garage that smelled of fumes and oil as Bane shouldered two large duffel bags I didn't recognize.

The car beeped as it locked and I glanced back to it. "Are you not afraid your car will get taken from here?"

"No. If it does, it does."

There was no telling how much money that vehicle cost, but that didn't seem to be a worry of Bane's. I followed Bane to the waiting yellow cab out front. Getting in, I was assaulted with the smell of stale cigarettes that turned my stomach. After putting the bags in the trunk, Bane got in beside me. Tucking myself into him, he wrapped his arms around me.

"Are you hungry?"

I shook my head. Food was the last thing I needed at this point. Silence engulfed us on our way to the station, which took about twenty minutes. The cab driver had the radio on to some sort of rap that only irritated my raw nerves. Bane soothingly stroked my arm and I felt his lips press against my head. "We'll get this figured out, angel."

"I know. I'm worried about my brother." Frankie was an ass, but he was blood. I was worried about him.

Bane let out a hard breath. "I'll try to find him. But, Maren ..." He paused and I glanced up at him. "I'm not letting him hurt you again."

A zing of something I hadn't experienced went through me. We were in the most terrifying time of my life and yet I didn't want my time with Bane to end. We'd been promised only a month, but things could be indefinite if we weren't able to figure things out. I had to keep my heart safeguarded. Being in this type of situation could easily lead to feelings.

The rest of the drive was silent as I tucked my face into Bane, engulfing myself in his scent. As we approached the city, horns honking became more frequent. The cab came to a stop at the train station. While I adjusted to the bright lights from the building, I squinted.

"Here, put this on." Bane handed me a red baseball hat and large black sweatshirt that must have come from his bag. While he paid the driver, I did as he asked. It felt new.

Bane put on a hat and sweatshirt also. The look was strange compared to his normal black sleek attire. The cabbie announced, "It'll be fifty-five forty."

After handing the driver some cash and instructing him to keep the change, we got out of the cab. The station had a few people milling in and out. Bane grabbed the bags and I followed him into the terminal. Overall, the place looked abandoned. A few old newspapers laid scattered about giving it an eerie feeling.

"Act like you know where you're going. Keep your head down and don't look up at anything. Otherwise, you'll draw attention to us."

Keeping a pleasant smile on my face, I looked forward as Bane guided me while the pale-yellow lights flickered.

It was hard not searching all the surroundings. Bane was able to see everything inconspicuously. "How long until our train?"

"Just under an hour. I purchased our tickets so all we should have to do is scan them from my phone. We're Chad and Jessica Parker."

Nearly fumbling at the implication of being married, I took a silent deep breath and let it out. I needed to lighten the situation up. "Wow, married. Just so you know, I'm not picking up your dirty underwear and you better put the toilet seat down after peeing."

Bane chortled and shook his head. "I'll see what I can do."

The train was more compact than I'd imagined as we climbed the steps to the second floor of the last car. I carried the backpack while Bane had two larger bags. The hall curved, revealing more hard vinyl grey walls. Doors made of metal were intermittently placed between compartments.

"This is us."

I was glad we were staying in a compartment car away from everyone else. It was hard not to be self-conscious of other people watching you while on the run. The room was tight and smelled of bleach tinged with an old newspaper smell. Along the far wall was a couch that turned into a bed with a fold down bed on top of that. A table for two sat against the opposite wall. Along the wall near the door, a bathroom was nestled in the corner. All of this fit into a space of about eight feet by eight feet. Quarters were ... tight.

"Home sweet home for how many days, Mr. Parker?"

"A little over two, Mrs. Parker." Another frown appeared on his face as he spoke and a little pain went through me at him not liking the thought. I knew it was stupid considering what this was. In the parking lot, he'd been more jovial about it. Mercurial mood swinger. I chose to ignore it and looked around the room again.

The door shut and a lock snapped. I felt the heat of Bane behind me and I stood my ground not moving back into him. That familiar need from the last time we had sex took root in my lower abdomen. The pent-up emotions I'd bottled away during all this needed an escape before they erupted. Sex would be my coping mechanism ... for now.

Bane's finger traced the edge of my collar bone as he

turned me to face him. The feather-light touch traced along the edge of my shirt. "Maren, if you want anything to stop say so. It won't change me helping you."

"Please don't stop."

He leaned down and murmured against my neck as I leaned back. Little goose bumps formed in the path of his fingers while a shiver passed through me. "I need to check the train. You have fresh clothes in the bag closest to us." I started to ask how, when he continued, "I called a department store on our way as we entered North Carolina. They got it ready. I told them to get you everything you'd need. I haven't checked it since they brought it to the car for me. Since it's late, there should be something to sleep in somewhere in the bag."

There was no telling how much this cost. "Thank you."

He nibbled my chin again and I could feel my desire growing as his stubble hit my skin. "I'll be back. Keep this locked. I'll knock like this when it's me." Bane did a succession of three quick knocks then two slow ones.

"Okay. I won't let anyone else in."

Bane grabbed a small bag from the duffel farthest from us and then left to check everything out. I shuddered thinking that after all that we'd done there could be more danger encountering us here. Jumping from a train at high speeds did not sound like something I wanted to experience.

All I wanted was to go back to a few days prior to being on the run—to the night that Bane and I first slept together. In all this chaos, I couldn't regret meeting Bane. Thinking about my life without the dark brooding man of few words seemed emptier.

Unfastening the buckles to the extra-large duffel, I peeked inside and nearly fell back in shock with the amount of clothes compactly packed inside. Stylish jeans, shirts, undergarments, a coat, and lingerie filled the bag. A black nightie caught my attention as I went through the stacks of clothes. Whoever picked out the clothes only chose sexually appealing outfits. A small giggle escaped.

Grabbing the silky piece, I headed to the restroom. As I was about to take off my shirt, the secret knock sounded at the door.

"Coming."

Opening the door, Bane gave me a straight face as he searched the room with his eyes. "All looks good." After locking the door, Bane added some sort of stiff wire to the lock while fastening it to a pole connected to the ceiling above that held the foldout bed. Testing the hold, he spoke. "Helps reinforce the door."

"Okay." The foreboding feeling of why we were here came back front and center. Hastily turning and wiping a tear that tried to escape, I entered the bathroom. "I was about to change. Thank you for the clothes. They're lovely."

As I closed the door, Bane called through it, "Good. I didn't have a chance to see what they picked, but I'm glad you're pleased with it."

Bane ran hot and cold. At times he was caring and a man who exuded a sexual prowess, and at other times he slid behind an impenetrable mask becoming an island state.

The space was limited in the restroom, but I managed to slip off my clothes and put on the black nightie. I ran my hand down the dark V of the lace that turned into a sheer organza fabric, showcasing the barely there panties. It was stunning as it slightly shimmered in the light. For the first time in a while, I felt sexy and wanton.

Stepping into the room, Bane typed a million miles an hour on the keyboard while he sat at the little table. To the right, the bed had been pulled down. Several little screens on the computer displayed different parts of the train.

Bane was dangerous. But, something about Bane hummed underneath my skin causing me to crave him more.

"I think I'm going to lay down for a bit." If Bane wanted me, he'd have to come and get me though I offered myself up on a silver platter in my scantily clad outfit.

Bane glanced up, about to speak, then stopped as he devoured my body. "I need to personally thank whoever picked out your clothes."

"Do you like it?"

I twirled and stopped short. Bane prowled toward me. "I'm about to fuck you in it."

Not having a chance to respond, Bane kissed me with a fierceness as he lifted me up while my legs hooked around his hips. A thud sounded as we slammed against the wall. Bane pulled a condom out of his pocket and put it between his teeth to tear open the foil. The ripping sound elicited a moan of want. Holding me with one hand, Bane managed to get his pants undone and the condom on.

Impressive.

The train moved as we tumbled to the wall near the door. The cups to my nightie were pushed down, hoisting my breasts up. Bane pushed inside me in one deep thrust as he sucked my nipple.

"Ahh!" I felt stretched to the max.

His breathing was labored. "Are you okay?"

"Yes. Keep going. I'll adjust."

The pace became relentless as the ridged length stroked my inner walls. Our breathing labored as we raced to a release that would help ease the tension of the day. This numbed me from all the other harsh facts we were dealing with. This was the escape Bane promised me. Euphoria.

I gave myself over to Bane as he hit the spot within me one more time, eliciting a pleasure-filled moan as I came around his dick. Bane growled as he bit my shoulder; that only lengthened my own orgasm, hearing him come undone inside me.

"Angel, fuck. I needed that."

"Me, too."

Breathless, we held onto each other as I let my mind stay numb.

CHAPTER

13

BANE

I TOOK A sip of bourbon as I watched Maren sleep in the suspended foldout bed. Her brunette hair feathered out on the pillow. She truly looked angelic and peaceful. *Angel.* I shook my head from my thoughts and checked the monitors again. All was clear.

I'd placed portable cameras at various parts on the train as well as a few trip wires. If anyone tried to land on the top of the train, I'd know.

Eric-fucking-Thornhill was alive. Anger simmered to the surface as I went through all the damning evidence of his betrayal that lead to Jasmine and Faith's death. My little girl had never been given a fighting chance to survive. It was because of me they'd both been sentenced to death. My presence alone caused that. I couldn't let someone else innocently die because of me.

Maren shifted and the black nightie rode up higher as the blanket fell down. My dick instantly hardened. I stared at her creamy white skin. For what we'd been through, Maren had been a trooper.

Earlier, when she'd referenced us being married, a sickening knot formed in my stomach for the things I wanted. *Once wanted*, I clarified mentally. Any thoughts of marriage or kids were gone. I didn't deserve those things. My fate had been sealed when I watched our unborn child die in her mother's womb.

Focus back on the task, Bane. This isn't a walk down memory-fucking-lane. The last thing I needed was for my nightmares to make themselves known. If I slept in forty-five minute increments I should be fine.

At some point when it was secure, I needed to call Sarge at Black Division and talk to Hampton. Sarge would blow a fucking gasket knowing that a traitor was alive.

Since Maren fell asleep, I'd searched public records to see if there was any chance of a twin. Nothing looked out of place. How did someone survive a bullet to the head? That was the damn fucking question of the day.

In Colorado, at my cabin, I had proper equipment with secure links to look further into this mess. Maren and I would be safe there. No one knew of the cabin. Eric and whoever else was involved were probably in the final stages of being organized. With the other fake tickets I'd bought in several states, they'd be looking for a needle in a haystack to find us. Once we got to the cabin, I'd feel better. Having Maren with me was a game changer.

"Bane?" Maren sleepily raised her head. "Come to bed, it's late."

I hadn't slept in the same bed with anyone since Jasmine. I wasn't sure if I could do it as my heart went to my throat. Was I betraying her memory?

Maren got out of bed and came down the steps, her lingerie riding up until she stepped away from the ladder. I finished off the rest of my bourbon. Coming to straddle my lap, Maren didn't say a word. Hell I wanted her again. Watching me, asking me for permission her hands roamed to the hem of my shirt. The shirt bunched and came over my head, baring my chest to her.

Prominent scars from the years of fighting looked like a war zone on my chest. Leaning in, Maren kissed them as her hands caressed my body. I was speechless as I fell under her spell, letting the warmth of her touch spread. My belt was undone, followed by the zipper coming down. The noise loud in our otherwise quiet compartment. I was commando and my dick sprung free, hard as a tire iron.

Petite fingers rubbed the tip as we looked down, watching the drip of pre-cum escape. Maren massaged it around. Sexy as hell. As I looked at her face, a shy smile graced her lips. The heat from her pussy beckoned my dick. Leaning back slightly, she pulled the nightie over her head, revealing perfectly perky tits.

She stood. And I went to protest, but her finger came to my lips. "Come to bed. Bring the condoms."

Gloriously, her naked, toned ass shimmied up the steps. I turned on the sound alert to my phone, shucked my jeans, and grabbed a handful of condoms. Over the next two days, I had a feeling neither one of us would be able to walk. By the time I made it to the ladder, I'd already sheathed myself.

Laying sprawled across the bed, gloriously naked, Maren opened for me. I touched her pussy making sure she was wet and ready. Earlier, I'd taken her when I'd become consumed by her. Seemed like Maren needed it as bad as me.

I felt the wetness and she groaned. "You're wet, angel."

"Because I need you."

Those words vibrated through me as I positioned myself above her, ramming in. Maren grabbed on to my shoulders and held on. When I was with Maren, nothing else mattered but bringing her pleasure. In and out. Faster. Harder. Sweat formed between our bodies. I fucked us to oblivion.

"Angel," I said as a prayer on my lips. The release was like no other, but left me craving more of her. The thought sobered me. Going to get off the bed, I disengaged our bodies.

Maren pulled me closer. "I won't bite. I won't get the wrong idea. You need to sleep."

Apprehensively, I took off the condom before lying beside her. Legs intertwined with mine as Maren cocooned herself around me. "I'm so glad I remembered those condoms."

I chuckled. Out of all the things in the hotel room, she packed the condoms. "Me, too, angel."

"Why do you call me that?"

"Because that was one of the first thoughts I had about you when we first saw each other at Discrete Encounters." I slid my fingers up and down her spine, melting her further into me.

She yawned against my chest. "Do you think we were setup from the beginning?"

That was what I needed to look into next. "I don't know how they'd of known we'd be attracted to each other like we are."

"I thought I'd lost my mind that day in Discrete Encounters with the magnetic pull I felt." It was hard to contain the smile. We were helpless against each other. If we'd seen each other anywhere, I was sure it would've ended with us in bed together. Once would not have been enough.

"Any regrets?" I hoped to hell she didn't regret anything.

Her hand came up and caressed my cheek, intensifying the moment. "I don't regret anything in my life. It's what makes us who we are—the good, the bad, the ugly."

I didn't respond because I was the *bad* and the *ugly* in people's lives. The sharp pain of remembering Jasmine being able to see past my faults sobered me. This was too much. After Maren fell asleep, I'd slip out of bed and catch some sleep on the couch.

Arms tightened around me as I came to. Light seeped through the drawn curtains. What time was it? I looked at my watch and saw it was after eight. Hell, I'd slept four hours. I'd slept with Maren. My instinct was to pop out of bed like I'd planned. Maren nuzzled into me, still fast asleep and I stayed put while I worked on relaxing my now rigid muscles.

Bane, calm the fuck down.

I waited for the guilt to assault me. It happened every time after I slept with someone—like I betrayed Jasmine. That feeling had yet to consume me like it normally did. The lack of guilt bothered me. I deserved to pay for what I'd done for as long as I lived. I hadn't pulled the trigger, but I'd led them to my family.

Discrete Encounters had been involved, but the question that bothered me was if Hampton set all this in motion. Or was Hampton a pawn in this game of revenge? It was shitty of me to think he'd betrayed me after all we'd been through, but I trusted no one. I hoped to hell that wasn't the case.

There was no one else I could call that I either trusted or wanted to drag into the middle of this mess. With Eric Thornhill still alive, there was no telling who else he'd sold me out to with the amount of intel I knew he'd given the drug cartel.

"You're tense." The sexy sleep-ridden voice had my dick stiffening and pushing away my other thoughts.

Not commenting, I rolled Maren onto her back and grabbed a condom from the pouch where I'd put the stash I'd brought to bed last night. Grabbing the wrapper, Maren tore it. "How many more of these do we have?"

"Not near enough."

Sucking on her neck, Maren fumbled as she tried to roll on the condom. "Bane, I can't concentrate."

"You'll get it." I moved farther down to her nipple, gliding my tongue around the area. Her hand fell from my dick only rolling the condom on halfway. I traded nipples while finishing the job for her. Maren was boneless to my assault. Lining myself up, I took her mouth as I pressed against her core, entering at an achingly slow pace.

As her heat closed around me we moaned in unison, seeking that release that let us escape.

Breakfast had been delivered. An array of muffins and fruit laid on the small table. There wasn't much in the choice of food on the train, but hopefully Maren liked some of this. I'd relocated the surveillance equipment.

Maren was in the shower as I checked all the cameras. None of the alerts went off through the night. I took a sip of coffee. What I needed to do would have to wait until Colorado. With the sound of the train, I couldn't make a phone call. And the connection wasn't secure enough to investigate in depth.

Coming out in fresh clothes, Maren sat at the table. Delicately, she tore the wrapper and ate. For now, the fewer people who saw us the better.

"Any progress?"

A frustrated sigh escaped. "Nothing new. I've combed over my saved files of Eric's death and there's nothing out of place. Everything down to the tattoo on his hand matches the photos."

I spun the computer around to pull up the two photos side by side only showing the hands. One was from the day Eric Thornhill supposedly died and the other was from my house when he'd looked into the camera.

It was a small tattoo of a double infinity symbol.

Cocking her head, Maren studied the photo. "Wow. They are the same."

"Yeah, it doesn't make a damn bit of sense." I scrubbed a hand down my face as the train temporarily stopped at a station. A few people boarded. Continuing, I added, "The timing feels off for everything. Why introduce us and then come after us right away? Frank was not in control of himself. Anger took over and eliminated his rational thinking. The guy in the back of the truck was clearly agitated with him when he came down. I'm not sure if he was meant to stall me or not expose his hand so soon."

Maren took a pensive sip of orange juice. The long-sleeve shirt hugged her tits. I wanted to take her again. Hell, my need was only growing and I needed to get control over it. "Is there anyone you can think of that would want to hurt you?"

"The right information in the right hands. Yeah, there are

a lot of people out there. With what I did, the job I had before walking away, I made enemies except my identity wasn't known." Rubbing my forehead, I knew I'd never be free of my past unless I completely vanished.

Maren's eyes grew a little wider. "Oh."

"Yeah, angel. I'm dangerous." There was no mistaking the truth in my voice.

"I don't think you'd hurt me. You're a good person, Bane." Her voice was small as she looked down. I wasn't sure if that meant she didn't believe her words or didn't want to see my reaction.

"No. I'm not. I'm as bad as they come, angel. But, I'll keep you safe."

I would not fail this time.

CHAPTER

14

MAREN

THE TRAIN STOPPED in Denver, Colorado. A whistle sounded letting the passengers know it was okay to disembark. After being cooped-up for two days, I was done with trains. We hadn't left the confines of our room the entire time. The nearly nonstop sex had been a distraction, but Bane was restless like a caged beast. In the two days we'd traveled, no new information had been discovered due to the limitations of Bane being able to connect securely. Technology was not my thing.

"Remember, keep your head down," Bane instructed me as I put the cap down on my head.

I wore the sweatshirt and ball cap I'd worn to board the train. "Yes. I'll stay close."

For the last hour, Bane drilled in what I was supposed to do almost sergeant like. He'd been colder and barely touched me since we'd woken up entangled together. With my back-pack secured on my shoulders, Bane came behind me with the two other bags.

Slipping his aviator glasses in place, Bane told me, "Stay close."

"I will." I followed Bane off the platform. The fresh air invigorated me. Though the air was chilly, I stopped myself from leaning my face back into the sun to absorb it. How I missed feeling the direct light against my cheeks.

The station was busy. There was a large group of adults following a group sign for skiing. Bane absorbed us into their group. Keeping my head down, the group animatedly talked around us about the slopes and their plans once they got to the resort. I envied their situation. The tourists were here for pleasure while I was here to stay away from some covert peo-ple that wanted to capture us.

All of the sudden, I felt exposed and leaned farther into Bane. "Are you okay?" His voice was low, concerned.

"Yes. I'm fine. I want to get out of here."

Winding our way through the terminal, Bane flagged a taxi.

As we got in, the driver asked, "Where to?"

"Twenty-third and fifth." Bane gave the directions with-out hesitation. Yesterday, I saw him poring over Denver maps while marking locations.

The cab driver sped off. "Yes, sir."

This cab was cleaner than the last one and smelled of cheap air fresheners. I stayed silent as we made our way through the city. Snow-covered mountains created the perfect scenic backdrop as we wound our way through the city. I'd never been to Denver before. Honestly, I'd never left the state of Georgia except for once when we went on a family vacation to Pensacola, Florida.

Looking at the far-off mountain range, I wondered which mountain we were headed to. I knew we were headed to a cabin in the woods. Another safe house. Hopefully this one proved safer than the last. To have this many escapes options meant one thing … Bane had more enemies than I could comprehend.

The cab stopped and Bane paid the thirty-six dollars in cab fare. Disembarking, Bane headed down the street. "We're catching another cab."

"Okay." This felt like a game of cat and mouse. With his authoritative tone, I didn't ask any questions. I wasn't in the mood to poke the bear.

Hopping in another cab, Bane gave another street intersection. We did this five more times. I felt like I'd gone in circles. Bane was distant as he scanned the streets. He needed more time than the average person to reflect. Since this morning, he'd slipped away and distanced himself from me. There were demons he battled. What Demons? I wasn't sure, but if I could help I wanted to. It was the least I could do.

The cab pulled to the curb of a restaurant. I was hungry, but doubted we'd be dining here. Bane grabbed our bags. "This way."

I nodded. Exhaustion from the stress and day's events seemed to seep into me. "Are we close?"

"We're getting the car. If they happen to find we came to Denver, using different cab lines and multiple stops will make it nearly impossible to trace us."

A chain-link fence started on the edge of a property that housed climate-controlled storage units. Bane punched a code and we entered the gravel lot. The area was quiet overall which was expected for a Wednesday afternoon. In the middle of the section we came to a door. Bane punched another code, raising the door. Another black shiny SUV sat. With the hood propped up, cables attached to the battery.

"Hop in. Let me unhook the trickle charge. Keeps the battery from going dead. I'm going to place an order for groceries while I finish packing the car."

I did as he asked, buckling myself. A sense of dread came over me. The last two times I'd gotten in a vehicle similar to this we'd ended up in car chases and a building on fire. On the wall there were shelves with more black bags. Bane grabbed three and put them in the back. Bane talked to the grocer as he walked around the room, grabbing a few things and depositing them in the car.

Getting in the vehicle, the call ended. "Thank you. I'll be by in twenty minutes to pick everything up. Yes. Thanks."

Cranking the car, we left the area. "I ordered us groceries. I figured you might like some fresh food over the MRE's I have at the cabin."

Meals Ready to Eat. I'd heard of those and they did not sound appetizing. "I'll cook us something when we get there."

"Sounds good." Bane focused on the road giving no indication to his mood. When he called me *angel* or promised to protect me, there was a softness about him. A softness I wanted more of, but disappeared today. With our situation, I should avoid those thoughts. We were escaping with each other. Nothing more.

Nearing the outskirts of town, Bane pulled into a small grocery store parking lot. He dialed someone. "I'm here. Black SUV. How much? Thank you."

A few minutes later, a pudgy man wheeled out a cart filled to the brim with white sacks of food. Popping out of the vehicle, Bane transferred the food to the back. There was some small chit-chat. Nothing I could make out. Paying the man,

Bane talked to him for a couple of minutes more before getting back into the car and driving off.

Bane mentioned, "Looks like there's a blizzard coming tonight. They're expecting eight to ten inches."

"That's more snow than I've ever seen." The normal pep in my voice was gone as we continued to talk about trivial things. In Georgia, it was rare to get snow. When we did, the city shutdown not having the proper equipment.

The road turned from four lanes to two and became curvy as we ascended into the mountain areas. Snow-covered trees encapsulated the road, almost creating a fairytale picture.

"It's beautiful here."

"It is. I think you'll like where we're going even under the circumstances. It's peaceful."

Turning right on a nearly imperceptible road, the brush dragged along the side of the car. I cringed knowing little scratches were happening to the pristine coat of paint. Cars seemed disposable to Bane.

As dusk set, Bane made another turn. Five minutes later, a small cabin sat nestled on a ridge. To the left was a shed Bane pulled into. Spider webs and dust covered the shelves. This would take a bit to clean out.

"It's been awhile since you've been here." It wasn't a question, but a fact from all the dirt.

"Nearly four years since I bought it and set it up."

Four years. I guess a safe house wouldn't be on your list of frequent visits or vacations. "Do you think it's still livable inside?"

He nodded as he looked out into the area. "This place is monitored through a secured network I own. Everything looked operable the last time I logged in. If not, I have the tools to fix it."

Grabbing my stuff, I got out of the vehicle and waited for Bane. Two snowmobiles sat to the right. After not being here for four years, how long would it take to get everything running? He grabbed a few of the duffels. "I'll get the rest once we get settled and the generator going. There's barrels of pure gasoline in the back of the shed that will keep the place going for months."

"Months? What about my jobs? I need to tell someone." We could be here for months? I wasn't sure how I felt about a lengthened trip in nowhere land. Especially with a withdrawn Bane. Would they worry about me? I wasn't sure. The turnover for the types of jobs I did were high. Sometimes people simply quit showing up.

"Angel, I don't think it'll take months. I have enough supplies here to survive. You can't call your jobs. I'm sorry, but you can't. We can't take the risk." There was the nickname again that came out of nowhere with a semi-softened tone. I chose to ignore it with everything else I tried to process. Since leaving the train, the reality of the situation continued to sink in. I'd been in a bubble on the train and now it was popped.

Bane was right, there was nothing I could do about the jobs.

Through the snow, I followed Bane. Only a few inches were on the ground. After tonight I would probably feel snowed-in with how much was expected to fall. As I looked closer, the wood cabin had a steel door and shutters. This was more than a cabin. Bane used a key and unlocked the deadbolt. Sheets covered the furniture and more dust showered every surface. There was less dust than in the shed, probably from everything being sealed better. Bane sat our things down. "Let me get a fire started to warm the place. Then, I'll get the generator going. We'll have power, water, and appliances then."

"Sounds good." Bane watched me for a second like he wanted to say more. Instead, he turned and busied himself.

The cabin was one large room. Wandering through the place, I realized this was going to be my residence indefinitely. After a little tender loving care, I believed this place could feel … homey. The kitchen sat at the far back with a dining area to the right. A desk with more technical equipment was to the far left. And the rest was open living space.

Bane went back outside without saying a word. In the middle of the far left wall, next to the fire place, was a door. I opened it and peered in. More sheets covered the furniture. A large bed sat against the wall in between two steel-plated covered windows. Along the left wall a dresser sat between two doors. I probably should ask for permission to look, but I didn't.

The left door housed a laundry room. A small washer and dryer along with a large dead-bolted cabinet sat undisturbed. As I came back out, I noticed my trail of footprints in the dust on the floor. Cleaning was a priority. To the right of the dresser was a medium-sized bathroom. The tub was rust-free unlike my previous place. I hoped one night I'd be able to soak. It had been a while since I'd relaxed in a bath since in my apartment I'd worn flip flops to the shower not wanting to touch the tub.

Coming back in the main room, Bane nearly had a fire going. "I like your place."

"It'll do." He stood. "Before I lose all daylight, I need to get the generator going."

"No problem. I'll make myself at home." On the way to the front door Bane stiffened and froze for half-a-second. I wasn't sure what I'd said, but I wasn't going to push. Without responding, he left. And all the softness from the shed was gone. Distant Bane was back.

I wasn't sure what to make of his actions. As I surveyed the room, I knew how to keep myself busy. Bane Bradley needed time to process some things on his mind. And I needed to make sure my boundaries were reinforced.

CHAPTER
15

BANE

"DAMN IT ALL to hell!"

The generator in the back of the cabin groaned in protest. I'd been working on getting it going for a while. Between the rubber rot in the fuel line and the carburetor, the generator had been a bitch to start. The problem now was the choke hanging.

"Work, you son of a bitch!" I took the pull start and yanked it.

Vroom. Vroom. Vroom.

The generator came to life and gained strength. We had power. I added more gas to the tank and sat for a second. I knew I'd been a bastard to Maren this afternoon. Those last two days on the train had been too intimate with us sleeping together at night after she'd coax me to stay after a round of serious fucking. Man, I had hardly been able to keep my hands off her.

Then, this morning. Fuck, this morning. I'd woken up wrapped around her like a vine. She'd been in my dreams last night as we laid on the beach and made love. Made love. No, we fucked. There was no love making.

Then, Maren called the cabin home. *Home.* There was no such place anymore. Those words got people hurt. This was a safe house. A means to an end. When I'd killed all those assholes after me this time, I'd help Maren disappear. Then, I'd walk away from her and not look back. There was no straying from the motto. The motto of not having anything in my life I couldn't walk away from kept everyone safe. If only I'd never gone to Alaska. Jasmine and Faith would be alive. Without me. But, nonetheless alive.

I leaned against the wood wall and let out a breath trying to rid my body of the restless energy. Now that the generator worked, I'd unload the car and get the place cleaned up. Looking at my watch, I noticed I'd been gone for a couple of hours. Shit. Abruptly, I stood and dashed to the cabin. It was dark. Maren was probably scared.

Entering the cabin, I came to a halt. Candles and a few lanterns were lit giving enough light to see. The place was spotless. Maren came out of the bedroom and screamed when she saw me. "Oh my gosh. Bane. You scared the shit out of me. I didn't hear you come in."

Her hair was thrown on top of her head. Dust streaked her face. She looked beautiful in the dim light. I wanted her.

Nervously, she continued, "I cleaned up the place a little bit. I hope that was okay. I found some vinegar, a broom, and a mop in the closet."

"It's fine. I got the generator going." My tone came out harsher than I intended. I flipped the switch and the power came on.

Maren tucked an escaped hair behind her ear. "Once we have water, I'll get the dishes cleaned. Tomorrow I can wash all the sheets that covered the furniture to get the dust out."

Going to the sink, I hoped the water pump still worked. Digging through frozen ground to fix it was the last thing I wanted to do tomorrow. I lifted the facet knob. It sputtered. Then water flowed freely through the nozzle. *Finally, a break.* "We've got water." My tone was hollow and ice.

Why was I being such a jackass?

I turned and Maren was within inches. "I'll wash the dishes."

"Maren, I don't expect you to be my maid. You don't have to do anything. The cabin looks great." There, that was better. More appreciative sounding.

Watching me closely, she asked, "What happened today? Why are you being so cold to me?"

Leaning against the counter, I scrubbed a hand down my face. "Maren, I like fucking you. Maybe too much. But, I don't want you to get any false pretenses. When all this is over, when I know you're safe, it all ends. We go our separate ways. I don't want living together to bring some false sense that something has changed."

Her eyes narrowed. "I haven't given you any impression that I wanted more, Bane. Not once! I've been a human to you and that's it. I'm not some desperate girl who doesn't know the score. I'm fully aware we're simply fucking. But that's fine, we can become roomies until you sort through whatever mess this is."

With an animated turn, Maren stalked toward the bedroom. "I'm going to bed."

The door slammed.

"Fuck," I muttered to myself knowing I deserved all that. Maren wasn't the one running hot and cold and sending mixed signals. I was.

Shit!

Tomorrow I'd try to make things right between us. It looked like it was the couch for me. That was better anyway. I'd get the car unpacked, computers up and running and catch a few hours of sleep. Distance was a good thing.

***

I pulled Jasmine, but nothing happened. Dead weight was all I was greeted with. Turning back, I had a sickening feeling I wasn't willing to admit. Before my eyes, Jasmine was slumped over as a red pool of blood spread into the white snow from her head.

Grabbing her shoulders, I brought her to me. "No! No! No! Baby, wake up!"

Jasmine laid before me. Lifeless. Dead.

Sobs erupted from me. "NOOOO!"

Everything worth living for was fading in this moment. I had to be there for my little girl as her movements faded. "Faith, I'm here! I'm here, Faith! Daddy is here!"

There was nothing I could do. Helpless. I prayed for a miracle as I begged, "Baby, don't leave me! Please don't leave me!"

"I'm so sorry. I'm so sorry."

Nothing I did brought Jasmine or Faith back.

"Bane! Bane! Wake up!"

I stirred as the darkness let go. A pressure shook my shoulders and my defenses went on alert as I sprung, putting the body underneath me. With a firm grip on the person's neck, I squeezed. Who the hell was with me? Who the hell entered my place? Whoever the asshole was would see what happens when you break and enter.

A gasp and a soft barely audible voice rasped out as the person squirmed beneath me, "Bane, it's Maren."

Realizing I was at the cabin, not in my house, I let go of Maren and fell back onto the floor. She coughed. I'd hurt her. Shit! A slight tremor took over me. Gasping for breath, I righted myself. I'd never been woken up from the nightmare before.

"Maren, angel, I'm so sorry. I—I—" Stopping, I wasn't sure what I wanted to say. The nightmares disappeared when I slept in the bed with Maren. I thought I'd be safe. Those words couldn't be voiced.

She knelt in front of me, keeping a small distance. "It's okay. I'm okay. My dad had nightmares like that. We couldn't wake him and had to let him come to. He served in the military, and from time to time, the memories of the past haunted his dreams. I won't wake you again."

Still afraid to speak and let my tone betray me, I nodded. I'd known Maren's dad had been a marine when I did a background check. A damn fine one. "Bane, why don't you take a shower and come to bed?"

"Maren—"

Cutting me off, Maren bent a little lower to meet my down-casted eyes. "Bane, it's fine. If you have one again, I won't wake you. The bed will be more comfortable."

I felt like a total dick for how I'd treated her earlier. First, I needed to shake the nightmare. Get it out of my system. Running it all out wasn't an option. I wasn't leaving Maren by herself. "A shower sounds good."

My skin felt cold and clammy. Maren didn't say a word as she got a towel out of the sealed container in the bathroom, laid it on the counter, then left. The water turned on and I waited for it to run. Soon steam filled the bath and I stripped out of my clothes. The nightmares always left me out of sorts.

I catalogued all the memories like I normally did to help me process the lost, but all I could think about was Maren. My body craved to be insider her to escape. I didn't want to remember. I wanted to forget.

Fisting my dick, I pumped it a few times remembering her tight heat. Base to tip I touched myself. It wasn't as good as the real thing, but it worked. The nightmare faded as I focused on the brunette beauty.

The shower curtain slid over and Maren came in naked. She looked down at my hand palming myself. The familiar heat passed through her eyes and my dick grew harder in my hands.

"Let me."

I let go of my dick. Her fingers came out, stroking the tip. Water beaded down her creamy skin. Needing to bring Maren to pleasure first, I reached for her. "No, Bane. This is for you. Only you."

"Maren—"

A finger touched my lips shushing me. "Let me do this for you."

Touching my balls with one hand, Maren moved them in an erotic fashion that had my dick pulsing. With her other hand she stroked me. I took her mouth, forcefully moving and pushed her against the wall away from the shower spray. The strokes came faster, my balls tightened, and I couldn't get enough of her tongue.

"Maren …"

I needed this.

I needed her.

Like this.

Right now.

She'd known how to soothe me.

The familiar draw came and let go as I came undone under Maren's touch. The kiss softened and I disengaged our mouths, looking down at my now semi-hard dick. Maren's stomach had my cum spread across it.

"You've got a good aim." She gave a little giggle as the substance moved down. It was fucking hot.

Something feral came alive in me seeing part of myself on Maren.

"This was for you tonight, Bane. Come to bed when you're done." The woman was going to drive me mad with lust.

Giving me a quick kiss on the cheek, Maren stepped under the shower spray and washed me off of her. All I saw was her spreading me into her skin.

I'd marked her. I'd fucking marked her. And worse part yet … I liked it.

CHAPTER

16

MAREN

CHANGING INTO MY pajamas, I brushed my now wet hair as the erratic beating of my heart slowed. Seeing Bane's evidence of passion on me was sexy. In the shower, I felt like I belonged to him. Before he could see it in my eyes, I'd rinsed off and left. I would stay true to my word and not make this into more than it was. Though my heart wanted to heal Bane, I knew I couldn't change him.

His tattoo was exquisite. It was the first time I'd been able to look at it. The geometric shapes formed a dragon. In the train, I'd only seen it a few times but couldn't tell exactly what it was. I wondered what the reason behind it was. Tattoos always seemed to have some sort of meaning to them. The dragon started at the left hip and wound up to his back finishing at the base of his neck where the tail was.

Remembering to take my birth control pills, I grabbed them from my purse. I normally took them as I got ready for bed. Taking them in the morning always left me feeling off all day.

"What's that?"

Bane's voice startled me as I looked at the pale pink compact in my hand. "It's … umm … my birth control."

"Oh. Good. Yeah, that's real good."

At a loss for words, I smirked at Bane. "You have sex with me every which way on a train and me taking birth control embarrasses you?" A small snicker escaped.

He shook his head in amusement as he dragged a hand over his head and yawned. Going to the freshly made bed, I pulled back the covers. "Let's go to sleep."

Without saying a word, I got in bed and Bane flipped off the lights. I felt a depression in the bed moments later. Bane was distant, but contemplative. Probably making a game plan for all we had to do in the morning.

"Night, Maren."

"Night, Bane."

How I wished he'd hold me like he had the last couple of nights when we were on the train. The space remained between us which was probably good for my head and heart. The darkness closed in as I succumbed to sleep.

Light peeped into the room as I stretched my muscles and reached across the bed. All I found were cold sheets, abandoned long ago. Through the night, I'd woken up from the heat of Bane's body as he held me. At some point during the night he'd moved close to me and I'd relished him holding me tightly. Staying awake for as long as I could, I felt his chest expand with each breath. Eventually, the soothing motion soon sent me back to sleep.

Through the walls, I could hear Bane watching footage of something. Probably security footage of one of the places we'd been. Bane had been keeping close tabs to see if anyone followed our tracks. So far we were in the clear.

After what he'd said in the kitchen last night, the shower incident, and him holding me through the night, I wanted to give him some space. Shower, first I'd take a shower.

The hot water felt soothing as I let it work my loose muscles. After the shower, I'd face reality again. And see if I could understand where Bane's head was at. The emotional whiplash was getting old.

Drying off, I dressed in a pair of jeans and green sweater that hugged my figure. It was time to face the grumpy beast as I headed into the living room. Several computer screens were illuminated along the back wall. The snug-fitted black shirt hugged his body as he stood over the table looking at documents.

"Good morning."

Bane took a sip of coffee. "Morning. Did you sleep okay?"

"Yes, I was very … warm." Bane stopped and looked at me before going back to work.

Irritating ass. If I stripped down, I bet he'd be all over me and calling me *angel* and what not. I scoffed as I went to the kitchen. Bane loaded the cabinets after I'd gone to bed last night in frustration. The kitchen was well-stocked with enough food to last us awhile. Deciding on something easy, I got out the ingredients to make pancakes. I could make a batch and freeze the leftovers for later on since Bane didn't seem to eat breakfast or he hadn't while we were on the train.

Bane casually would peek glances at me, but would quickly focus back on the task at hand. As the batter sizzled in the skillet, I rolled my eyes. Whatever crawled up his ass drove me insane. Finding the peanut butter and syrup, I slathered both on in modest amounts before taking a bite.

The silence interrupted by irritated sighs brought an angry boil to the subsurface. Finishing the last of my pancake, I cleaned up the kitchen. I came and stood at the table where Bane alternated looking between maps and his computer.

"So are we back to ignoring each other?"

Bane paused, confusion passing over his features. "I'm not ignoring you. I'm working."

"Right. You've said all of like five words to me this morning. Much different from the train or was that because I let you fuck me every five minutes?" Clearly his words from last night still rubbed me raw, even after the intimate moment in the shower.

Bane's jaw set. "You say you know the score, but you're acting like a clingy emotional girlfriend that needs attention. If all we were doing was fucking it wouldn't matter if I said nothing to you." That smug look nearly sent me over the edge. There was something completely off with him since we'd arrived. This version was an asshole.

Involuntarily, my hand slapped his face. With his jaw tense, he rubbed the now reddened area with his hand. "Fuck you, asshole. You're the only one I can talk to out here in the middle of nowhere. I'm sorry I'm not a stone-cold trained secret agent person!" Turning on my heel, I stalked toward the bedroom. Before I closed the door, I looked back at Bane who stood there with a stunned look. "Don't worry, I'll stay out of your way."

"Maren—" I shut the door and leaned against it before he could finish and tears pricked the back of my eyes. Until this moment, I had never felt cheap with Bane. Technically, we were each other's escape, but I demanded respect. I would not be demeaned.

Restless, I started the first load of laundry before I laid down on the bed. I wasn't tired, but I refused to go back out there. Bane made no attempt to come apologize. *Jerk.* Someone had done a number on Bane in his past unless it was the years of doing whatever he did that hardened him.

After tossing and turning for who knows how long, my mind slowed and I let myself fall to sleep.

Stretching, I glanced at my watch. It was after lunch time. I'd nearly been immobile since coming into the bedroom. Moving the clothes from the washer to the dryer, I washed a new load. There were probably still two to three loads that needed to be done from the sheets that covered the house.

Ready to leave the confines of the bedroom, I made my way out into the living area. No one was out there. The computer screens against the wall were black. There was no telling where Bane was. The fire crackled in the fire place and the vinegar smell from cleaning dissipated. Peeking out the window, the grocery store man had been right. The snow looked significantly deeper. I'd never been in snow that deep before.

My lips turned up in a smile as I thought about making a snow angel. We'd never gotten enough snow in Georgia to make a good angel since we could always see the tips of the grass still. Heading to the bedroom, I grabbed my heavy coat, hat, and gloves, courtesy of my new wardrobe I'd acquired on the way to the train station.

Opening the door, the cold brisk air greeted me. I welcomed it, letting it refresh and invigorate me. With my boots on, I stepped out into the snow and nearly squealed in excitement as I sunk into the six or so inches of pure white powder.

Like a school girl, I took off running through the small yard. We were in a heavily-wooded area. The snow was powdery as I kicked through it. Nearly out of breath, I stopped and looked at the beauty. It was pure, clean and refreshing. Closing my eyes, I held out my hands and leaned back as I fell back into the snow.

Moving my legs and arms in and out, I made my first-ever snow angel. A giggle escaped as I enjoyed the moment. Dad read a story about a little girl who loved to make snow angels. This was better than I'd imagined. For a second, I pretended there were no problems as I fluttered my limbs about. With my eyes closed, I felt a shadow stand over of me. I stopped moving as the butterflies danced in my stomach. He came for me.

"I was an ass, I'm sorry."

The deep voice stirred within me. Peeking my eyes open, I found Bane looking at me with an apologetic face, his shades tucked into the top of his shirt. "Yes, you were."

"What do you want from me, Maren?"

"To lay down and make snow angels with me."

Bane looked at me quizzically. I nodded my head to the side. It would be his decision, I wouldn't press. The cold snow seeped into my pants, but I wanted to see what Bane decided. In a sense, this would give me an answer on if we were to stay at arm's length apart or continue having fun together. After long minutes he moved to my left where he sat. "You want me to make snow angels with you?"

"Yes. Only if you want."

A small wrinkle marred his forehead. It was hard fighting the chill that set in my bones, but I waited. Hesitantly, Bane laid back and glanced at my position as he mirrored it. A smile spread across my face.

"Now what?"

"Move your hands and arms like this." I demonstrated and Bane followed my movements, a happy expression crossing over his features.

Stopping, we were eye to eye. "Are you ready to see our angels?"

"Sure thing, angel."

My smile grew wider at my nickname and how fitting it was. I loved the name angel from Bane. My only other nickname had been ruined by my brother.

Carefully standing, we turned to look at the angels before us. Our feet and arms touched, joining us together where there was no separation between us.

"You bring out feelings I shouldn't have. I can't have them."

I turned to Bane and grabbed his hand, bringing him out of whatever thought he was lost in. Snow started falling heavy. Any trace of my snow angel would be gone within a few hours. "Why?"

The look of pain that crossed his face tore through me. The scars were deeper than I'd imagined as his tormented eyes looked deep into mine. "Because everyone I've ever cared about or loved has ended up dead. I'm cursed."

My hand went up to Bane's face. "You're not cursed." He tried to protest or that's what I assumed, but I put my index finger to his lips. "I'm not here to change your mind or who you are. Only you can do that."

I removed my finger.

"Then, what are you here for?"

For once, I saw uncertainty and fear in the strong man. "To give you the escape we want. Let this last for as long as we're on the run. When it's over, I'll disappear. We'll go our separate ways. Stop pushing me away. There's nothing to push."

Bane leaned his forehead to mine. "You have to promise me you won't get attached. Maren, I have nothing in my life I can't walk away from. It's not something I plan to change."

"I don't want you to change. I understand." Our cold breaths mingled with each other.

His lips moved to touch mine, barely. "Are you sure you want this, angel?"

"Yes, for as long as it lasts. Yes."

Kissing between words, my libido was in overdrive as Bane's walls crumbled and he let me in, fully feeling his tender side.

"Nothing more can happen between us. I don't want to hurt you, angel."

"You won't. I promise."

CHAPTER
17

BANE

I CLOSED MY eyes as I absorbed the feeling of Maren's lips against mine. *Could I give myself this little bit to enjoy being with someone?* The walking away part would be no problem. I'd conditioned myself too thoroughly to not be able to. Maren seemed like she understood.

Fuck! I wanted this ... whatever *this* was. She'd promised me and I believed that Maren would hold true to her word. Having those few minutes in the damn snow making those snow angels gave me a feeling of ... happiness. An internal war happened within me as I tried to come to grips to allow myself this time—however long it was.

Fervently, my mouth moved with more urgency against Maren's. I would not be a dick to her again through this time we had. Maren's body became pliant against mine. As we began to make our way to the cabin, I unzipped her jacket needing to feel more of her. Something happened and Maren tumbled down to the snow-covered ground. I didn't care and followed her. We didn't stop our onslaught of each other, needing to devour one another. The snow fell around us and Maren's body shivered.

If I fucked her in the snow, we'd end up with frostbite. Pulling back, Maren protested with a moan that had my dick begging to get inside her. "Let's get inside. We'll get sick if we get naked in the freezing temperatures. And I want you naked."

Maren pushed off me. "Hurry, then. No messing around."

I sat back on my heels and chuckled as Maren sprang up and dashed to the house. She turned to me with a no-nonsense look on her face. "Bane, I mean it. I expect my first orgasm to happen in less than three minutes."

Hell, I never backed away from a challenge. I sprinted in after Maren. Inside the cabin, Maren had her pants off, but struggled to get her shirt and jacket off at the same time with her hands up in the air, the fabric completely obstructing her view.

Perfect opportunity.

By my guesstimate, I had about two and a half minutes left in the challenge. I prowled toward her. The shirt was completely over Maren's head while her hands were up in the air, flailing, trying to pull it off. Adorable. Absolutely-fucking-adorable.

Scooping Maren up, she squealed. "Bane, I can't get my shirt off. Help!"

"All in good time. I can't lose the challenge."

"What?"

I didn't respond as I made my way to the table. Setting

Maren down, I bent her over the wood. Her pussy glistened.

"Bane—" My name died on her lips as I knelt and licked her core. She tasted like honey and I wanted more. Much more.

I sucked her clit and she moaned through her shirt, writhing at the friction and pushing against my face for more. Grabbing her hips, I kept her from moving. I had less than a minute left to work her into an orgasm. Sucking on her while moving my tongue around to lap up her sweetness, Maren convulsed in her orgasm. The sweetest sounds of satisfaction filled the air.

After taking everything she had to give, Maren slumped on the table forgetting her entanglement with her shirt. Standing Maren up, I helped her out of her clothes. "How was that three-minute orgasm?"

With her glossy eyes, I knew she was satisfied. "I feel like jelly."

Teetering on her legs, I scooped Maren up as she nuzzled into me. A sweet scent filled my nostrils. Her soft body melded in my arms. I wanted to be in her now. "Are you up for more?"

"I need more, Bane."

I blew out a breath as Maren laid against me, sleeping lightly. In twenty minutes, I needed to get up and research any leads and prepare an evacuation protocol if someone breeched the perimeter. Maren would need to practice what to do. Most people froze in the moment. If rehearsed, muscle memory kicked in.

Also, I needed to call Damien Wales in case they went after his family. I doubted it, but I would never forgive myself if something happened to Allison or their two children.

While Maren had been rightfully mad as hell at me for pushing her away, I'd been out making sure the perimeter was secure. All trip wires and cameras were fully functional and transmitting. Later, I needed to make sure the snowmobiles were working. If it was anything like the generator, there'd be some lines to replace and who knows what else.

Should I be going after the people? I wasn't sure. If I did, Maren would be left here defenseless. Until I had a better understanding of where everyone was, I would stay here with her. Fuck, I hated sitting around.

Sleepily, Maren looked at me. "You look like you're thinking hard. Any regrets to what we're doing?"

"No. None." I looked up to the ceiling. "I'm going through everything I still need to do. There's hours of research ahead to see if I can figure out what's going on. None of it makes sense."

Wrapping her arms around my middle, she snuggled into me deeper. "Let me know what I can do to help."

"Thanks, angel, I will." I kissed the top of her head. "I need to check the computers and make a phone call."

"Okay, I'll make dinner. I saw we had some fresh salmon in the fridge. Does that and green beans sound okay?" Maren made no attempt to move. I wanted to stay in bed, but I needed to work.

"Sounds perfect."

I disengaged our bodies and threw on a pair of sweats. Maren watched me in the reflection of the mirror and I enjoyed the lust in her eyes. Still, there was an innocence about her even after all the hardships she'd endured.

Leave Bane. Or you'll end up in bed with her again.

The living room put enough space between us to allow me to clear my head. Stoking the fire, I added another log. So far the fireplace had been adequate to keep us warm without having to use the heat.

Sitting at the desk, I prepared to call Damien Wales. He needed to put his staff on high alert in case Eric and his team tried anything. I doubted Eric would go after a multi-billionaire who I previously worked for and had negligible interaction with publicly after I quit. I heard the shower turn on and decided now was as good of time as any to keep me from joining Maren.

I pulled out the phone and dialed the secure private line that rang into Damien Wales' cell.

"Wales." Curt as ever.

I switched to my security advisor no-nonsense tone. "Wales. Bane. Are you on your secure line?"

"Yes. Good to hear from you Bane. Alli and I were talking about having you over."

My heart clenched as I thought about telling Wales the news. "I wish I could, but I'm calling for a reason that's not pleasant."

There was a change in his candid tone. "Are Alli or my kids in trouble?"

"No. But, I need all your staff to go on high alert and increase security to the top level."

"What the fuck is going on, Bane?"

Here went nothing. "You know I came from a Black Ops group."

"Yes, we never talked in-depth about it, but you said it was in the past."

I blew out a small breath he couldn't hear. "It was, until a traitor to the division I served in turned up alive. He's supposed to be dead. I saw them execute him not five feet away. Right now he's after me, but I can't take the chance he'll come after your family. Jeremy needs to create a false threat and increase security. There's several scenarios I worked up he can choose from."

"Just a second. Let me get Jeremy on it." Damien spoke to Jeremy on another line issuing rapid fire commands. I'd enjoyed working for Damien. He always let you know exactly where you stood. I felt like an ass having ever put him in this situation. Damien came back on. "Bane, I need you to level with me. Do you think they'll come after my family?"

"I don't, but it's not a chance I'm willing to take. Damien, I'm going to hunt those motherfuckers down and take care of it. After that, I'll be disappearing to make sure that this can never happen to anyone who knows me again." I knew it had to be done, but I hated leaving them. They'd been the family I never had but wanted from a distance.

The line stayed silent for a minute before Damien said, "I understand. All I ask is that you say good-bye. You've been like family and saved the woman I love. You kept my past mistakes from taking away Alli. I almost lost her. If there's anything I can do to help let me know. I'll do whatever I can."

"Thank you. I'll get this taken care of. If you run into any problems, call this secure line."

Maren came out wearing one of my long T-shirts that came down to her mid-thighs. She was beautiful. Long slender legs, tiny waist, beautiful brunette hair piled on her head. Giving me a smile and wink, she made her way into the kitchen. Damien's voice brought me out of my mindless eye-fucking. "I'll keep you posted. Bane, I don't meddle, but everyone deserves to have someone they love in their life. I know from experience."

Not everyone.

I wasn't touching the last statement with a hundred-foot pole. "Thanks, Damien. I'll keep you posted. Let me know if anything happens on your side."

"I will."

I hung up the phone and watched Maren as she moved around with easy grace. Perfect was one word to describe her. Deep down, I knew that I looked forward to enjoying the time we had together and letting my walls down. Keeping them fortified all the time was exhausting. Shaking my head, I pulled up all the information I could find on Hampton.

There was no doubt Security Branch was being monitored. Eric was a cold-hearted bastard, but he was smart. With Hampton's wife being sick, I couldn't drag him too far into this mess. I'd sent flowers to the hospital. It wasn't hard to find where Felicia was being treated before all hell broke loose.

It was important to figure out how far this thing went since Security Branch had obviously been used to get me to Discrete Encounters.

Opening my timer, I set it for five minutes as I dialed Hampton. "Hello." The gruff older voice answered tensely.

"Hampton. Bane."

He coughed. "Bane. Thank you for the flowers. Felicia appreciated them. I tried calling you yesterday for another job I have, but couldn't reach you."

"Yeah, I disconnected my number. I need some time off to get my head on straight. How's Felicia?"

Hampton was exhausted. I pulled up the hospital Felicia was staying at as he answered. "Better. She's eating and her white blood cell count is looking good. I think we'll be able to leave in a few days. Felicia's exhausted and ready to be home."

"I bet. Quick question. I was thinking about the job at Discrete Encounters. Did you find anything odd?"

He paused. "No, why?"

"Well, they claimed to have a top-notch security system but it had more holes in it than a leaky sieve. Before I disconnect from everything for a bit I was simply wondering." I listened for any sounds of the hospital in the background, but didn't hear any. There was a hotel connected and Hampton could be there. Without becoming obvious, I'd have to investigate the records on my own.

"Umm … they came into the office the day before I asked you. Sounded desperate. Made me a great offer if I could pull it off. Then, I called you."

Made sense. If they were watching Hampton, they'd know his wife was sick. The first choice to call was always me. "I'm probably crazy. Thanks, man. Tell Felicia I'm thinking of her."

"Will do. Take care."

Hanging up, I steepled my fingers underneath my chin and was glad I'd made the choice not to tell Hampton about Eric. Maybe in a week or so if I wasn't able to get answers. Plus, first I needed to talk to Sarge and tell him. Otherwise, I'd have my ass thrown in a sling by the Black Division. They were not someone you wanted to piss off.

Protocol stated to call in as soon as possible if there was a breach in security. Eric being a traitor was a major fucking breach. Even though I was out of Black Division, I was still bound by certain rules.

Eric Thornhill hated Hampton with a passion. They'd never agreed on missions and how to handle situations in the field. Hampton wanted to limit casualties while Eric wanted as many bodies as possible. Going through every moment of the committed memories during the interrogation, I thought back to the day I'd questioned Eric and he confessed.

Eric sat in the metal chair with both hands and feet cuffed and zip-tied to the side. Blood dripped down his face from my earlier few punches. Not once had Eric agreed to any of the charges against him, claiming he was being framed as well.

Complete and utter bullshit.

"Eric, I can make the pain stop. Tell me who all you sold me out to and you won't die."

He wiped his chin on his sleeve, spreading the blood. "I didn't sell you out."

I stood, throwing the chair against the wall. Sarge stood watching me get in Eric's face as I yelled, "Liar! I have a dead fiancé and child because of you!"

"I didn't sell you out!"

I took the wand Taser in my hand and held it to him—enjoying the immense pain radiating through his body. The electricity flowed through Eric as he pissed himself for the third time. The skin smelled burnt, but I pressed it in further. "Tell me or I won't stop next time."

"Fine!" He spit through gritted teeth.

I released the wand while Eric breathed rapidly. "I did it. I sold you out, motherfucker. And guess what? I'd do it again."

Sarge swung at Eric as I went to unleash hell. Three guards rushed in and held me. Sarge looked at me. "Go get your shit together, Bane."

I looked at the guards. "Take the traitor down to the execution hall. I'll be there." Sarge didn't argue with my commands. He knew better. It was part of the arrangement to get me to finish the six missions I'd agreed to. They still had four left to ask me to do.

"You fucker!" Eric yelled.

I shrugged and walked out the door as I called over my shoulder, "I lied."

A day I thought as victory had been fake. Part of me felt like I'd been cheated out of the revenge I deserved. The bitter taste flooded my mouth. I wanted Eric Thornhill dead.

Turned out, Sarge's punch dislocated Eric's jaw. Only his muffled sounds were heard as Hampton pulled the trigger and I watched with absolute joy while the man who caused Jasmine and Faith's murders died. If it had been my choice, he would have suffered—slowly.

But it all had been for nothing. All of it. Eric was alive. And Eric deserved to die. I would make sure this time around he didn't escape. Who had helped Eric from the inside? Was Hampton involved since he'd pulled the trigger? I saw the blood.

"Dinner will be ready in about thirty minutes." Maren's voice brought me out of my unfocused gazed as I went over the details of the past—hoping something would stick out as being out of place or wrong.

I focused back on Maren as she gave me a sweet smile. "Sounds good. I have one more phone call to make."

"Okay. I'm going to go switch out the laundry and wash some of our clothes."

Maren seemed to know I needed privacy. I dialed Sarge's direct line and set the timer. In case anyone got through all the decryption coding, I'd cut this off at five minutes.

The line picked up. It was customary for Sarge not to say anything until we identified ourselves to him. "Bane Bradley, number five-one-three-six-zero-bravo." All my files listed me now as the name I went by. I'd been forced to give it to them prior to leaving Black Division to be with Jasmine.

We had several identification numbers. The one I'd given said I wasn't captured and speaking on my own free will.

"Bane." The cold calculating tone brought back many memories of getting missions without an ounce of emotion. All Sarge cared about was getting a mission done.

I cleared my throat. "Eric Thornhill is alive. He has a team assembled and has tried to take me captive. I've evaded him and I'm now holed-up in a safe house until I figure out what's going on."

"Fuck! Are you sure?"

Opening the files I had of Eric, I pulled them into a file as I spoke. "Yes. I can upload the identifying images to the secure location. All prominent features are a match to the pic on file after his execution."

A cold tone came over the Sarge. He didn't like losing. "Send me the info. I'll upload our findings at zero six hundred tomorrow morning. We should keep contact to a minimum in case we have another rat."

"Yes, sir." There were still three minutes until we had to disconnect.

"Do you need anything, Bane?"

I ran a hand over my smooth scalp. "No, I'll be fine. I'll continue to upload anything I find."

"Okay. We'll get this asshole taken care of."

"Yes, sir."

The line disconnected. Quickly, I uploaded the files. Scrubbing a hand down my face, I tried to decide what my next move was going to be.

CHAPTER
18

MAREN

COMING OUT OF the bedroom, Bane looked at a file with his normal frown in place. Dinner would be ready in about twenty minutes. I wasn't sure what to make of the phone call. Bane must have called whoever he used to work with about Eric. With several screens pulled up, I knew Bane was running Eric Thornhill through some sort of facial recognition program. He'd done it on the train a few different times. So far, everything came back as a match.

I sat down on the edge of the table. "Found out anything new?"

"Not yet. I am hoping tomorrow we'll have a breakthrough. I called Eric's and my superior when we worked together. It's a liability for his division also. We'll see. Sarge had been there and saw the death. The person who'd escorted Eric to the execution chamber died nearly five years ago on a mission. For now, I think it's best to lay low and see what Eric is going to do. As the days pass, I hope he gets sloppy like he did at the hotel."

Bane took a breath. "What I do know is Sarge's boss, Alex, is retiring. Sarge stated he wants this tidied up prior to him leaving Black Division. None of it makes sense. There's something else going on. Sarge thinks so too. Eric always blamed Alex for his wife's death. Maybe the announcement of the retirement set him off. The only thing I can think of is that I ruined his plans of revenge for who knows who else when I discovered he'd become a traitor."

"It sounds like nothing is or was as it seems." Bane nodded, lost in thought. Frankie came to mind. I hoped my brother was okay. "What do you think is happening to Frankie?"

"I'm not sure. You can't call him, Maren. No contact. He's working for the men after us."

Biting my lower lip, I tried to keep the tears at bay. Blood was blood and I still loved my brother. I needed to hear his voice. "But maybe we could get more information out of him. Maybe they're hoping I'll call. Frankie's not trained."

Bane cracked his neck to the side. "Maren, not right now. I'm not saying no, but there are still too many unknowns. With you, I'm not taking any unnecessary risks."

Bane's true look of concern caused me to relent. Frankie made his bed. Hopefully he was okay, but I knew I'd be disappearing from his life forever when this was all over. The sting of leaving him was less than I thought it would be. It still stung, but I'd made the choice freely before all this started.

I stood and Bane watched me closely as he leaned back in his roller chair with his shirt off. Moving to his lap, I straddled him and felt his hard-on press against my barely there thong through his sweats. He was commando underneath and I wanted him inside me.

"Angel, are you wanting something?" The sexiness of his voice sent a round of butterflies through my stomach as his hands caressed my thighs.

Answering him silently, I pulled off my shirt to reveal my braless state. A condom was tucked in the top band of my thong. I put the condom wrapper to my teeth and tore it. Yeah, I wanted something.

The answering sex-ridden grin from Bane spurred me on. Hell, he was muscular. His abs contracted as I ran my hands down his stomach making it to my goal. My arousal heightened. Adjusting his sweatpants, his dick swung free. After playing with the tip and spreading the pre-cum, languorously I rolled on the condom. I was rewarded with a feral groan.

Play time was over.

As I was about to dismount and remove my thong, Bane pinched my right nipple. I arched as my sensitive nipple spiked with pleasure keeping me in place. Fabric tearing sounded through the room and I felt my desire. "Bane—"

"Slide on, Angel. Take what's yours."

Positioning myself above Bane, I slammed down on his dick causing us to curse at the sensation.

In this moment, he was mine.

I was his.

We consumed each other.

Using my legs, I propelled myself up and down while increasing the momentum.

"That's right. Clench that pussy around me."

I bared down on him as the engorged head of his dick rubbed against my walls. Both of Bane's hands came up and pinched my nipples simultaneously—hard. I screamed as my orgasm took over. An animalistic noise came from Bane as he released himself. Our breathing heavy, I slumped against his chest. Fingers trailed up and down my spine as I heard his heart beat return to normal.

"You're fucking amazing, Maren."

I smiled into his chest. "I think the same about you." The timer for dinner went off. Standing, Bane's thick dick slid out of me, covered in my pleasure. I wanted him again.

Striding to the kitchen, Bane called after me, "Do you want your shirt?"

Looking over my shoulder, I sexily replied, "Why? I'm hoping you fuck me again right after dinner."

Behind me as I moseyed toward the oven, I heard the chair moving. Bane prowled to me and I loved it. My hand came up to turn off the knob for the oven. Bane's hand covered mine and a shrill of pleasure filled me. "I think we can wait a few more minutes to eat."

Facing him, I nipped his lip. "What did you have in mind?"

"You."

A week passed and nothing new had been discovered that I knew about. Bane spent countless hours looking at documents, satellite snapshots, different security feeds, and documents from the past. It had been two weeks since I'd met Bane. We'd fallen into a comfortable pattern which I liked. It was easy. But, I knew time with each other would be drawing to a close at some point. It was hard keeping my heart guarded because Bane opened up to me.

I didn't know all about his past, what he'd done, or what happened to him. However, I saw the person inside—his soul. Deep down, I knew Bane wanted something more. He wanted to live and be happy, but he didn't allow himself.

The morning light came in through the windows. Bane laid on his stomach, his dragon tattoo facing me. It was a maze of intricate lines forming the geometric dragon that I never grew tired of staring at. With the head starting in the middle of the left side of his back, the body wound up with the tail finishing at the base of his neck. It was strong and powerful—like Bane.

I traced the claws, working my way to his body. "You like my tattoo." The morning-gruff voice brought a smile to my face.

It was true. I traced it all the time when we were lying together. "I do. What does it mean?"

Bane rolled over and searched my face, something passing over his features I couldn't place. Something warred within him. "It signifies raw power. Dragons are guardians of things and known to be wise. A dragon's soul must at all times be tempered with wisdom to keep those safe around him. They must always be prepared. I got it about six years ago. It's a reminder to never become complacent."

From the pain passing across Bane's face I knew this was the result of the demon he faced. I didn't press but knew this was tied into his nightmare from the first night we were here. We hadn't talked about the nightmare since it happened. But I knew he lost someone. Since that night, he'd slept with me and I seemed to help keep whatever ghosts of his past that haunted him at bay. Maybe my presence soothed him too.

"What are we going to do today?" For the last week, we hadn't left the cabin at all except the occasional stroll outside.

Bane had the snowmobiles working but he hadn't allowed us to go anywhere on them. Our groceries were running low. I hoped we'd be able to go into town.

Bane stretched. "What would you say to us heading into town to get some groceries and calling Frank?"

I couldn't answer for a second as I processed him wanting me to call Frankie. "What?"

"We haven't gotten anywhere with the leads we have. Let's call your brother and see what he has to say like you suggested. It may give me an idea on where to look next. If he's with them, Frank has been coached, but I'm hoping we may catch a break."

"Why are we going into town to make the call? I thought the cabin was safer."

"If someone is listening in, I don't want them to know I'm having to communicate by a satellite phone. They'd be able to tell so we need to use the regular cell."

"Sounds like a plan." Nerves sat in my gut as I thought about talking to Frankie. Through all this, I'd somewhat stayed in a state of denial, mentally giving reasons why Frankie would get in their truck. He was forced. He was coerced. He was threatened. He was protecting me. This was what I hoped.

After this phone call, if Frankie picked up, I'd know the truth. Getting ready, I knew I was quieter than normal, but Bane gave me my space.

Heading to the car, I plowed through the fresh snow. If only people could spend all of their days making snow angels. I loved the isolation here at the cabin, but I missed the warmth of the Georgia sun. City life never suited me. Inside the garage shed, Bane's car had chains added to the tires.

I blew out a breath as I got in the vehicle trying to relieve the anticipation of the phone call. Without a word, Bane got in, cranked the car and we made our way down the mountain.

"Maren, it's okay to be nervous."

My leg bounced a million miles an hour. "I know. I just … it's just … I don't want it to be true."

"I don't want it to be either, angel."

"What am I going to say? How do I act?"

Bane looked pensively out on the road. "Don't give any weather or geographic indicators. Talk to him like nothing is going on. Ask him if he got the money to pay his loan shark."

"Did you send him money? There's no way my two days with Discrete Encounters covers the debt."

Bane glanced at me for a second. "I would have, but didn't since I'm pretty sure Eric and his crew have him. But, your brother is obsessed with money. It may knock him off guard enough to give something away." More knots formed in my stomach. "Maren, if you're uncomfortable with this, it's okay."

"No. I need a minute. Suspecting my brother of betraying me and confirming are two very different things. After all of this is said and done, I'll have no one." Bane went to say something, but locked his jaw. "I need to do it. I'll be okay, I promise."

Nodding, we continued to drive as I got my thoughts together.

At the edge of town, Bane parked the car in an old church parking lot. For the last hour he'd been prepping me for the phone call as he went through various scenarios. It must be tiring to be a secret government agent person. Bond was the only thing I could honestly relate to him. Except there was no *M* giving out orders or a *Q* giving us special spy equipment. It was us figuring this out—alone.

Bane pulled out a cell phone, cords, and a laptop. While he did techy-type things, I looked out the window and watched a few flakes fall. Snow was beautiful as it freely fell from the atmosphere to the ground. I went over the basics of how to act on the phone call.

Remain unemotional.

Don't allow yourself to be surprised.

Think before each word you say.

Prepare for the worst.

The list went on and on. Bane's hand touched my leg. "Angel, I promise there's other ways if you don't want to."

There was no time to second-guess my decision. "Is the phone ready?"

Bane handed me the phone. "Just hit send."

Hitting the button, the phone rang out in the car since it was on speaker phone. With each ring, I felt myself becoming more nauseous.

"Hello." I missed my brother's voice. I'd missed him more than I thought.

I cleared my throat. "Frankie." The clock timer for five minutes counted down on the dash of the car.

"Sis, no one thought you'd call. Are you okay?"

No one thought I'd call? I didn't have friends. This confirmed my worst thought. Bane nodded for me to continue. "Yes. I'm sorry I haven't called since the incident in the hotel room. I've had to lay low."

"I know. Where are you at?"

Bane shook his head as a reminder and I sidestepped the question. "Are you still in Atlanta?"

"No … I mean … yes."

That was enough to confirm that Frankie was indeed lying to me after all the time we'd spent together. "Hey, I need to stay low for a little bit longer. I snuck away for a bit to make sure you got the money I wired to pay Tommy Tricks. It went into your account."

Silence.

More Silence.

Then, Frankie erupted on the other end. "You fucker! You said there hadn't been any money. I want what's mine. I told you I'd help get that asshole."

There was a shuffle and a commotion.

Then another voice came across the line. "Eric—"

The line went dead. I stared at the phone with sadness and empty feelings. Tears flowed freely down my face. Frankie hadn't cared about me at all. What happened? A sob broke free. I couldn't take it anymore.

Air.

I needed air.

Now.

What happened to our brotherly-sisterly love? Gasping, I leapt out of the vehicle as my stomach heaved, expelling everything into the pure white snow. I wanted my innocence and purity back from childhood. Bane was at my side in an instant.

"I'm here, angel." I had to be strong. This was not a time to break.

Bane held my hair as I continued to be sick. *Why, Frankie, why?* My hands shook uncontrollably as I worked on getting control. *Calm down, Maren. This isn't news.* Deep breaths, helped the heaves subside. I held up my hand. "I'm okay. I needed a second."

I looked at Bane and he looked murderous. From his

touch, I would have never known.

"What's wrong?"

A chill went through me as Bane's steel voice cut through the air. "The voice that said Eric's name at the end of the call, I think is a colleague of mine."

"Who?"

"Hampton."

CHAPTER
19

BANE

I'D KNOW THAT voice anywhere.

Fucking traitor.

I trusted that motherfucker and he betrayed me. My insides shook with rage. Hampton played me. That lying sack-of-shit played me for who knows how long. I wouldn't know for sure until I cross-analyzed the voice on the phone with his. I'd recorded our conversation the other day in the cabin. Felicia was at the hospital. I'd verified the admittance records.

Motherfucker.

Maren leaned back over as dry heaves racked her body. I felt ill for her, knowing how the sting of betrayal felt from your own flesh and blood. My mom had been the worst. As a kid, she'd forced me to con women out of money or I'd be beaten black and blue for days. That was until I stood up for myself at fifteen. After that, she never laid a finger on me again. But, I was still called *bastard* until I left for the Marines.

Standing, Maren turned into me and sobbed. I hated this for her and felt like the bastard I was for suggesting she call. There wasn't a breath of space between us as she clung to me. My body craved to be the comfort she needed, but my heart fought it knowing this was going to all come to an end sooner or later.

Crack.

My mind went into defense mode as I watched the branch on the nearby tree fall to the ground. We were exposed out in the open like this. One well-placed sniper and either one of us could be taken out if someone had been tracking us. "Maren, I need us to get back in the vehicle. We need to get back to the cabin."

Shopping would have to wait until I further assessed the situation.

Nodding, I swooped her up and rapidly got us in the vehicle. Scanning the streets, nothing seemed out of place. There was hardly anyone out on the road which made identifying possible tails easy. There was no way they'd know I was in Colorado, but it wasn't worth the chance if somehow I overlooked something. Maren looked out the window as silent tears came down her face.

She needed comfort and I wanted to give it to her.

The tree snapping brought too many memories of Jasmine dying back. It was too close to feeling like a gunshot. So many unanswered questions as to what was actually going on. Guilt plagued me for getting Maren into this situation.

As we drove, my mind tried to fit the pieces together as to what was going on. An involuntary shudder went through her body.

"Maren, for what it's worth, I'm sorry I came into your life and caused all this."

She sniffled and looked my way. "I'm not."

I was rendered speechless and something thawed within me. *Focus, Bane. History cannot repeat itself.* Jasmine and Faith came to mind as I remembered what it felt like as my baby fought to survive. My heart ached. Had Hampton been involved with Eric's survival? Or was something else at play? Hampton had never seemed like a traitor and there'd been pure satisfaction in his eyes when Eric had been executed. What did they have on Hampton? Or had I completely misread him as a person?

Hell, I needed answers and all I was getting was more fucking questions.

I glanced at Maren again. She needed space to process as she watched out the window. Sarge sent me files the day after we'd talked as promised with a detailed dossier of his experience.

Eric Thornhill was a fucking thorn.

A few days after our conversation, a detailed brief had been uploaded with all of Eric's whereabouts for the last six years. He'd been living in Mexico under the identity of David Churchill for the last five years. A year ago, he came back to the states.

Sarge believed he was closing in on Eric's location in the Midwest. I assumed Hampton and Frankie were with him. Being centrally located meant that if they found me, they'd have a better chance of getting to me quicker.

For now, I wasn't disclosing to Sarge that I'd heard Hampton there. Something deep within me … call it instinct, kept me from going there. If I was wrong, Hampton would pay the price.

When Eric was located, I was meeting up with the Black Division for one last hurrah. It would be surprising if anyone was still there that I'd worked with considering the survival rate. This time, when we located that son of a bitch, I was going to be the one to put a bullet in Eric Thornhill.

Maren didn't know about these plans. I'd make sure she was safe before I left.

"Bane, how do you get past the hurt?" Her voice caught as she spoke.

Maren knew from my nightmare alone that I had issues. I looked at her and her red rimmed eyes softened me. "For me it was time and revenge."

"Did revenge help?"

Had it helped completely? No. Hell what did I know about healing. "Probably not. But it gave me something to focus on. Maybe it never goes away but only dulls with time."

"Have you tried forgiveness?"

"Forgiveness?"

Turning my way, Maren watched me, truly curious. "Yes, forgiving yourself for what happened to cause your nightmares. You're a good man, Bane."

"Some things aren't worth forgiving. Would you forgive Frankie after all he's done? He tried to whore you out for money."

My words caused her to flinch and I regretted them, but couldn't retract them. Maren challenged the very core of my existence. "Yes, I would. I'd forgive but never forget."

Well hell, I had no words as we drove the rest of the way to the cabin in silence. Her words made me reflect. Forgiveness from the unforgivable. Was it deserved?

Maren knew I needed the silence as we got out of the vehicle and made our way into the cabin. I needed to make sure it was Hampton's voice I heard on the other line before I threw out any accusations. I got my laptop and sat it on the arm of the couch as I downloaded the voice into my recognition software. Grabbing a blanket, Maren laid across my lap. The touch brought me comfort.

Before long, Maren fell asleep. The progress bar was nearly done. I debated if my decision to not tell Sarge about Hampton was the right one. If I did, that meant I'd have to disclose Maren or lie. Lying was a worse offense than omission. The risk wasn't worth it. I'd deal with Hampton on my own if he was indeed working for the other side. I hoped to hell he wasn't.

The screen flashed green.

I clicked and it was one hundred percent confirmed to be Hampton.

Son. Of. A. Bitch.

Scrubbing a hand down my face, I had no idea how far this rabbit hole actually went. Glancing down at Maren, her eyes moved behind her eyelids rapidly. A grimace came on her face, then relaxed. Simply she whispered, "Choose me."

If only I could.

Another week passed. Eric was either in Missouri, Kansas, or Arkansas.

The more I thought about Hampton, I wondered if they had something on him. Maybe they were forcing him somehow. The only problem was ... Hampton hadn't used any of our code phrases when we talked the last time.

I'd never expected Eric to still be alive, so I guess that proved my judgment lacked in this case. Why after all this time? Putting your faith into anyone always fucked a person over.

Of course, I assumed that Eric and Hampton were still together. It was a gamble, but it was the best I had to go on.

Yesterday, Sarge confirmed they were in Kansas. The team combed through the state to find his exact location. It was only a matter of days before hell rained down on all of them.

Initial briefings were rolling in as the mission was defined. As soon as the location was found, I was going to meet Sarge and a group of Black Division Ops to kill them. There was a no-kill order as the Black Division wanted to question Eric and his team. But accidents happened and I planned on there being no survivors.

Trying to keep Maren unknown to the Black Division hindered my movement. I had to move slower and take fewer risks. If I didn't survive this, I needed to make sure that Maren was set and able to disappear. Nearly all the pieces were in place.

And maybe, just maybe, part of me didn't want my time to end with her. I enjoyed this semblance of a life we'd created. Fucked up, I know. Last night, I'd uploaded the possible locations I thought Eric could be to the secure server. It was untraceable from both ends in case someone was compromised.

Against my chest, Maren purred, "Morning, handsome."

"Morning, angel. I think we definitely have to make it to the grocery store today." It'd been a week since our attempt to go. I should have waited until we had the food to call Frank, but I wanted answers.

Honestly, I don't think Maren wanted to leave. She liked the escape the cabin provided. Even through all the stress, I'd been able to provide her what I'd promised. And hell, I was fine with that. She moved to straddle me. "Tell the truth, is it because we noticed we were running dangerously low on condoms last night?" Her tight heat slid down my body.

My dick sought her. "That may be a huge driving force. If I could keep you here naked I would."

The words were out of my mouth before I thought about them. The tip of her pussy touched my dick. "Would that make me your sex slave?"

Thank goodness she hadn't gotten those crazy in love eyes with what I'd said. "I think I could make that work."

Slightly pushing against Maren, I felt the inside of her. Fucking amazing. I needed more. I went deeper.

Maren gasped. "That feels amazing." Then, she went stiff probably realizing I wasn't wearing a condom. "I won't come inside you, angel. But this feels incredible. I'll stop if you want me to."

"No, don't stop."

A slow rhythm consumed us as I memorized her pussy clenching around me—skin on skin. Hell, I wanted this. Flipping us over, I drove into her harder. Once, just once, I'd have her come around me without a condom on. Maren writhed beneath me.

"Faster."

I pushed into her at a relenting pace. And then that look of euphoria passed over Maren's face as she moaned. With my balls drawing up and the tingly feeling spreading out at the base, I knew I was about to come. I wanted to mark the inside of Maren, but I'd promised. Pulling out, I poured my come out onto her stomach.

Best. Damn. Experience. Ever.

I collapsed to the side, completely wrung out. After a few minutes Maren propped up on her elbows. She giggled. "You're all over me."

"I like being all over you."

"Me too."

Again, we became silent as we approached the precipice that we knew was coming at some point. This would be ending and we'd never see each other again. Stretching, Maren got up. "I'm going to take a shower before we head into town."

"Sounds good."

I let her go alone so I could get a hold of all the confusing thoughts going on in my head.

Groceries were put away. Maren was inside reading a book I'd asked the grocer to add. Some new romance book. The grocer said his wife loved it. I knew cabin life had to get old without any entertainment, but Maren was a trooper and never complained. Today, I was going to do something hopefully she'd enjoy.

Picking up the walkie talkie, I radioed Maren. "Hey, angel. Can you meet me out in the shed? Dress warm."

Within ten seconds, she responded. "Sure thing. Need anything else?"

"No. I've got it all."

About ten minutes later, Maren came through the doors in her heavy gear. She looked adorable as only her nose and mouth showed. "It's so cold. For future note, you should make any safe houses you have in warmer climates."

I chuckled. "I do have a couple in warmer climates." Her mouth gaped open. "It's harder for someone to check the place out. With the constant fresh snow there's no way not to leave footprints and because of the echo from the mountain it's nearly impossible to approach by air without being heard."

"Yeah … I'll leave the super-agent stuff up to you. What did you want? My book was getting good."

Shaking my head, I responded, "I thought we could take the snow mobile out and look around."

Maren's eyes lit up like I knew they would. She'd asked several times, but I hadn't felt comfortable leaving. With things coming to an end in a week, I wanted us to have this memory. She jumped and clapped. "Where do I sit?"

"In front of me. Hop on the right one. I'll grab the backpack."

Donning the backpack, I sat behind Maren and pulled her flat against my chest. "Put these glasses on."

"Okay." Maren's face was now completely protected.

Cranking the snow mobile, we left the confines of the shed. The machine roared to life as I let her go full open. Maren chortled as she held on to my legs. We were free of all the bullshit and strings life attached to us. If I could freeze this moment, it would be one of those perfect times to stay suspended in.

Coming to the cliff, the sun crested before its final descent, sending beautiful rays of red and purples across the sky. "Oh, Bane. This is perfect."

I wrapped my arms around her. "It is."

"I'll always remember this moment. Just like this. The sun setting, you wrapped around me. Thank you."

"Me too, angel. Thank you."

For the first time in a long time, I felt complete and the memories of the past were at peace.

CHAPTER
20

MAREN

WE'D BEEN AT the cabin for a month. It had been a week since our snow mobile experience. I was certain in that moment something changed between us, but Bane hadn't told me that we'd try to make it work after all the drama was over.

It was the middle of the night. Bane left the bed about an hour ago to check some things on the computer. For most of the night, I'd tossed and turned feeling out of sorts and like Bane was withholding something from me. Deep down I knew our time was coming to an end.

Turning over, I looked at the red glowing numbers.

I tried to think warm happy thoughts, but I was jittery. At dinner, I'd barely eaten anything from the weird feeling pulsating through me. Bane read something on the computer this afternoon and became more quiet than usual. For some reason, I hadn't worked up the nerve to ask him about it. Hell, I knew it was going to be something I wouldn't like.

The door creaked open. "Bane?"

"Yeah, angel. Did I wake you?"

I was going to miss that warm soothing voice. "No, I can't sleep."

Cocooning himself against me, I grabbed him around the waist. "Can you tell me what's going on? I know something changed today."

He took a big breath. "They've located Eric Thornhill. A mission is being put together to take him out tomorrow evening. I'll be leaving at noon to meet up with the team. You'll be safe here."

My heart caught in my throat. "Afterward, what will happen?"

An awkward silence filled the air and I dreaded the next words that I knew loomed ahead. "I'll find a safe place for you to live. Get you a new identity. You'll be set and never have to worry about money again."

The words were like a knife to my chest. I wasn't supposed to fall for Bane. I had tried to safeguard my heart.

I had failed.

My chest tightened. This was ending. Tears threatened to make their presence known. I had to remain strong. We were in our final days together.

Our relationship was over. Wait, we never had a relationship. In Bane's touch I felt something deeper. He cared for me. I knew it. Whatever happened to Bane had a death grip on him.

Pushing away reality, I responded, "Sounds good. We can talk about it when you get back."

Nothing else was said. Bane tightened his grip on me and kissed my forehead. A restless sleep ensued while I tried to sear into my mind what it felt like to be in Bane's protective embrace before it ended.

Bane slept peacefully beside me and my stomach roiled with nerves. I was going to be sick. All night long I'd thought about us and how I could tell Bane I wanted a shot to see what this could be. It wasn't fair that I was going back on my promise to Bane.

I'd fallen for him. Hard.

My heart was taking control and refusing to let my mind walk away from this attraction. What if he died? What if I never saw him again after today? I knew there was an envelope with details for me, but I'd refused to look at it because that meant Bane would be dead.

I felt sick. *Calm down, Maren.* I was going to be sick. Shoving the covers aside, I made it to the toilet in time before I expelled what I had left. My nerves were at an all-time high as I tried to quiet them.

"Angel, what's wrong?"

I wiped off my mouth and flushed the toilet. "Nerves."

Bane wet a washcloth and handed it to me. "I promise you'll be fine today."

"It's not that." A small sob erupted as I wrung the wash-cloth between my hands. "I don't want this to end. I don't want *us* to end. I'm falling for you, Bane."

The shutters came down over Bane's eyes as he shut him-self off. "In less than forty-eight hours we'll be over. This was the deal from the beginning."

More tears fell down my face and Bane became angry. "Maren, I'm leaving in five hours. I'll be back and then we'll have two days together. You can't do this right now. For fuck's sake, I need my head on right. I should have never agreed to this arrangement. I knew it. Damn it! This was all a mistake."

Bane slammed the bedroom door which jolted me as I stared at the tile on the floor. With the finality of the door clos-ing, my heart shattered in a million pieces. I had been stupid to let my guard down. What had I been thinking?

It was over.

Standing, I brushed my teeth. Maybe I'd be able to stay in the bedroom until Bane left and wallow in my humiliation there. Here was to hoping. Ugh. Why had I opened my mouth and said anything? I should have never broken my promise. But, my heart would have forever wondered *what if* had I not said something.

Life was a bitch.

The ickiness from the morning visit to the toilet wore off as I got control of my nerves. There was nothing I could do and I refused to beg. I wanted someone to want me for me and nothing else. Eventually, I would find the love that Mom and Dad had. Someone would want to share their life with me because they loved me.

Finding a heavy sweater and jeans, I put them on. The more clothes, I wore the more it would be a deterrent from having sex. Any more intimacy and I wasn't sure if my heart would survive the fallout.

Bane busted into the room. "We have to go! NOW!"

Adrenaline shot through me as I grabbed Bane's hand. Bane grabbed our coats off the rack as we left the cabin, not taking the time to close the door. Running full speed to the shed, Bane threw open the door. I didn't say a word as my heart nearly beat out of my chest. In all the discussions on what to do, I never imagined it would come to fruition.

Someone was here. The nausea hit again as I thought about someone doing something to either one of us. Bane had been insistent on practicing and discussing protocol if someone was to breech the perimeters. I'd never believed that this would be something we'd have to deal with.

Bane jumped on the snow mobile and I quickly sat on back.

"Hold on, Maren. Don't let go of me for a second."

"I won't."

The snow mobile roared to life as my heart raced faster. They'd found us. What if Bane had been gone today? I buried my face in his back as Bane took off at a dangerous speed. He whipped the snow mobile around to head behind the shed. Bane needed to focus. Me freaking out on the back wouldn't help the situation.

Keep your eyes closed, Maren. Don't look. It doesn't matter. Bane will keep me safe.

I couldn't help it, I looked back. No one was there. I breathed a sigh of relief until another snow mobile came roaring out from the side of the woods.

"Bane!"

"I see him. Hold on!"

The throttle whined as Bane turned it farther. With one hand, Bane pulled a gun from somewhere up front. He slowed minutely, the gun raised, and fired. I glanced back to see the guy slump off the machine. The snowmobile veered back into the trees as its rate of speed decreased.

Looking around I didn't see anyone else, but felt completely exposed and buried myself further into Bane. Anyone in the tree line could take a shot at either one of us and we'd be finished. Bane bee lined for the trees. After we'd been in the trees for a few minutes, he slowed and looked around. A large boulder sat ahead. Pulling behind, the engine silenced.

"There was only one intruder that registered on the cameras, but I need to make sure."

Bane pulled out his phone and flipped through different screens like he did often when we were together. "None of the other pressure places, trip wires, or cameras are registering anything. That's odd."

"Why?"

He checked a few more things. "Because they know it would take a team to take me down. This was a scouting trip. The man only tripped the outermost wires. Normal protocol has the perimeter closer than mine is. It's a hell of a lot to keep up with, but gives enough warning to escape."

Scouting meant one thing. They were coming. Bane could have been gone. The nauseous uneasy feeling came over me again. I shivered. Bane looked me in the eyes. "Let's get to my other vehicle. In these frigid temps we won't last long out here without the proper gear. I'm going to keep you safe, angel."

It was freezing as I worked to keep my teeth from chattering. The snow mobile came to life immediately. As we drove cautiously, Bane stayed tense as he scanned the area. The speed was more moderate as we weaved in between the trees.

After an hour of driving, I was frozen to the core. An opening came into view and I heaved a sigh of relief. The cedar smell calmed me as I took deep soothing breaths. Buildings came into view as Bane stopped. None of the snow had been disturbed from what I could see.

Lowly, Bane spoke, filling me in. "This is one of my places. It has a vehicle inside the shed. I've been out here once about two weeks ago to make sure everything worked. It can't be monitored since it doesn't have electricity, but we'd see if anything had been disturbed." Bane brought his hands up to the side of my face. "Remember what I told you if we were to get separated."

"O-o-okay. I do." The cold became almost too much to bear.

Bane looked back at me with concern. "Let's go." Bane ran in a half-crouch and I attempted to keep up with his pace. The air eerily silent. Not even the birds chirped. Bane looked to the left and to the right of the building before going to the door on the far right side. It seemed like no one had been here, which eased my nerves as Bane's tracks from the time before he'd came were gone from the snow.

Coming to the door, Bane unlocked it. "Stay here. Let me check it out."

Wrapping my arms around myself, all I wanted was to be in the vehicle with heater on full blast. A commotion started as I heard men tussling. There was a grunt, then Bane's booming voice. "Maren, run!"

The reality momentarily rooted me in place until the words connected with my brain. I turned and headed for the trees where the snow mobile was. Where was I going to go? I had no idea. Wait. Bane told me to always use the compass and head south. It would take me into town. That was part of the protocol we'd discussed numerous times.

Making it to the snowmobile, I stopped when a man in a white outfit sat on it with his gun pointed at me. Not any man—Eric Thornhill. His picture had been on the computer screens for endless hours. I'd recognize his crew cut hair and leathery tanned skin anywhere.

I gasped and turned to run in the other direction.

"Don't think about it, sweetheart. I have Frank back at the cabin. Do you want to be the cause of his death?"

Frankie. I stopped and faced him again, feeling the goose bumps on my skin raise in apprehension. The man hopped off the snow mobile and wrenched me into his grasp. "Let's go see how loverboy is faring."

As if he was being summoned, Bane came running out into the open. A gash on his chest and knuckles bloodied. "Maren, are you okay?"

The gun cocked to my head and my heart stopped beating, rendering me speechless. "She'll be fine as long as you listen. I have no problem putting a bullet in her head like I did Jasmine."

The blood from Bane's face drained as he watched me. Who was Jasmine? I felt light headed and swayed. Eric's grip tightened on me. "Keep it together, sweetheart. Now you're responsible for not only Frankie's life, but Bane's also."

Bane talked. "Deep breaths, Maren. You can do this." I nodded and focused on my breathing. The darkness leaving the edge of my vision.

"Let's get back to the cabin. Put these zip ties on your wrists after you dump your weapons, Bane. If we find any on you when we get back, I'll hurt the girl." For a minute, Eric let me go and threw the plastic ties to Bane. Cautiously, he picked them up, watching Eric. Bane hesitated for a moment. "Don't fuck with me. I won't hesitate taking another woman away from you."

"I'm going to kill you, motherfucker," Bane said as he deposited two guns and three knifes into the snow. The blood darkened around the cut on his shirt. Bane was hurt. I checked him over closer and it appeared to be more of a surface wound.

Eric laughed. Actually laughed. "Like you did the first time …"

Fire emanated from Bane as he watched Eric with nothing but pure hate. "Let her go. I'll come without any issues."

Dramatically, Eric paused like he was thinking about it. "I don't think so. You see, Maren has a bit more to play in getting what we want."

A small frown, nearly imperceptible appeared on Bane's face as he stared at Eric with no emotions. Binding his wrists and pulling the ties tight with his mouth, Bane held his hands up to show how secure they were.

"Very good. Now walk northwest. Stay fifteen paces ahead or you'll be responsible for what I do to her."

Bane's jaw locked tight, but he did as he asked. The snow crunched beneath our feet as we walked to what felt like our death sentence.

CHAPTER 21

BANE

THE HUMMER CAME into view a hundred yards away. Thank goodness. Maren's teeth were chattering and she was dragging her feet from the sound of it. She needed to get warm before hypothermia set in. I hadn't dared look back in case that bastard hit her for me disobeying. At least Maren would be out of the cold here in a second, and I could hopefully get a better assessment of the situation.

"Bane, wait outside the passenger door. Maren's driving. If you try anything … I'll kill her."

Fucking asshole.

I nodded my understanding and did as asked. For the first time since we'd started walking, I got a glimpse of Maren through the windows. She was freezing as she shivered and looked exhausted. Our eyes met briefly and I saw fear in them.

She got in the car, defeated. Eric got in the backseat and put the gun to the back of Maren's head. She squeezed her eyes tight and a tear seeped out. I balled up my fists as I got my anger under control. Nobody touched her like that.

My angel tried to be strong, but this would be hard for anyone who hadn't been conditioned. Eric motioned for me to get in. The plastic ties bit into my wrists like a bitch. A small trace of blood seeped out the sides. The pain helped me stay focused. Getting in, Maren trembled as she turned the key to crank the car.

"Can we turn on the heat, Eric? She's freezing." However he answered would help me determine my course of action. If he said no, it'd be a sure indicator that our lifespan was coming to an end and quickly. I'd have to take more risks to keep her safe—which was worth it. If not, I'd bide my time until an opportunity presented itself.

An opportunity *always* presented itself. Most people weren't able to see it in stressful situations.

A few minutes passed. "Yes. No sudden movements, Maren. Then follow the road until we come to our first left. From there, we'll be on the road to the cabin. Keep a steady pace, not over thirty miles an hour."

"O-o-kay."

All I wanted to do was kill the asshole behind us and get Maren somewhere safe where I could make her warm. I'd been a total prick this morning to her and I regretted every word. I'd wanted to say, *Yes, I want to see where this goes too.* All my hard work to not get attached to someone had backfired. With all the careful planning, I was in the same situation as before. I'd messed things up with Maren. Jasmine's face flashed in front of my eyes. I couldn't imagine seeing Maren like that. I couldn't imagine her being pregnant and losing another baby.

It'd kill me. There was no doubt about it. Maren was my angel—sent to save me from the hell on Earth.

I had been too late before. What if I was too late now?

I kept stoically still and watched the road in front of me. Maren kept a steady pace with two hands on the steering wheel. I watched her closely through my peripheral vision. The chattering of her teeth lessened—slightly.

Eric and I never got along for whatever reason. Shortly after joining the Black Division, Eric lost his wife. They'd been vacationing and he'd been called out on assignment. The mission went terribly wrong from what I knew. Details weren't shared. I never would have imagined him being capable of betrayal.

Deciding to give Eric a sense of victory, I asked, "So how'd you make it into the building?"

Eric scoffed. "You played right into my hands. He told me it wouldn't be that easy, but turns out he was wrong."

He? Eric was working for someone and not an organization. Who was the question? I imagined everything would reveal itself shortly. Hampton no doubt would make an appearance. Soon I'd know if he was a traitor or if Eric had something over Hampton.

There was no use in continuing to prod. If Eric thought I needed the information, he would withhold it. If I didn't continue questioning, I had a higher probability of getting more answers. Eric had a weakness—his need to brag.

Eric continued, evidently pleased with himself. "It was brilliant. You bested two of my best men back there. I thought they'd at least cause you a little more damage. Seems I thought too highly of them." Eric goaded me into a pissing contest. I didn't care. All I wanted was Maren safe, even if that meant sacrificing myself. Maybe then the tone of my sins would be forgiven.

Maren flinched every time Eric spoke. The gun scraping the back of her head. I should have left well alone until we got to the cabin, but I needed information. Fuck. Eric kept talking. "We dropped the two men out about three miles to the west. They had small stilts fashioned like animal prints. When they got a clear line of the shed, they zip-lined to it, got inside. The retractable line went back to some tree in the woods leaving minimum to no trace. With the continuous snowfall their paths was erased within two days. They've been in that building for the past five days."

That meant they'd known where we were for at least a week, maybe longer. This cat and mouse game had been orchestrated well and thought out. Maren turned left and headed up the mountain. The car became silent as my mind sorted through different scenarios. If I could manage to get my phone out of my pocket, I could set off an explosion to maybe buy me a window of opportunity. I had a few different areas rigged.

The cabin came into view and only one other Hummer. "Bane, you'll get out first. Walk to the cabin and stop at the door. No sudden movements. I'll have Maren."

Maren parked the car. I got out and headed to the front door. From behind, I could hear their approach. With the smoke coming from the chimney, someone was inside stoking the fire. Answers were about to reveal themselves. There had been no additional track through the yard from what I could tell. It looked like three sets of footprints headed to the door. The yard looked undisturbed. The numbers were on my side if there were only four total to take out. I'd take some damage, but it was doable.

"Walk in slowly." All I wanted to do was turn and hit that

asshole so hard it would crush his jugular, but he'd have time to pull the trigger. I couldn't lose Maren.

I turned the knob. The main room was vacated. "Take a seat in the chair in the middle of the room. Don't move."

Keeping me isolated and away from everything was smart. All I need to do was keep a calm head and an opportunity would present itself. I was sure of it.

I took my seat resting my hands on my lap. Untrained people thought it best to tie someone's hands behind their back. That was a mistake. It put the hands out of sight. Near, the fireplace sat another chair. Eric pointed to it. "Take a seat, Maren. Face Bane."

Maren trembled and I fought the urge to go to her. The place had been set up for a show of some sort. I was positioned to see most of the room. My senses were on high alert as I watched everyone closely. With a shaky voice, Maren asked, "Will you let my brother go now?"

The plea in Maren's voice broke my heart as I watched her beg Eric. "Bring him out."

The bedroom door opened; Frankie walked out with a gun held to his head. With … Hampton following. My chest heaved at seeing who I thought was one of my friends. The thought Hampton could betray me stung. I waited for any sign from him that this was a double-cross. None came as he stared without emotion back at me.

"Tell me, did you know Hampton was involved? Was I able to get the phone turned off before his voice came through the line when your whore was talking to Frankie?" I fumed at Eric's jubilation with his insult and my demise. I stared down Hampton, but he couldn't meet me in the eyes.

Fucking coward.

"Ahh … I take it this was the surprise I hoped it would

be. Good."

Frankie looked shaken standing in front of Hampton. With him being a loose cannon that could make things worse fast or he'd get himself killed. For once, Frankie seemed sincere as he asked, "Maren, are you okay?"

"Yes." I could tell by the shaking in her voice she was far from okay. At least she was near the fire where she could continue warming up.

Frankie went to walk toward her, but Hampton jerked him back. Panicked, Frankie, confessed, "I shouldn't have done all the things they asked. Switching out your condoms ... pills ..."

The blood drained from my face as my head shot over to Frankie. Hampton hit him upside the head.

Bang.

Maren yelled and I looked at her. There didn't seem to be any wounds as she recoiled in her chair. The sound ricocheted through the room as Frankie dropped letting out a blood curdling scream.

"Frankie! No!" Maren bolted from her seat, but Eric caught her wrenching her back. A gasp escaped her lips.

In one movement, Eric shoved Maren back into the chair and I saw red as I stood. No one touched her like that. No. One.

The hammer cocked which sobered me. Eric held the gun to her head while giving me a malicious smile. I sat back in the chair. He'd kill her without a second thought if I pressed or stepped over the line too much. I needed to save the moment for when I would get us out of here.

"Sit, Maren. It's a leg wound. He'll be fine." Without hesitation, Maren obeyed the orders. Eric alternated the barrel of the gun between us. "Either of you move and I'll shoot him again."

Hampton remained impassive as he watched the scene. Any hope continued to diminish as I waited for a sign that I wasn't going to receive.

Maren shook as Frankie grabbed his leg in agony. He'd live. Leg wounds hurt like a son of a bitch and slowed someone down, but they were survivable.

Eric crouched in front of Frankie. "Ruin my surprise again and it'll be worse." Scoffing, Eric muttered, "Amateurs." He turned to address Maren and me. "I hoped to reveal this little secret in a bit, but seems Frankie let the cat out of the bag."

The mischievous grin on Eric's face made me sick. I had a feeling where this was going and I hoped to hell I was wrong.

Eric kept his gun pointed at Maren. I wished he would aim at me and leave Maren out of this. "Maren's birth control pills were replaced with blanks for two months prior to meeting her. She was one of the many targets we thought you might be interested in based off of accumulated data we had of likes. The condoms were replaced, something engineered by our team. Completely permeable. Basically, this entire time the two of you have been having unprotected sex."

That was the reason Frankie had been in our motherfucking room that day. Damn it all to hell.

Maren swayed in her chair. "A baby."

Eric caught her shoulder. "Keep it together, sweetheart."

This cannot be happening.

No.

Not again.

I can't lose another baby.

Seeing Maren's lifeless body like Jasmine took over my

vision. I had to shut my eyes to clear my head. This was not happening again. Maren had been throwing up; we'd been fucking like mad … unprotected. She was pregnant. I knew it.

Dryly, I spoke. "Get her some water. She's in shock."

Hearing my voice completely defeated, Eric looked at me. "Hampton. Get her some water. I think he's right."

Hampton did as he asked, leaving Frank writhing on the floor. He was useless. Hampton handed her the water. "Take small sips. It'll keep you from getting nauseous."

When Hampton turned my way, he blinked his eyes consecutively five times, stopped, and then three more.

Our sign. Finally, our fucking sign. Hampton hadn't flipped.

I said every prayer I could think of. If there were only three guys, including Frankie, as suspected, my odds improved dramatically.

All I could do was stare at Maren's stomach. I always knew this time meant more than what I gave it credit for. Shit! The situation was spinning out of control—everything I had fought against. I needed to save her and our child if she was pregnant. If we made it through this, I was going to give it all I had. It was time to fight for something I wanted—for Maren. I should have told her this morning how I felt. Regret filled me.

"Maren, be a dear and go piss on this. Let's see if I'm about to congratulate the two of you." Maren's eyes were closed for a brief second. What was going through her mind? I wasn't sure what I wanted. I knew I wanted Maren and children, but not forced upon her. She'd never believe I wanted her for her. Damn it all to hell!

Maybe she wouldn't be pregnant. Maren reopened her eyes, tears threatening to spill over. Eric mocked her. "It's okay. If you're not, we have some backup plans. Bane's next steps will decide the outcome of this situation."

He handed Maren a pregnancy test from the table behind him. A tear fell from Maren's face.

"Motherfucker!"

Eric turned to me, truly satisfied that he'd gotten a reaction out of me. "I thought you'd be happy Bane. I'm giving you something back you lost." I kept my gaze on Maren trying not to let his words affect me as Eric said, "Hampton, take Maren to the bathroom."

On shaky feet, Maren stood and walked to the bedroom. She gave me a sad smile and my heart broke. This was all because of me and not being able to stay away from her. Hampton followed, which only left Eric, Frank and myself in the room. Eric paced victoriously in front of me. "I'm sure you're wondering how we found you. I won't make you try and figure it out. In Maren's birth control pills we put a tracker. Did I mention that her pills had fertility enhancements added to them?"

He laughed like a hyena as he took in his victory. Eric had never been able to handle that I was faster, better, and more agile than him in the field. Overall, I had been a better agent.

I was going to take great pleasure in killing Eric when I had the chance. But for now, I sat still while Eric gloated more. "I didn't mention the fertility part, did I? Shame on me. Well, we made her as fertile as possible." He cocked his head. "I digress. At first, we were going to come after you more aggressively. Then, when I searched the hotel room, I realized the condoms and pills had been taken. Frankie said Maren had an extra pack in her purse. We knew there was a two month supply. There was still a chance that Maren could get pregnant. If you had a baby to lose from the get go, I knew you'd be more willing to cooperate, considering you know what that already feels like."

Eric brushed some imaginary lent off his jacket, truly enjoying this sick mind fuck of a game he played. "About a week ago we turned on the tracker to get your location. It had been turned off up until that point. It wouldn't have registered on any of your equipment. In case you were monitoring, we turned it back off. Each day we checked and you hadn't moved locations. It was brilliant actually. With Maren on her second pack of pills, we were running out of time and hoped you'd fucked her enough to impregnate her."

"What do you want from me?" My voice came out tight and barely contained. I was losing patience with this dog and pony show. This asshole was gambling with the life of the girl I wanted and potentially my child. The end game had not been revealed yet.

Maren appeared back in the door, clearly shaken. Hampton was behind her. Without warning she ran to me, throwing her arms around my neck. "Take the knife from the front of my pants."

Without hesitation, I took the small sharp knife from her. It had to be Hampton's. "I swear I'll get you two out of this. I'll keep you guys safe. I swear it."

Hampton wrenched her back but not with enough force to hurt her. It was for show. "Hampton. Bring her back over here."

Another gun shot went off and Frank cried out. "Fuck, man. Not my other leg. Maren, make it stop!"

A sob erupted from Maren. "Please stop. Don't hurt him."

I positioned the knife to where all it would take was a bit of pressure and I'd be free. Frank continued to wail in the background. "His fate rests on you not misbehaving, Maren. Be a good girl and I won't hurt him."

She nodded and looked back at me. My heart broke. Unfortunately, in this game there were calculated risks and injuries happened. The sooner I got us out of this mess the better.

Eric's left eye had a twitch. Same tell-tale sign from when we worked together. He was lying, of course. Maren stood next to Hampton.

"I think it's about time to check." Eric took the pregnancy test from Hampton and looked directly at me.

"Congratulations, Daddy. We won't have to artificially-inseminate Maren now."

Holy shit! Maren was pregnant with our baby. *Our baby.* I was going to be a dad. I watched Maren's hands go to her stomach.

I will protect you little one. I swear I won't fail my family this time.

Whatever was about to come out of Eric's mouth would be a lie. By the gleam in his eye, I knew he planned to take Maren and the baby away from me again. He was going to use them as leverage. All the cards weren't on the table yet … not by a long shot.

CHAPTER
22

MAREN

I GRABBED MY stomach.

I'm pregnant.

We're pregnant.

We're having a baby.

I'm going to be a mom.

I could barely comprehend the thought. Bane and I had been tricked. I glanced at Bane and he was intently watching my stomach.

In between birth control packs, it wasn't uncommon for me not to have a period. I'd spotted a little, but that was normal. It never crossed my mind that I could be pregnant.

Was he happy about this? This morning he'd told me there was no future for us. My heart broke in two. Now, I had a life within me. A life made with two people who gave something to each other. Silently, I made a vow. *I'll love you always and forever. We'll find a way through this. Your daddy swore he'll get us out of this. It'll be okay if it's me and you, kiddo.*

Would Bane want to be part of this baby's life? I wasn't sure.

Frankie writhed on the floor and my heart ached at the sight of my brother in pain. It had been necessary, but I'd always wonder if there was another way. In the bathroom, Hampton snuck a knife and instructed me to run to Bane. Apparently Hampton was on our side. I trusted no one except … Bane.

There was a man still in the bedroom that hadn't made his presence known. When I'd walked in, I'd nearly yelped but the gun pointed at me froze me in my place. The scar running along his face would be something that haunted my dreams. Whoever he was, he was bad news.

My head hurt and I felt woozy. I swayed. Bane went to move but stayed rooted as he remembered himself. Hampton spoke as he grabbed my arm to support me, "Should she sit? The last thing we need is for her to fall and hurt the baby. The entire plan hinges on that baby."

Baby.

Baby.

Baby.

"Fuck, your right. Sit, Maren. Keep drinking."

Bane watched me intently and there was relief in his eyes when I sat. The small sips were refreshing and helping. I was tired and hungry. *Pregnant.* I had to be barely pregnant, like a few weeks pregnant. Besides the nausea this morning, I hadn't experienced anything I'd heard about pregnancy.

Frankie moaned again. How could he have intentionally

done this to me? To the baby? He knew what he was doing. Why? It had to be for money.

Bane's raspy voice broke my thoughts, "So what is all this about? Did you get her pregnant to kill her in front of me again, like Jasmine and Faith?"

Jasmine and Faith. Wife. Baby. Dead.

"No, it's always been about you coming back to Black Division." The voice came from the doorway and it was the man who had been in the bedroom.

Bane looked as if he'd been struck. "Sarge. What the fuck?"

The man walked toward the middle of the room. My natural instinct was to recoil from him as I got a good look at the scar that ran jagged along his face. The dark crew-cut hair only added to the menacing look.

The man Bane called Sarge took a chair from the kitchen table and dragged it to the middle of the room. The metal dragging along the floor caused me to look away and cringe. "When you left Black Division initially, I knew it was because of that cunt, Jasmine. I wasn't going to let some piece of tail take my best asset. On your last trip, I'd followed you. Saw you two confess your love to each other. Figured you'd return there with that romantic notion you told me about living your life and maybe starting a family."

Sarge scoffed, "Men like you aren't meant to be happy, Bane. Men like you are meant to fight—cause chaos and destruction. That's what you do. The plan to kill Jasmine had been in place from the moment you asked to leave. After Jasmine and the baby's death, you came back. We'd agreed to only six missions, but I figured you'd become addicted to it and want to stay. You didn't."

This wasn't happening. How could this be real? Bane

spoke, barely holding it together. "How's Eric still alive? I saw a bullet go through his head."

Sarge cut right to the chase. "We looked far and wide for someone with genetic similarities to Eric. It was Eric in the exam room. When I punched him, we pretended it dislocated his jaw. That man Hampton shot in the head was some dumb fuck we'd found who'd pass facial recognitions after having some surgeries. His jaw had been broken, so he wasn't able to speak. The tattoos were done to match Eric's exactly. The incoherent moans of pain before Hampton pulled the trigger were probably him trying to say he wasn't Eric."

Bane worked hard to control his breathing. Hampton looked unaffected from what I could tell. Of course, he probably knew all of this prior to today since he'd been with them. After a few moments, Bane's eyes took on a deathless stare, unleashing all the hate hidden in those depths. I shuddered. "How'd you know I'd go for Maren?"

"We didn't. Over the past two years, there have been hundreds of women we put in your path. They'd all had their birth control switched. We needed you to fall for one of them. The security girl in your building, the mail delivery girl, people at the bars you visited, several girls on work projects were all purposefully put in your path. You fell for none of them. That is until … Maren. When you went for her, we worked fast to get the condoms switched out."

My head spun. All along I'd been used to get a baby in order to keep Bane in line.

Sarge stood. "So here's how this will play out. You'll be allowed supervised visits with Maren and the baby in between assignments. Any funny business and they'll die gruesomely. If you fail to complete your mission, they'll die. I will get my way with this, Bane. I will win. Do you want to lose another child?"

I was going to be held captive for the rest of my life, wondering if Bane would survive the next mission and come home to us. A sob wanted to spill free but I pushed it down. The last two times I'd done anything, Frankie had been punished. What would happen to Frankie? There was no way they would let him leave here.

Sarge nodded to Eric. "Let's clean this up."

Those words were bad with the way he said them and I glanced at everyone to see what was going to happen.

Eric lifted his gun to Frankie and I cried out, "NOOOO!"

Bang.

The gun went off and Frankie screamed. They needed me alive to keep Bane in order. I knew they wouldn't hurt me or the baby. I scrambled to the floor as Bane yelled, "Maren, don't!"

Tears filled my eyes as I looked up at Sarge. "Please, he's dying. Let me go to him. I'll cooperate."

Sarge nodded as I held Frankie. His eyes fluttered open. "Hey, Sis. Remember when you were fifteen and after you finished homework we'd each get a scoop of vanilla ice cream?"

The memory flooded back. I'd sit on the black countertop as Frankie and I sang songs together. We had special cups for our vanilla ice cream and chocolate syrup. Those were special memories as we talked about our day. I whispered, "Yes."

He was trying to put on a brave face like he had when I'd be hurt as a kid. The corners of his lips turned down slightly and trembled. On a shaky voice, he commented, "I did some things right. Do that with your kid. I know I've been a shitty—" He arched in pain and took a deep breath.

My gut twisted. After all the terrible things that happened

over the last few years, the Frankie I had once knew existed. The brother I loved finally came home and now I was losing him … forever.

A sob erupted from within me. "Frankie, I don't want to lose you. I can't."

"I love you, Maren. Always have. Always will."

There was nothing I could do as I watched the life slowly seep from Frankie's body. His body was relaxing as he fought to stay awake. Tears streamed down my face. "Frankie, I love you."

"I know." He took a deep breath. "Even after everything. I got twisted up in the wrong things." His eyes started to close.

"Frankie!"

They shot open and he gave me a loving smile. "I love you too, Sis."

I rubbed furiously away the tears that were falling down my face. I needed to stay strong. "Say hi to Mom and Dad for me."

His voice was barely audible. "I will. You're going to be a great mom, Maren."

Time was running out as I felt Frankie's body becoming more relaxed. He still breathed. I gave him a kiss on the cheek. "I forgive you. I love you."

"Thank you." I think that's what he said. His eyes closed, but I would not leave him until he breathed his last breath. I would be here for him. Unexpectedly, I was yanked to my feet.

I fought whoever held me as Bane yelled for me to stop.

Sarge spit out the words as he said, "He's still alive."

Eric didn't care as he forced me to sit in the chair. Frankie moaned as Eric spoke. "He won't be for long."

Uncontrollable hysterics took over me as I watched Eric hold out his gun and walk with a swagger. There were still a few precious seconds left I could have with my brother. Bane yelled, "Maren, angel, look at me. Look at me." I glanced to him. "Don't look. Look at me." I nodded. "I will keep you and the baby safe."

Bang.

Flinching at the sound, fear shot through me. The ringing of the gunshot wouldn't stop. I screamed as I stared at Eric. "You bastard! You bastard!"

Eric raised the gun and Bane stood. Sarge said, "Eric, stand down."

I sat. At this point, my actions were making the situation worse.

Eric spit beside my foot, clearly agitated he'd been reprimanded. He tried to rile me. "You're the one carrying the bastard, sweetheart."

Sarge faced us. "Enough! Both of you!" The tone scared the shit out of me and I closed my mouth and glance toward Frankie's body.

He was gone.

Forever.

Then, all the commotion started. Bane leapt from the chair tackling Sarge to the ground. Hampton grabbed Eric. Bane's booming voice echoed through the cabin. "Maren, to the bedroom!"

I fell off the chair and crawled. Yelling, cursing and gunshots went off around me. Making it to the door, I looked back. Sarge and Eric were on the floor with Hampton and Bane standing above them. Hampton had blood dripping down his arm. I slumped in relief. They'd been subdued.

"Check him," Bane commanded. As soon as the words were out, a gun was in Eric's hand, pointed at me. I curled into a ball. Our baby. I have to protect our baby.

Bane cried, "Angel!"

Bang.

Thud.

I peeked my eyes open, checking myself. I was fine. Hampton kicked Sarge and Eric in the head, knocking them out cold. But, Bane wasn't. Bane laid on the floor in a heap. I died a thousand deaths as the father of my child laid on the floor unmoving.

Please don't do this to me.

"Bane! No!" I crawled over to Bane. I couldn't lose him too. Not Bane. Not the father of our child. No!

I rolled his body over. Blood seeped from his shoulder. Banes eyes opened and landed on me. "Are you okay? How's the baby?"

"We're okay. You saved us."

"Finally. I was able to save my family." *Family. We are a family? Where did we stand?* I searched Bane's face and only relief was there as he looked over me. His eyes landed on my stomach and he swallowed hard. Oh, how I wanted those words of being a family to be true. But, the memory from this morning in the bathroom flittered unwantedly into my mind and I couldn't let my guard down.

Bane turned toward Hampton. "Are they secure?"

"Yes."

"Good. The bullet went through. I need you to cauterize my wound. We need to see what these motherfuckers have on us and how deep it goes."

Hampton moved to the fireplace where he put the poker in the red hot flames. Was he crazy? I interrupted, "Bane, you need a doctor."

Bane's hand came up to my face, "I'll be fine. We'll cauterize the wound. After we get what we need, I'll go to a doctor. I've had worse."

That thought sickened me. Hampton handed Bane some booze and he shook his head. "No, I want to be completely alert when I question them. I can handle it." Hampton started to protest. "No! I need to be on top of my game. What did they have on you?"

Pouring rubbing alcohol on the wound, Bane didn't wince. "They'd been using Security Branch on a few jobs and I caught on. Before I had a chance to warn you, they took Felicia. They had her for about a week prior to Discrete Encounters. When I gave you the signal, my guys confirmed they had my wife safe via my pager while I was in the bathroom with Maren. There've been several moving pieces to try and limit any casualties."

My eyes drifted to Frankie's dead body. Bane watched me as more tears fell. Bane nodded to Hampton. Hampton grabbed a blanket from the couch and covered his body. "Angel ..." I looked back to Bane. "I need you to go to the bedroom while Hampton cauterizes the wound."

"I—"

"I know you want to stay here, but please, the stress can't be good for you or the baby. I'll be in there in a second."

Baby. I was still trying to comprehend we were going to be having a baby. I was pregnant. I hadn't fully had a chance to comprehend it all. Kissing his forehead, I stood. Bane watched me until I disappeared behind the bedroom door. Sitting on the bed, I rubbed my stomach.

This is happening. All of it. Later, I'd have time to mourn the death of my brother. It was too much to process right now. Not ever knowing what happened to make him change when I turned eighteen will be hard. I always thought I'd be able to sit and have a serious conversation with him. Time changes things. It's unpredictable.

I heard grunting from the other room and my teeth ground together. Bane was in pain. Pure pain. Moments later, burnt flesh permeated the air. *The smell.* Oh geez, that awful smell had my stomach roiling. Toilet, I needed the toilet. Barely making it, I expelled the water I'd drank. My throat burned as I stood and brushed my teeth. I finished and looked at my reflection.

Did I look different?

I felt different. My world had been turned upside down in a matter of moments. Nothing would ever be the same. I was going to be the mom of Bane's child.

The queasiness came over me again as another wave of burnt flesh smell hit me. Hopefully this sickness was from the situation and not the pregnancy.

Quickly, I wet a cloth and put it to my nose for a filter. The door opened and Bane walked in, concern clearly etched on his face when he saw me in the bathroom. "Did you get sick?"

Through the cloth I spoke. "The smell." He wore a white bandage so I couldn't see the freshly cooked flesh. *Stop thinking about it, Maren. You'll make yourself sick.*

"I'll be right back." Bane left the room.

Going to the bed, I laid down with the cloth still covering my mouth and nose. There was no way a smell so sickening would be gone at this point. No way.

Bane entered with a bottle in one hand and a protein bar in the other. Confusion raced through me as to where we stood and what I thought about everything as he laid the two things on the table. "Try to drink and eat this when you can." His thumb came up and rubbed my face. "You're in shock and need the nourishment. I need to go make sure my family will be safe. Stay here. I'll be in the shed."

I mumbled, "Be careful."

"I will."

With Hampton standing at the door, Bane left the room. I wanted Eric and Sarge dead. They were truly vile people. Villains like them weren't supposed to be real. They planned to use me and the baby to keep Bane in Black Division. Was there anyone else who knew about the plan? Bane would get to the bottom of it all.

Frankie. I'd lost my brother today. Turning on my side, I let all the emotion out as I tried to think if there was something different that could have been done to save him. Frankie had been a liability all along. If only he'd walked away from whatever they'd offered him. But then, I wouldn't have met Bane. I wouldn't be pregnant.

Baby. Family.

How did I feel about this being forced upon me? I wasn't sure. But, I would love and cherish this baby forever. There was no going back. I cared for Bane, but as of this morning he was willing to walk away from me forever. Now, because of the baby, he wanted to keep me around.

There was one thing I knew I wanted. To be loved for me and not because I was carrying someone's baby.

CHAPTER

23

BANE

MY EYES FELT heavy.

My limbs couldn't move.

There was something important I needed to check on.

The fog needed to clear so I could think.

A sweet angelic voice broke through my conscience. "No, he's still asleep. I'm fine. I've been sleeping on the couch. Yes, I promise I've been eating. Yes, they haven't left the door. Okay, I'll call you if anything happens. Thanks, Hampton. Means a lot. Talk to you soon."

I cracked open my eyes and caught sight of Maren. "Angel." My voice was hoarse and my head hurt like a fucking semi drove through it.

"You're awake!" The loud excited voice was like a hammer bashing me in my head. I pushed further into my pillow.

The relief on Maren's face brought a warmness to me.

Baby. She was pregnant. I remembered that important thing that had been plaguing me only moments ago.

She was at my side in a second. The darkness closed in on me. I needed to know one thing. "Are you okay?"

"Yes, we're fine."

We're. Does she mean the baby? I had to verify. I had to make sure. "The baby, too?"

"Yes, the baby is fine. The doctor checked me out." Her voice sounded confident. Maren wouldn't lie to me.

My eyes closed as I whispered, "Thank, God."

I fell back into the oblivion.

Opening my eyes, I saw Hampton sitting in the chair Maren had been in before. I scanned the room as dread seeped in with the antiseptic smell. Had she left me? She couldn't leave me. I'd been such an ass the day Eric found us. Things needed to be set right between us. "Maren?"

There was no answer from her voice. She wasn't here. Where was she? I tried to sit up and Hampton pushed me back down. "Take it easy. She's at the hospital. The doctor's examining her."

He sidestepped my question. "Why? What's wrong?"

A firm hand stayed on my chest. I was two seconds away from ripping the damn cords off of me and finding her.

"He's being cautious with all the stress she's been under."

That was closer to the truth, but not all of it. "What the fuck happened, Hampton?"

Running a hand through his white hair, he blew out a

breath, only raising my anxiety. "She started spotting. John thought it best to do a thorough examination at a hospital."

John Willbanks. I remembered telling Hampton to take me to him. He was a doctor who saw people off the books for a price. No questions. Just cash. I was in his home. I recognized the room. Not much changed since the last time I was here five years ago.

I tried to sit up. "Bane, lay your ass back down. I have three of my best guys with her. Do you remember what happened?"

My pulse rocketed under my veins. The heart monitor confirmed it as the beeping increased. All I could think about was Maren. "Let me talk to her and then I'll think about all that other shit. I need to hear from Maren that she's okay."

Of all people, Hampton knew what I had been through. The fear from what happened with Jasmine bulldozed its way to the surface. Happiness wasn't something I deserved. Something was going to take away my last chance at love … I knew it.

Hampton handed me the phone with the number already dialed. It rang twice before she picked up. "Hampton, I was about to call."

Her voice instantly soothed me. It sounded normal. If something happened she'd be upset. Wait … was she upset about the baby? We needed to talk. What if she didn't want the baby? What if she tried to abort it? I took a steadying breath realizing I was overreacting. Maren wouldn't do that. Through all our time together I knew her as a person.

I swallowed hard. "Angel, it's me."

A page with someone's voice went through the speakers and came through the line. "You're awake! How are you feeling?" She sounded calm and excited to hear from me. Thank goodness.

There was no hiding how stressed I was. "How are you and the baby?"

"We're fine. The doctor left and said the amount of bleeding was normal. I'm supposed to take it easy for the next few days. If any more spotting occurs, I should come back."

I heaved a sigh of relief. "Good. Are you on your way back?"

"Yes. As soon as I get the discharge papers. The doctor estimates I'm almost five weeks along, which means I got pregnant one of the first times we slept together."

Even if I'd been strong enough to stay away after the first time, chances were Maren would have my child inside her. Some things were meant to be. I'd been drawn to Maren like a moth to a flame. There had never been a chance for me to stay away. It was all clear now looking back.

"Bane?" There was hesitation. Had I responded to what she said? Fuck, I messed this up. When she got back, I'd clear the air—set things straight.

"Yeah, angel?"

"I'll be back in about twenty minutes."

"I need to see you."

"I'll hurry, Bane."

I laid back and remembered the questioning of Eric and Sarge. It had been brutal as I pulled their finger nails out one by one, ensuring no one else knew about Maren, Hampton, me, or the pregnancy plan. As I'd assumed, me coming back to Black Division wasn't the real reason to get Maren pregnant. It had been a way to get me to cooperate based off my history with Jasmine. Playing off my fears to subdue me until they got what they wanted.

Bastards.

They needed intel only I had, on several contacts I'd used through my years at Black Division. Operatives didn't give out their field allies. It was understood. Most of the time, having the outside resources was what kept us alive.

Alex, Sarge's boss, wasn't retiring. That had all been lies from Sarge. After Sarge and Eric had all the pieces of their puzzle together … Alex would have an "accident", leaving Black Division to Sarge.

To get their finances in order, Sarge and Eric were involved in several illegal gun smuggling operations. Up until this last year, they'd kept the operation small and under the radar. Then, when they decided to take the side business to the next level they needed my Middle East contact. My contact could get information on anything or anyone. He was still alive.

Sarge hoped with Jasmine's death I would come to the wrong side of the line. I hadn't. And I'd walked. Knowing I wouldn't be swayed to join them, they'd let me walk. That's why there had been a large gap in the years since they'd contacted me.

From what I could tell, Alex had no idea all this was going on.

The squad who'd tried to raid my safe house in Atlanta had been killed days before they came to Colorado and that's why the team had only been Hampton, Eric, and Sarge. There were to be no loose ends. Hampton's men killed the ones holding Felicia.

They'd planned to kill Hampton and Felicia as soon as Maren and I were safely in route to our destination.

Fuckers.

Sarge knew better than to beg for his life. He'd taken the bullet stoically. Eric spit and had been an asshole to the end.

All of this—the loss, the pain, the sadness—was to try and keep me in Black Division.

Regrets.

I'd always regret my decisions that cost me Jasmine and Faith. They'd forever be part of who I was. But, maybe, just maybe, I was being given a second chance at life.

Forgiveness.

Could I forgive myself? I hoped so. Maren entered my life like a ray of sunshine showing me that there were things worth living for. She'd accepted me for who I was regardless of my scarred soul. Maren wanted me as I was. Stupidly, I'd pushed her away. I needed to prove myself to her.

"You look deep in thought. Do you remember it all?"

I nodded at Hampton's question. The reason they'd gone after Hampton was to get to me. They needed his help to get me into situations. Before Maren, there was nothing to lose in my life. Hampton was a casualty because of his association with me.

We'd put all the bodies inside the cabin and set it on fire. The same had been done at the shed. There'd be no way to trace the identities after Hampton removed the teeth in case dental records were used. With the combustible resources we'd used, the fire should've burned hot enough to leave no traces of the body. Hell, it'd be hard to tell how many people died there.

After all that had been done, we'd gotten in the car and drove off. Shit, I'd lost a lot of blood and pushed beyond my limits to keep my family safe.

"Yeah, I remember it all."

Maren cried while I held her until I'd passed out in the car. Her brother had been left in the cabin to burn. The memory of her staring at the cabin in complete silence would haunt me forever. There was no other choice and I hoped to hell she forgave me for it.

Hampton interrupted my thoughts. "She's a strong girl, Bane. I'm sure she's hurting, but she's putting up one hell of a front. Just remember her world's been rocked. Give her time to adjust."

"I know."

How much time would she need? Would I even be able to convince her I was the right choice? Would I be able to let go of the past so I could love with my whole heart? That was what Maren deserved.

As promised, about twenty minutes later, Maren walked through the door with a sweet smile on her face. Hampton gave her a hug and indiscreetly left. "You're looking better. How are you feeling?"

Sitting next to me on the bed, Maren looked me over as I grabbed her hand. "Better. What did the doctor say?"

The baby and Maren were all that mattered. I'd survive. Maren touched her stomach. "The baby is perfect from what they can tell. All my blood work came back good. The spotting happens in some cases. They said not to worry, but if it happens again to come back. He put me on vitamins and folic acid. I need to have my next visit in about a month wherever we end up."

Relief coursed through me. There had been an underlying fear of Maren not keeping the baby. With her plans for the future, I knew she was keeping the baby. Of course she was keeping the baby. My head was a mess from all the drugs. My thinking was delayed—slowed.

I leaned back trying to stay casual. "Have you been sick anymore?"

"No, not so far. Just queasy from time to time."

"Good." Then a thought occurred to me as I shot straight up wincing from the pain. "What name did you use at the hospital?"

Gently, she pushed me back down. Her sweet aroma enveloped me. "Don't worry. Hampton has been taking good care of me. No one knows my real name, not even John Willbanks. I used Kendra Childers from the bag I was supposed to use when we walked away from each other. You'd packed it before you set the cabin on fire."

Oh, fuck. I could hear the hurt in her voice. "Maren—"

She held up her hand and gave me a loving kind look. "It's okay, Bane. I get what we were, I do. You can be as involved as you want in this baby's life since we're now connected. But if you still need to walk away, I'll understand. We were pawns in their game."

"No, Maren, you don't understand."

I tried to explain, but she cut me off again, not listening. "Bane, until you found out I was pregnant you were willing to leave without a glance back. I heard the resoluteness in your voice that morning. You choosing to be with me at this point would be out of obligation. I'll never be Jasmine."

This was not going to plan. "Maren—"

"Bane, I get it. It's okay. From the beginning you were upfront with me. I stepped out of line the morning before everything went down. That was my fault for not keeping my promise."

Her words hurt. Was I using Maren to replace Jasmine? No, I wanted to ask her to stay with me before we found out about the baby. I wanted Maren. Jasmine had been my past. Maren was my future. I'd come after her if I'd had the willpower to leave in the first place. Resisting Maren wouldn't be possible.

With her jaw set, I knew Maren's mind was made up. Hell, if I was her, I'd believe I was a second place prize too. Shit.

Taking my hand, she gently rubbed the scabbed knuckles. "We're going to be connected for a long time. I want us to get along. For our child's sake. Just let me know what you want to be involved in and I'll make sure you have all the details if you decide to stay."

"Everything, Maren. I want to be involved with everything."

A beautiful smile graced her lips. While I was involved with the baby, I'd work on convincing Maren that I wanted her to. She was worth the effort to try and make a go of it. She was worth opening my heart up again to the potential of being hurt. The connection was stronger with Maren than it had been with Jasmine. If something happened to her, I'd be finished. There'd be no coming back for redemption.

"Can we go back to Atlanta?"

Panic set in. There was no way I could take a chance with Maren in Atlanta so close to where this all started. Eric and Sarge seemed to be telling the truth, but I'd been fooled by them before. "Not right now. I need to make sure the intel we got from Sarge and Eric is correct. Maren, I'm going to need to keep you close to me for a while. If there is still someone out there, I can't take the chance with you."

"Or the baby." Did she think this was only because of the baby? Of course she did. Maren's hand touched the side of my face as she rubbed her thumb over my lips hushing me. "I get it. I'll need a life of my own eventually, but for now while things are settling this will work."

The words stung, but were deserved. I was gnashing my teeth at the thought of some other fucker even daring to touch

Maren. *Calm down, Bane. This is going to take patience. I'm the one who fucked up.*

Not acknowledging having a life without me, I responded, "I think we'll be able to leave tomorrow."

Maren stood and walked over to the chair by the side of the bed. "Where are we going? Please make it somewhere warmer."

"How does Brandon, Florida sound? It's near Tampa." I knew someone who had a place there. It wasn't necessarily a safe house, but it was remote and would provide escape options. With the baby, Maren needed to be able to get to a hospital if something went wrong. Until it had been a few days without any spotting, I would be on edge regardless of what the doctors said.

Maren yawned. "That works for me."

"I'll work with Hampton to make the arrangements." I breathed a sigh of relief. I'd have her with me for a bit.

"Sounds perfect."

Slowly her eyes drifted closed as she held her stomach. We still hadn't discussed how she felt about the baby. Hell, we still hadn't discussed much at all.

CHAPTER 24

MAREN

BANE AND I hadn't talked about the obvious elephant in the room—what we felt about having this baby. He wanted to be involved, but was it out of obligation or because he wanted to be part of the child's life? I hoped it was the latter. If not, the baby would be better off without someone who wasn't truly committed.

I wanted this baby. I loved this baby. It was a part of something special we'd shared together, created by the two of us.

We'd touched down about an hour ago and were in another black SUV driving through smaller towns. The green of Florida was a welcome sight from the cold snow. Part of me missed the cabin. The other part was still healing from losing my brother. So many mistakes had been made through the course of all this. I'd never know why Frankie did what he did, but I knew he loved me when he died.

People lose their way sometimes. Only the lucky ones find their way back. Before Bane, I'd merely been surviving and enabling Frankie in his gambling addiction. Now, I had a chance to reclaim my life back. A tear slipped out as I thought back to Frankie's last moments. He had been the only family left.

The past can't be changed as it was set in stone. The future was a blank slate waiting to be etched in stone.

Three men followed us who were part of a team Bane put together. His friend from a previous job, Jeremy, recommended them. They had one mission. Protect me.

Even though the idea of being a mom was still new to me, I couldn't imagine losing my child. There was a connection I felt, an indescribable love from someone I never met. I didn't know the specifics of Jasmine and Faith's murders, but to lose the love of your life and your baby at the same time explained why Bane was the way he was about commitment—keeping everyone at a distance.

We drove passed a food stand. A little boy had a Popsicle that the mom handed him. It brought a smile to my face. That would be me soon. "Do you have another safe house here?"

Bane was relaxed as he spoke. Only his eyes gave away how tense he was as he scanned the area. "No. This one is a friend's. He owed me a favor. It has several escape options. We can get out easily by land, air or sea." My stomach churned as I looked out the window. I hoped our running days were over. "Angel, there's no reason to think anyone is still out there. I'm only doing this to make sure."

Hearing my pet name melted my insides and lowered my resolve. I had to remain strong. To enter in to this for the sole reason of a child would eventually make us unhappy. Two people should only be together for one reason—love.

It took six years for Eric to reveal himself. How long would we have to wait? Honestly, at this point, I didn't want to know the answer, but I needed an idea. "How long will we be here until you think it's safe to find a place to settle? At some point I'll need to find a job."

Bane's eyes got wide. "Maren, you can stay with the baby. I can provide for both of you."

"Bane, I'll need to provide for the baby too."

He didn't say a word. I let it go. Eventually, when it was safe, we would have to discuss me having a life. The other day he'd ignored me when the mention of me working came up.

We turned down a dirt country road. Orange groves lined the road. It was beautiful as I took in a deep breath and was rewarded with the orange smell. A white house with a front porch came into sight. It was well kept and warmer than the cabin had been. I missed the cabin. It became like a home as Bane and I pretended to be the loving couple. The memories stabbed at my heart like a knife. I distracted myself with talking. "This wasn't what I imagined."

"It's not a safe house, but it's set up like one. Security is optimal for what we need. It's not as rough as I go." He chuckled. "I like to be completely isolated when I'm laying low. But, I think it's best if we're not."

"For the baby." My hand came out and touched my stomach. I couldn't wait to feel the baby kick.

Bane looked at my stomach and a sweet smile graced his lips. "Yes, for the baby."

Tingles erupted over my skin at his loving voice, but I needed to know where he was with all this. "Bane, are we going to talk about what you think about all this?"

"Yes." That was all I was getting. This was frustrating. To my relief he continued, "Maren, I want us to be alone when we talk about everything. We've been surrounded by people or driving. This is something I don't want you to think I'm taking lightly. I want you to see all of me, not the version I let others see."

Wow. I hadn't been expecting that. Was it bad what he wanted to say? I touched my stomach. *Little one, we'll be okay if it's bad news. I know how to survive. We'll be okay.* Even though Bane said he wanted to be involved with everything, it could have been the drugs talking. In the light of day, he may have changed his mind. Glancing back at Bane, he intently watched the road. It wouldn't be long until all of our cards were hopefully out on the table.

Bane parked the car. The swing on the front porch called to me. I couldn't wait to sip tea and watch the sunset if that was allowed. "Let them check the house first and then we can get out."

I hated this part of going places. The same happened when we boarded the private plane to come to Florida. Watching other people disappear behind doors, expecting someone to be there, wracked my nerves.

The three burly men got out of the car and proceeded to the house. Bane wore an earpiece that he communicated with the security team on. Nothing came from the house as I glanced back and forth. A few times he nodded to himself, gave instructions or confirmed something. My nerves were on edge as I acutely watched what was going on around me, waiting for someone to come out of nowhere like they had at the cabin.

My hand gripped the door. A few minutes later the men came out. Bane grabbed my knee and I jumped letting out a yelp. "It's okay, Maren. I didn't mean to scare you." I nodded. "We're clear to go in. Are you ready?"

"Yes."

Getting out of the car, Bane came behind me, putting his hand on my lower back. There was no doubt I missed his touch, the feeling of him inside me. *Stop it, Maren.* I could not continue the unhealthy relationship we had for a few orgasms. It wouldn't be good for the baby when my heart broke from Bane not being able to give me what I needed—his love. I knew his heart belonged to someone else I could never be.

The love of someone's life could never be replaced. I didn't want to replace Jasmine, but I didn't want to live in her shadow either.

I focused back on the house. This was my new home. My only home for the time being. I'd never go home again or see Frankie. It was all gone. It was hard to wrap my head around it all, but I had to be strong. All along I knew the time to leave would come when I was at the cabin. Reality of that decision was harder than I'd expected.

The men greeted us on the front porch. "All is clear. Everything is as you instructed."

"Thanks, rotating shifts twenty-four seven. I want hourly reports for now." Bane's direct tone would have me shriveling in the corner. He'd always been warmer to me.

The one with the lighter hair of the three stepped forward. "Yes, sir."

The men intimated me with their cold tones and gestures—almost like robots. Ushering me in the house, Bane closed the door behind us. It was as simple farmhouse with an open floor plan and warm colors. It smelled of a citrus cleaning supply of some sort. Good thing my stomach agreed with the smell. Breakfast on the plane nearly did me in with the smell of sausage.

Walking toward the other end of the house there was a small hallway with four doors. Three looked to be bedrooms and one a bathroom.

"You have new clothes in this bedroom." I walked into the room Bane gestured to. It was the master bedroom. The light-pine furniture was sparse in the room. Walking over to the closet, I opened the door and found the clothes Bane referenced. They seemed to be comfy in nature and light fitting. It had been such a long time since someone truly took care of me.

This is only because of the baby. Don't confuse the lines, Maren.

Bane's body pressed closed behind, eliciting goose bumps that longed for his touch. I fought my body to lean into him. His body heat seeped into me. "I know you won't be showing for a bit, but I wanted to make sure you were comfortable. If there is anything you need, I can get it for you."

"This will be perfect. Thank you." It was amazing I hadn't become a stuttering mess in my response.

It was hard fighting my bodies reaction to want to turn into Bane's embrace, but it would only lead to one thing—Kissing. The kissing would lead to another thing—clothes being shed. The clothes being shed would lead to—hot sweaty sex.

Stop it, Maren!

I needed to get my hormones in check. Hell, it wasn't my hormones it was my attraction to Bane.

Hot breath tickled my neck. "Want something to drink."

"Umm … yeah that would be great."

Hearing Bane leave, I sagged against the wall. Would one more time hurt? Yes, yes it would. Having a child, his child, growing within me would make sex different. It wouldn't be sex for me. Taking deep breaths, I worked on calming my erratic pulse.

I can do this.

I pushed off the wall and headed to the kitchen. Bane had two glasses of ice water poured. Wordlessly he moved to the cream colored couch and placed the drinks on the pine coffee table. Bane sat in the middle of the couch which meant we'd be sitting next to each other regardless of what side I chose. It was too soon to be in that close. My newly built walls would surely crumble.

Taking the glass, I sat in the recliner across the way. A frown formed on Bane as he nodded to himself. "Maren, I'm going to cut right to the heart of the matter. I know this isn't what either one of us planned, but I am happy about this baby. That morning in the bedroom I wanted to ask you to stay, but my fucked up past kept me from doing so. This baby kept me from losing you. It's been a long time since I've cared about anything."

Tears formed in my eyes as I heard the words, but the pain of rejection still scarred my memories. I mashed my lips together and wiped away the moisture that accumulated on the outside of the glass. If I spoke, I would cry.

"Maren, you're not a replacement for Jasmine. I swear. What can I do to convince you?"

The sincerity in Bane's voice seemed to ring true, but so had his words when he hadn't wanted to continue the relationship. I was confused. Clearing my throat, I responded with a semi-hoarse voice. "Bane, I need time. I think you're doing this because you're scared of losing the baby. It won't happen. I would never do that to you."

Bane stood, his muscular frame in control of his every

movement as he moved toward me. He knelt in front of me. "I know you wouldn't. I'll prove it to you. I'll convince you how I feel. Words won't work right now."

There was nothing I could say as a tear slipped down my cheek. I hope he was telling the truth, but I didn't dare hope.

CHAPTER 25

BANE

IT HAD BEEN a week since we'd arrived in Brandon, Florida. It was the middle of the night while the clocked ticked on the wall. Each night, I semi-slept in the recliner that faced Maren's room. In the early morning hours, I'd go to the kitchen to make coffee after messing up the sheets in the guest room.

All I cared about were keeping Maren and the baby safe. So far nothing happened that would make me think we were in danger, but I refused to relax this time around like I had before.

Out here, in the living room, I could hear everything that was going on. Also, I didn't want the nightmares to come back and disturb Maren. So far, they hadn't come back since I'd begun sleeping with her in Colorado. Minimizing my sleep to only an hour or two at a time ensured that they wouldn't return.

I was miserable being away from my angel at night.

So far, I hadn't made much headway with Maren. Sure, we were friendly and talked about the baby. But, everything stayed on the surface level. Anytime I tried to delve deeper, Maren avoided the topic. Plus, she was incredibly tired. I'd studied up on the first trimester and knew it was normal, but I worried every second of the day that something would happen to either of them.

I sighed as I watched her door, wishing I was in there with her. What could I do? Her walls were getting stronger every damn day. There was no doubt that she still wanted me. Attraction, desire, want, or caring wasn't the problem. Trusting me was. I wasn't sure what my next step should be so I treaded water. Staying in place wasn't moving forward, but at least it wasn't backward.

My eyes grew heavy. If I only shut them for a little bit, I'd get the needed sleep to make it through the night. As my eyes drifted close, the door opened sending me into an upright position. Maren walked out toward the kitchen. There was no avoiding her seeing me in the moonlight. She froze. "What are you doing up?"

"I—I—I" Fuck, I was at a loss for words.

Maren walked up to me, her bare legs had me wanting to run my hands up them to the core of her body while she writhed beneath me. "Are you sleeping out here?"

"I wanted to make sure you guys are safe."

She knelt in front of me. "Bane, you have three guys watching this place twenty-four seven."

"I know, but I wanted to make sure. Out here, I can hear everything."

Maren's eyes searched mine in the moonlight. I felt like

she had a direct window into my soul. "Have you been doing this since we got here?"

"Yes."

A long silence permeated the air. Maren stood and held out her hand. "Bane, you need to sleep."

I knew I was running on fucking fumes. "I will. I promise"

Maren kept holding out her hand. I took it not knowing where this was going. Silently she led me to her room. "Do you want to stay in here with me? It's nothing sexual, but you need your sleep. Will that help?"

"Yes."

My body craved to be near Maren, let alone inside her. I missed her. Maren dropped my hand. "Let's get some sleep."

Slipping into my side of the bed, I fought the urge to pull her to me. This was the most progress I'd made all week, and I wasn't going to do anything to mess it up.

Through the night, her sleepy voice wound through the air. "Night, Bane. Thanks for caring about the baby. I'm glad you want to be involved."

"I care about you both. I care about you, Maren."

A hand came out to grab mine. "I care about you, too."

I swallowed and knew what I needed to do. Before I had a chance to second guess myself, I spoke. "I was fresh out of Black Division. My first stop was Alaska which was where Jasmine lived. I'd met her in New York City when I was on a two week leave between assignments. The day I landed I found out Jasmine was six months pregnant. Our last time together, she'd gotten pregnant. There was no way to reach me with being on assignment and getting debriefed out of the division."

Taking a deep sigh, the memories came back as I continued, "I already knew I wanted to marry her. Had already bought us a house. The baby was an added bonus. I was ready to embrace the family life. The second morning I was back I took Jasmine to the spot I told her I loved her the first time. I proposed and then the familiar sound of a sniper shooting came through the air."

I closed my eyes as the most painful part of the story washed over me. "Turning to get Jasmine, I noticed she'd been shot in the head. I felt the last kicks of my child within her as our daughter fought to survive. There was nothing I could do. They died because of my ties to the Black Division. If I hadn't of gone to them, they'd be alive."

Sniffles stopped my story. Maren squeezed my hand. "Maren, it's why I vowed to never be close to anyone. It's why I denied myself from telling you that I wanted you to stay. For us to have a chance to figure things out. Then, the baby was like the miracle I needed to keep you in my life."

Anticipation filled me as I waited for her response. All I wanted was to have a chance.

The bed shifted and I felt Maren scoot closer. "The baby is a miracle, Bane. It's our miracle. I get it, I do. I'm scared about being a mom, giving you another chance, living through this threat that I see hanging over us as we wait for the next thing to happen. It's a lot to process."

A thought occurred to me on what I could do. I squeezed Maren's hand. "Let's get some sleep."

"Okay." I could tell that was not the response she expected. Showing her would be better than telling her.

Through the night, we never let each other's hand go. It was the first time in a week I'd slept.

Morning was upon us as I finished putting the bagel and cream cheese on a plate with Maren's orange juice. For now, she kept her breakfasts simple for the slight nausea she had. Thank goodness she hadn't been too sick. Some smells bothered her more than others … especially meat.

I nudged open the door to see Maren's brunette hair splayed across the pillow while she peacefully slept. *My angel.* She'd unknowingly snuggled closer to me through the night and whispered my name. Music to my ears as I cherished the way her body felt against mine.

She stirred. Normally she woke up around seven. It was seven twenty-three. I laid the tray on the nightstand. "Morning, angel. How does breakfast in bed sound?"

Wiping her eyes she smiled sleepily at me. "I haven't had breakfast in bed since before my Dad died. This is a treat. Thank you."

Every moment of every day I was going to try and show Maren how special she was. "You're welcome." Taking a deep breath, I prepared to say what I'd been thinking about when my phone rang. Only a few people had this number. Pulling it out of my pocket, I saw it was Hampton. "I need to take this."

Maren took a sip of orange juice. "Of course."

Standing, I answered. "Hampton?"

The familiar voice answered me, "Hey, Bane. Division stopped by. I would imagine they'll be at your doorstep at any minute."

I knew they'd come, but I thought out of courtesy they'd call me first. Those fuckers had gotten my location and then kept Hampton engaged in conversation until they were too close for anything to be done. My earpiece buzzed and security came across the line. "Sir, three black vehicles have turned down the dirt road. Are they cleared?"

I muted the phone with Hampton before answering, "Yes. Stand down. I'll be out to greet them."

Unmuting the phone, I said, "Hampton. They're here. We'll talk later."

"Sounds good."

My heart thundered in my chest. I wanted to grab Maren and run away. We'd make it out of here, but then I'd look guilty as hell. The last thing I needed was to have the wrath of the Black Division rain down on us. We'd be on the run for the rest of our lives. I wanted a different life for Maren and our child.

With someone like Sarge vanishing they'd be turning over every stone to find him. Plus, there was a chance they knew about the communication with him. It surprised me they hadn't come before now which was a good sign hopefully.

Of course, I had a plan if we did need to escape. Being afraid of stressing Maren out with the spotting, we hadn't discussed the possibility of Black Division visiting. Maren took a bite of bagel and stopped when she saw my face.

"What's wrong, Bane?"

I sat on the edge of the bed. "Division is about to be here in maybe a minute. I doubt they know. They're going to wonder why I have security and I'm going to tell them you're pregnant. They'll figure it out when we go to the next doctor's appointment as I'll be watched for a bit to see if there's anything out of place. Just go with everything I say. We need to be dating, okay?"

She nodded. The stress on her face was what I'd been trying to avoid this entire time. Fuck. I should have warned her this was a possibility. "Angel, get dressed. I promise I won't let anything happen to you guys. Okay?"

She nodded her head rapidly. "I'll be right out."

I kissed her on the forehead. "I'll keep you both safe. Trust me."

"I do." I knew she trusted me with her safety, her heart was another thing.

Quickly, I left the bedroom and grabbed a cup of coffee. The more normal I appeared, the better. Making it out on the front porch, five black unmarked SUV's pulled up. Only six men deployed out of the vehicles. There were probably twelve to fifteen. Another good sign. From the middle car, Alex came out wearing a dark business suit. He looked the same as when I was in Black Division with his white, slicked-back hair.

Alex had been Sarge's superior.

"Bane. Mind if we talk inside?"

I took a sip of coffee. "Of course not. My girlfriend is in there. Besides these three men …" I gestured to the two guys on my left and one on my right. "I'm alone." My guys were relaxed in their posture, but were watching my every move in case I signaled to them. They were good. Hopefully, with me identifying everyone up front, it helped sell that I had nothing to worry about.

The fact was, I had everything to lose.

"Mind if we go in alone?" Alex still prodded me with questions to see my reaction.

And he meant, *mind if we go in without your men.* "Of course not."

Alex looked a lot like Hampton with his white hair and tall lean build. Regardless of rank, everyone in the Black Division was fit—conditioned to take on a fight in a moment's notice.

I hoped to hell that this worked. It had to work. Outwardly I stayed unaffected, but I was a nervous wreck on the inside. Only two of the other guys followed us in. It meant they trusted me or didn't believe I was part of anything. My record was impeccable. Maren came out dressed in jeans and a long-sleeved shirt. Her face took on a glow and I smiled at her.

"Alex, this is my girlfriend, Maren. Maren, this is Alex—a friend from the past." Maren knew not to talk about the Black Division from previous discussions.

She glanced at the security guards who accompanied us in. Alex spoke. "For my protection, dear. They're like secret service men."

Maren stuck out her hand. "Oh wow. It's nice to meet you, Alex."

"Likewise. Do you mind if I speak a few minutes alone with Bane?" His voice was silky smooth, but I could tell he assessed her every move to see if she hid anything. So far, Maren hid her emotions well.

"No, not at all." Walking to me, she gave me a quick kiss on the cheek. "I'll be in the bedroom."

Maren left the room. Alex remained standing and so did I. Hopefully that meant this was going to be a short visit. If not, he'd done a hell of a job separating Maren and me.

CHAPTER
26

MAREN

I CLOSED THE bedroom door behind me and heaved a sigh of relief. My palms sweated. Leaning against the bedroom door, I tried to hear what they were saying. The voices were too low. Why was Division here? Were they on to us? The possibility always lingered in the back of my mind. The last thing I wanted was to be separated from Bane. If something did happen, I wasn't sure if he could get to me.

There was no reason to have those types of thoughts. Bane found a way and nearly died. I shuddered at the thought of something happening to him. I spoke lowly, "We'll, be okay little one. Your daddy is going to make sure."

To busy myself I made the bed and then finished off my bagel. I wondered how long it would be until I got the baby bump as I looked at my still flat stomach. There was a life in there. It was still amazing to me as I tried to think of myself pregnant.

From what I read I would begin to feel the flutters of the baby around four and a half months. I couldn't wait. Turning around a man stood in the window staring at me with his hands cupped around his face.

I screamed, "AHH! Bane!" and backed toward the wall. The man wearing the black solider uniform disappeared from the window as the door busted open.

"Maren, are you oaky?" Alex was close behind as Bane drew a gun searching the room. More soldiers came close behind Alex. He held up his hand.

I stared out the window. "There was a guy staring at me with his hands cupped to the window. I had my shirt raised looking at my stomach. It startled me. I'm okay."

Bane glared at Alex who walked out of the room. His lips came to my ear. "Everything is fine. I won't leave you again."

I didn't say a word as I hugged him and took in his manly woodsy scent. This was all too close to what we'd gone through not long ago. The fear and loss was still too close to home. I took deep calming breaths. The last thing I needed to do was alert Alex that more was going on than appeared. Footsteps came back into the room. "Is she okay?"

"Yes, just shook her up a little."

Alex's voice was directed to me. "I'm sorry, Maren. He's back in the car. It will be dealt with."

Pulling back, I gave Alex a quick smile and got my emotions under control. "I'm okay. The hormones have me a little more emotional and jumpy than normal."

Alex gave me a smile. "I hear congratulations are in order."

"Yes, we're very excited." Glancing up to Bane, he

looked down at me with … could it be love? Little flutters filled me as the possibility seemed more likely from Bane's actions. I hoped our paths were going in the same direction. I wanted to give Bane a chance—to be a family.

Alex nodded, pleased. He was different than Sarge had been. He shook Bane's hand. "We'll be in touch. I need to get going."

"Thanks for stopping by."

Leaving the room to follow Alex, I blew out an imperceptible breath as we made it to the door. Was it that easy? I remained in the living room as Bane stepped out the front door. I'd only been up for less than an hour, but felt exhausted from this morning's activities. Overall, I was more tired than normal from the pregnancy. Cars cranked and Bane stepped inside, holding his finger to his lips. I nodded and laid on the couch.

If we weren't able to talk about anything, I'd close my eyes for a few. A blanket covered me and lips pressed to the side of my cheek. "Angel, I'm going to work on my laptop for a bit. Rest."

"I will."

That was all it took for me to fall asleep.

I woke up with the sun high in the sky when I glanced out the windows. Bane sat at the kitchen table with his laptop, doing who knows what. "I feel like I could give the dead a run for their money with how much I've been sleeping lately."

Bane closed the laptop and gave me a smile. "You're creating a life. It's normal until the first trimester ends."

"How do you know all this?" Bane constantly seemed to

know more than me when it came to this sort of thing even though I read about what to expect all the time. *Faith.* Instantly, I felt like an ass. "I'm sorry. I forgot. That was insensitive of me."

Coming to sit on the coffee table in front of me, Bane grew serious. "I wasn't a part of Jasmine's pregnancy except for two days. I've been reading up on everything while we've been here this last week, making sure I'm doing everything I can for you."

The warmth spread inside me as a smile spread across my face. "You're showing me up already."

He chuckled and his voice resonated. "There's nothing I could do to show up the mother of my child."

I sat up and Bane took this as an invitation to sit beside me. Against his shoulder, I asked. "Can we talk?" What I wanted to ask was, *are we safe?*

"Yes, we're safe. We'll be monitored from afar, but we are safe. Alex asked why we were here with security. I explained you were pregnant, we were dating, and that I wasn't taking any chances this time around given my history. He understood and wanted to know how I'd explained it to you."

Oh, I was glad that Alex hadn't pushed for information from me. Bane coached me on the standard answers, but I didn't want to be questioned by someone at Black Division. After my experience with Sarge, I had a rather dismal view of the group. "What did you say?"

"What I'd told you—that I'd made some questionable enemies while I worked for an oil company in the Middle East. That I lost my first child and all you cared about was keeping the baby safe."

How many lies had Bane told Jasmine? Or did she know the truth? It wasn't my place to ask. If Bane wanted to volunteer the information, he would. "Did he ask anything else about Sarge?"

"Yes, he wanted to know what happened. He knew about my communication with Sarge. I told him Eric Thornhill came after us and you believed it was someone from the Middle East. Sarge had been contacted. Originally, I'd been set to meet them, but I received a message from Sarge that Eric had been eliminated. I never left your side, saw Eric or Sarge."

Everything seemed too easy. Maybe Bane and Hampton's incessant planning paid off. The answer was obvious, but I had to ask. "What happens if they find out we're lying?"

"They won't, angel. Hampton and I have covered our tracks. We'll be fine. If something goes wrong, we'll disappear." Being on the run wasn't something I wanted to do for the rest of my life. Hopefully, it wouldn't come to that. "How about I cook you something? We could talk."

That was an abrupt change of topic. Talk? We always talked, but I enjoyed spending time with Bane. Talking helped lessen me missing the intimacy we'd once shared. "I'd like that. What do you want me to do?"

Bane led me over to the bar where he directed me to sit at one of the two high-backed chairs. "How about grilled cheese?"

I giggled. "Really? Grilled cheese?"

"It's one hell of a grilled cheese." He wagged his eyebrows.

My stomach rumbled. "I can't wait."

Bane moved around the kitchen with ease. Grabbing the bread, mayo, butter, cheese, and a skillet he got to work. "When I was a boy I loved grilled cheese. They were easy to make."

"Did your mom or dad teach you?"

Bane grimaced. "I never knew my father. My mother could hardly be considered one."

My heart hurt for Bane. So much pain in his life. Was this his way of opening up to me? "I'm so sorry, Bane."

"It's in the past. I've dealt with it. I've made a vow to make sure my kid knows what unconditional love is like." He paused as he prepared the sandwiches. "As soon as I was old enough, I left and joined the marines, which led me to the Black Division. Seems the group that saved me nearly destroyed me also." The pan sizzled with butter. I couldn't believe how open Bane was being. "No one ever knew this except now you."

No one? Jasmine was having his kid. Surely she knew. I couldn't bring myself to ask. It was trivial. She was dead and he'd loved her. I understood, but it made it hard to navigate these conversations at times knowing I wanted to be the center of his world. The damn hormones kicked in as I tried to keep back the tears.

Bane placed the grilled cheese in front of me. I took a deep breath as he knelt beside me. My heart hammered. "Maren …" I focused on the sear marks of the bread. The last thing I needed to do was cry. "Maren, please look at me." I did. "Not even Jasmine knew about all that. She didn't know any specifics about the Black Division. She didn't know about the darkness that's inside of me. Only you."

"Bane—"

He put his finger to my mouth. "I wanted you to have a little more of my past to explain why I reacted the way I did. Love doesn't come easy for me. Giving myself to someone is even harder. I've lost everything I've ever loved or wanted … except you and the baby. I'm terrified if I get too close or don't stay focused that the same thing will happen to you."

Removing his finger, I stayed silent as the tears fell down. Bane sat beside me and took a bite of his grilled cheese. I followed suit as he watched me. The flavors burst across my tongue. "Oh wow, the sandwich is delicious."

The cheese melted in my mouth with the savory butter bread.

He gave me a wink and I saw the carefree side of Bane that was rare. "It's all in the mayo that's used."

I giggled again. "Well, I can see these being in high demand through the pregnancy."

Bane beamed. "I'd like that."

———

A few days passed since Alex paid us a visit. No one triggered any of the alarms that surrounded the property. My mind eased, but maybe that was what they wanted. It was tiresome constantly wondering what was going to happen.

Bane tirelessly checked everything and kept in contact with the security. They had to be making a pretty penny being with us nonstop. Money wasn't an issue with Bane. It was hard to imagine me being in my apartment with all the bugs. So much had changed … for the better.

The security team had been on regular scouting trips to check for snipers. Every time I heard the word I felt queasy knowing that was how Jasmine was killed while Bane felt his child die in her womb. There were no words to describe the pain I would feel if I was left without Bane or our child.

Through the days and nights, Bane and I continued to share more about ourselves on a more personal level. We knew all of the surface level stuff about each other, but he was going beneath the surface. His mom had been a terrible person with what she'd done to him. I knew it all and it only drew me closer to him.

Not leaving the house made me stir crazy as I tidied the living room for the hundredth time this morning. Bane was outside on the porch talking to one of the men. I never saw them except occasionally out a window. On the mantle, I straightened and angled all of the decorative pieces a new way to see if I liked it better. Getting out of the house was about to become a necessity instead of a want. Bane walked back in the room wearing a short sleeve black T-shirt and jeans. "Want to take a walk?"

I froze as I adjusted the throw pillows. "Are you serious?"

There was more to Bane than I ever realized and I was falling for him. Dangerously falling for him as my heart became engulfed with the feeling. It was dangerous to feel this way and I was terrified of being hurt again.

"Yes, I thought the fresh air would do all of us some good. I know you're going stir crazy." Eyeing the pillow in my hand he suppressed his chortle.

Nothing more had been said about Jasmine. I was also scared that Bane wanted me around simply because of the baby. I wasn't sure where we stood or what we wanted out of this. Maybe Bane was thinking it all through deciding what he honestly wanted.

"I'd love to."

Slipping on my shoes, I followed Bane out the front door excited to feel the sun against my face, the wind in my hair, and hear the birds chirping. It was a beautiful day. Bane grabbed my hand as we walked down the driveway with the gravel crunching under our feet. Holding hands felt intimate with Bane over these last few days. When we slept together at night, he would hold my hand. I loved it.

The citrus smell filled the air as I filled my lungs.

"What scares you about being with me?"

I momentarily paused and looked up at Bane. His dark eyes showed the raw pain he exposed himself to. The truth needed to be out there in the open. "That you are only trying to be with me because of the baby. If the baby wasn't here, you'd have left me without a second thought or would leave me if something happened."

Bane shook his head. "It's not about what I've done. The innocent people I've accidentally killed. The chaos I've caused. The deaths I'm responsible for."

We'd spent hours talking about Bane's past. "No, none of that scares me. You survived, but you never strayed from the line."

He took a deep breath. "Maren, there is only the line. It doesn't matter how far you cross it. The line is the line."

I thought for a minute on how to respond. "I get what you're saying, Bane, but if you really believe you crossed the line … I believe the reasons matter. You've saved so many lives. The world is a better place because of you." We kept walking in silence as we approached the edge of the grove. A blanket laid out on the grass. "What's this?"

"I thought we could sit out here and talk like we have been."

Laying on the blanket, I looked up at the sky. Bane followed my actions. Peace. I felt peace. The clouds were plentiful as they danced through the sky like white cotton balls. Moments like this made it easier to get through the more stressful situations.

Reliving a memory, I said, "During the summer, my dad would lay a blanket out in the back yard with Frankie and me.

We'd stare up at the sky and make shapes out of the clouds that passed by. Dad always said you could tell a lot about yourself with what you saw."

Bane stayed quiet as he looked up at the sky and grabbed my hand. That excited nervous butterfly like feeling came over me. In the last few days, the small touches seemed more intimate than all the sex prior to Eric capturing us. Something changed between us. If things became more intense than they had been and Bane decided to walk away, I would be shattered.

Bane brought me out of my inner thoughts as he asked, "What do you see today?"

Gazing up at the clouds, I waited for one of them to take shape for me. "I see a giant bowl of ice cream loaded down with chocolate syrup and sprinkles." I laughed. "I guess food is starting to always be on my mind."

His thumb caressed mine. More clouds lazily passed by. "I see a dad reading a story to a child."

I rolled over on my side. "Bane, you deserve to be happy."

His dark, penetrating eyes looked at me without saying a word. So much emotion passed over his face as his thumb caressed my cheek. "I'm afraid that it's all going to be taken away from me again. I'm falling for you, Maren. Over these past few weeks you've seen the real me. No one has ever seen the real me."

Something inside of me needed to feel Bane as I moved closer, our lips a breath apart. "I've fallen for you too, Bane. But we have to be sure we're together for the right reasons— not because of our great chemistry or the fact that we have a baby on the way. We'll only end up hurting the baby if we're together for convenience or out of obligation. It's easy to be lost in our feelings while we're isolated from the world. Now, that you've opened yourself up to the possibility of being happy, you may not know what you want yet."

It was hard saying the words and I wanted to retract them. The truth was I didn't want to share Bane with anyone, but for this to work he had to be free to choose and not feel pressured. Bane's lips came out and touched mine. "I'll prove it to you."

His tongue touched my lips. I missed his taste as need raced through me. Deepening the kiss, our tongues danced with each other. Bane moaned a deep reverberation that reached my core. Snaking his hand up my shirt, I wanted him inside me. I pulled him closer to me and Bane positioned himself in between my legs. It didn't matter that we were in the middle of an orange grove, I didn't care. All I wanted was him, inside me.

Tender lips caressed my neck as I arched into him gasping for air from the intense kiss. Bane's hardened length ground against me through his jeans. Desperate, I clawed at his shirt to bring him closer. Then, everything slowed. I tried to speed him up, but he pulled back. "Angel, I want you."

"I want you too."

He put a little more distance between us, enough to help clear the fog. "I won't let this be about sex. When we have sex again it will be because you know I want you for you—not because I can't control my dick. There will be no doubt in your mind that I'm in this for the long haul."

My breathing was erratic. I was turned on, but his words blossomed inside of me. He was right. If we had sex, I'd always wonder. Bane knew me well. I closed my eyes. "This is going to be hard."

Tracing his nose along my jaw, every fiber in my being screamed for us to lose control and deal with the consequences later. "It'll be worth it."

Oh geez. This was not helping matters. I hoped my mind caught up quickly and believed what Bane was saying.

CHAPTER 27

BANE

MAREN WAS SEVEN weeks pregnant and we were about to head to the doctor's office in town. How the hell I'd managed to not sink inside of her for the last week or so was beyond me. I wanted in her tight heat, but needed to wait. I had to make sure she knew this was not about sex.

Fuck. I hoped the opportunity presented itself sooner rather than later.

My dick was in a constant state of feeling like a sledge hammer. And trust me, my angel made it hard to resist. I knew she was tempting me. Hell, she wanted it. Last night I'd read that a woman's sex drive increased during pregnancy. Maren needed some kind of relief before she sent me over the edge and we did something we weren't ready for.

Fuck, I was screwed. My hand was not cutting the job in

the shower. I felt like a pansy-ass sneaking off, spilling my cum down the drain like a teenager who couldn't control his cravings. As the days ticked by, Maren became more provocative. There was only so much strength a man had.

I was losing this battle.

Maren was in the bedroom getting ready. It was safest for me to be out here with my hot cup of coffee looking out the window, pretending she was not in our room naked. Thank goodness the pregnancy knocked her out fast asleep as soon as her head hit the pillow. In the morning, I slipped out of bed before she could try to seduce me into changing my mind. It wouldn't take much. I had a plan and I wanted to follow through.

All I needed was the opportunity.

I'd received a message from Alex. He'd found what he believed to be Sarge and Eric's bodies. Well, he'd found what we wanted him to believe were their bodies. We'd removed their teeth prior to setting the cabin on fire. While I recovered, Hampton found two corpses of similar build and replaced the cadavers' teeth with theirs.

It was amazing what we knew how to do from training at the Black Division. Heat destroyed organic material. There would be no trace as to who was left at the site after we were done.

Hampton staged it to where it appeared a small grenade went off, setting a chain reaction near a boat dock which was next to a tank of gasoline. They'd assume Eric and Sarge were in a standoff. Sarge would be a hero and Eric a traitor. The thought was foul, but it kept all of us out of the spotlight. We'd rigged the substitute corpses to only have a piece or two of the tooth survive so Black Division could extract mitochondrial DNA.

Once the identification was one hundred percent confirmed, it would be behind us. Alex hadn't mentioned me coming back. I didn't trust anyone, but I think it had been Sarge's hidden agenda all along—not the Black Division. At least that was what seemed to be the case.

Time would tell, but they wouldn't catch me unprepared this time.

Maren and I had some serious decisions to make. Hampton did too. One thing at a time. This thing with Alex needed to wrap up first.

The door creaked open. I took a deep breath as I readied myself to keep my dick in my pants. My body craved to be closer to Maren. *I'll have her and the baby in my life if I do this right ... forever.*

Taking a sip of coffee, I turned and spewed it out, choking. "Fuck!" Maren dropped her towel, revealing her body.

Hurt flashed across her eyes as she scrambled to pick up the towel. Her emotions were all over the place lately. Quickly, I sat the cup of coffee down and went to Maren. "Angel, you look breathtakingly gorgeous. I wasn't expecting it."

"Why don't you want me?"

Keep control of the situation, Bane. The desire was evident in her eyes. She needed pleasure. "I want you more than you know. I've whacked off more times than I can count to thinking about you in the shower."

"Then take me."

"Not yet, but I'll pleasure you, angel. I know you have needs." I ran my hands down her neck and she leaned back. If I took her to the bedroom, I wouldn't have the willpower to survive. Gently, I coaxed Maren to the edge of the couch. She braced herself with her arms.

With my left hand wrapping around the back of her neck,

she leaned back. I trailed my free right hand down her sternum. Her legs moved together. It wouldn't take much to send her over the edge. Her nipples beaded as I brushed over them with my fingertips.

Hell, I was going to need five cold showers after this. I leaned down and sucked one beaded point into my mouth as my hand glided down her stomach. There was a small bump. Her body was changing. I knew it intimately and fucking loved it.

My hand dipped inside her wet folds and Maren arched, putting more weight on my forearm. "Don't make me wait, Bane. I've needed this for a while."

I felt guilty for ignoring her needs, but knew the end result would be worth the torture for us. My thumb pushed against her clit, eliciting an erotic moan as I felt her wetness. Maren was past ready as warmth radiated from her. I massaged her walls as they tightened around me while giving her nipples little bites. She was more sensitive than normal and responded to my touch.

Touching her just right, she arched and cried out as her orgasm took over. She was beautiful with the soft glow that emanated from her. Sagging, she languidly opened her eyes. "Best orgasm ever."

I chuckled, knowing I could do better than that, but didn't want to stoke the fire for my own sake. Giving her a quick kiss, I whispered against her lips. "I'm sorry I've neglected you."

Maren kissed me. I wanted to take her over the couch and drill her into it. She was getting closer to accepting I was in this for the right reasons, but she wasn't there … yet. I pulled back. "We need to leave in about twenty minutes to make it to the doctor."

"Give me one more. I'll hurry."

There was no denying my angel as I touched her. My heart knew I felt more than I'd ever felt before.

In the hospital gown, Maren looked around the room. I hadn't been in a girlie doctor's office before. The place was filled with fake model vaginas and ovaries. I mean, what the fuck? No wonder there were guys in this field. Hands in pussies and surrounded by all this shit. It was a bachelor's walking wet dream.

I'd made sure we saw a female doctor. There was no way in hell some asshole was touching Maren. No fucking way. There was no doubt I'd snap his neck.

Excitedly, Maren asked, "Are you ready to hear the heartbeat?" I'd never heard one before.

I swallowed hard. "I am."

Maren grabbed my hand. "It's going to be okay."

All the time, I imagined different scenarios that would take her and the baby from me.

The door opened and a middle-aged female doctor walked in. "Hello, I'm Doctor Kelly Chase. How are you doing, Mrs. Childers?"

Maren glanced to me worried. I gave her an easy smile, remembering I'd forgotten to tell her I'd registered her under her alias, Kendra Childers.

She relaxed. "I'm good. I've been tired, but that seems to be normal. Two weeks ago I saw a doctor in a town we were visiting for spotting. He said that it was normal and not to worry unless it happened again."

Doctor Chase made a few notes. "Has it?"

"No. Everything seems normal. I'm taking my prenatal vitamins and folic acid."

"Perfect." The doctor flipped through all the paperwork Maren filled out. "Everything looks good on your charts you provided. Let's hear the heartbeat and check out everything. Are you ready?"

Emphatically, Maren answered, "Yes! I've been waiting for this appointment anxiously."

Maren gave me a glorious smile. The doctor instructed Maren to lean back. I stayed near Maren's head and held her hand. The doctor checked Maren's cervix. Yeah, there was no way I could have survived this with a man. Withdrawing, the doctor took off her gloves. "Everything seems right on track for seven weeks. Let's listen to the baby."

My heart caught in my throat as I waited to hear the sound of another life I'd been part of creating. A little goo was added to Maren's stomach. A little microphone-type thing was held to her stomach. After a few different positions, a whooshing sound came through the little speakers. "That's the heartbeat."

That was my baby. My baby was alive. My baby was real. I hadn't let myself fully embrace it all. I wanted a life with Maren and this child more than anything.

Tears formed in Maren's eyes as she looked at me. "That's our baby. We created this, Bane."

"I know, angel. It's perfect."

The doctor positioned it again and again. A frown forming on her forehead. I went on high alert, but tried to stay outwardly calm as Maren turned toward the speakers, listening to the thrumming sound of the heart. The doctor spoke. "I want to do an ultra sound. Let me go check with the nurse to get you squeezed in while you get dressed."

"What's wrong, Doctor Chase?" Maren caught on to the doctor's tone.

Doctor Chase gave Maren a comforting smile. "There's nothing wrong. I'm picking up an echo on the heart and want a better look."

My heart plummeted. I knew this was too good to be true. There was something wrong. Maren's lip quivered after the doctor left. I had to be strong for her. "Angel, let's wait to see what the doctor has to say. She wants to check it out. Let's get dressed."

She nodded and I helped her back into her clothes. The doctor popped back in the room. "The nurse is able to fit you in if you're ready."

Grabbing her purse, I followed Maren out. She rubbed her stomach and I saw her lips moving, no doubt talking to the baby. It hit me, this was my moment. I put my hand on Maren's shoulder stopping her. "Doctor, I need a second if you don't mind."

The doctor glanced back at me. "Is something wrong?"

Was something wrong? Yes, there was something potentially wrong. I tried to have faith, but it was hard as the name connected me straight to the memory of my child who hadn't made it.

"I need to speak to Kendra for a minute. It'll be quick." I'd nearly slipped and said Maren's name.

The doctor opened up a door on the side, revealing another exam room. I brought Maren in and closed the door to give us privacy. "Bane, what are you doing?"

"I need to tell you this one thing before we go in there."

"What?" I could tell Maren was aggravated and wanted to get the ultra sound.

This was my moment. I grabbed her shoulders making sure I had her full attention. "Maren, regardless of what the doctor says or finds I want you—all of you. This isn't because of the baby. I need you to know whatever they tell us, I'm not letting you go. I was a fool for trying to keep you away the last day at the cabin."

Maren cried and grabbed onto me. "I don't ever want you to let me go."

My heart burst as I finally got the girl I wanted. I was never letting her go regardless of what happened.

A light knocked rapped on the door. "Mrs. Childers, we'll lose the spot if we don't go now to the ultra sound room."

Maren sniffled. "We're coming."

I grabbed her hand and gave her a quick kiss. "Whatever happens, we'll face it together."

Walking out of the room, the doctor gave me a quizzical look at Maren's tears. She handed her a tissue. The doctor kept a pleasant smile on her face. Maren needed to understand I was all in.

I had my angel. She was mine. Only mine. The only thing that would make this day absolutely perfect was if everything was okay with the baby.

Positioning herself on the table, Maren lifted her shirt. Her hands shook as I soothingly stroked one with my thumb. A large screen flickered at the end of the room. The doctor watched the screen. Black and white fuzz filled it as the technician moved the wand across her stomach.

"Doctor, please tell me what's going on." The plead of Maren's voice nearly undid me. I wanted to choke the answers out of the doctor.

She turned and smiled to us. "I'm sorry to have scared you, but it's best to wait until a number of theories can be confirmed. The reason I heard an echo was because there's not just one baby."

Maren interrupted the doctor. "What are you saying?"

I was frozen to the spot. Did the baby have a third arm? Four legs? Two heads? My mind spun out of control with possibilities.

"You're having twins."

We asked at the same time, "What?"

The doctor gave us a gentle smile. "Yes, you're expecting twins."

"Two babies." My voice was in awe as I approached the screen. The doctor talked and pointed to two little lima bean-shaped objects in Maren's belly. Our babies. They were perfect. Beyond perfect. This was a miracle.

I repeated myself, "Two babies."

The doctor nodded to us. "Congratulations, Mom and Dad."

I was speechless as it sunk in.

Two babies. Two.

I rushed to Maren and kissed her for everyone to see, not caring that we had an audience. "I love you, angel. Thank you for giving me this."

Finally, I had let my guard down. Maren knew how I truly felt and it was fan-fucking-tastic for it to be out there. I waited as she searched my eyes and tears filled her own. What if she wasn't in love with me? Fuck.

The door shut and we were alone. I went to speak, but she cut me off. "I love you, too," she cried. "Did you mean what you said in the office before we came in here?"

Kissing her lips, I poured my love into her. "I did. Maren, when you're ready I want you to be my wife. I love you." I hadn't planned on saying it that way, but I'd learned to seize the moment. Waiting only led to regrets.

She wiped a tear from her eye. "Are you asking me to marry you?"

"I am. If you'll have me." I felt exposed as I waited for her answer, not knowing if I'd rushed this too fast.

Maren sat up and looked at me with her beautiful eyes. "Are you sure you want this? I don't want you regretting it later. Marriage is a lifetime commitment for me. We can take this slow if you need to. I'm not going anywhere."

Grabbing her beautiful face between my hands, I held her. "I will never regret spending my life with you. I've fallen in love with you over seven weeks."

This was the least romantic way to start our life together, but Maren got me. She watched me closely and my eyes never wavered from hers. Grabbing my face, she kissed me. "Yes. I'll marry you. I love you, Bane."

CHAPTER
28

MAREN

TWINS. WE WERE having twins. I held my stomach. There were two babies inside of me. Looking over at Bane, he looked happy as he pulled me to him while we laid in bed naked and entwined. The memory of his lips kissing me slowly brought goose bumps to my exposed flesh.

We'd made love for the first time. He'd held my hands as he slid in and out of me, uniting us in a way I never thought possible.

"What are you thinking about, angel?" His finger trailed down my arm. A voice of pure contentment.

For the first time, I felt what I had been missing for so long—a family. "Us. Making love. What it felt like to have you inside of me without any barriers."

Bringing me closer to him, Bane kissed my neck. His

warm breath tickled my neck. "I'm going to make love to you every day."

"Hopefully, there will still be some fuckings, too."

Bane nipped my shoulder. "Definitely."

A somber silence fell over us. "Maren, I'm scared of losing you. Of losing them."

Quietly, I added, "I'm scared of losing you. Of you realizing this life with the babies isn't for you." If Bane decided this was too much it would destroy me.

"This is it for me, angel. I'm all in." There was conviction is his voice. "No turning back. You're mine forever."

"I'm all in, too. I'm yours … forever."

A peace filled the air. Fingers trailed down my stomach. "We are going to have double the trouble."

Glancing back, Bane smiled as he chuckled. "I can't wait." He nuzzled my neck. "How fast do you want to get married?"

Married. I couldn't believe Bane proposed. "I don't want a formal wedding." The movement on my stomach stopped. "What do you want, Maren?"

"If you want something more, I'm fine with it. Okay?" I turned toward Bane. This was new territory for us on so many levels.

Bane searched my face. "I'll tell you if it's not something I want. I'll always be honest with you."

Running a finger down his chest, I told him what I wanted. "I want us to commit ourselves to each other. No wedding. No pastor." It wasn't conventional, but it fit us.

"Where?"

Excited flutters coursed through me. "Here. Now. But that's only if you want."

"Now? You're okay committing ourselves while being

naked?"

I giggled. "It may not be conventional, but I want us to be together."

Bane pulled me closer to him. "I, Bane, promise to cherish you for the rest of my days. I'll never leave or abandon you. I'll protect you and our family with every fiber of my being. I'll be yours forever."

We were doing this. Right here. Right now. I kissed him. "I, Maren, promise to love you with every ounce of my being. Be a good wife and mother. Be there for you in the good times and the bad. Let you be my everything and be yours in return."

Bane rolled on top of me as I felt the tip of him enter me. The connection between us intensified as I asked, "So, we're married?"

"We're married." He pushed in and I could sense victory coursing through him. "I love you, wife."

"I love you too, husband."

My world was complete.

Christmas was approaching in less than a week. I neared three months into the pregnancy. Sex was amazing. I couldn't get enough of it. Marriage was more than I'd ever thought. My stomach had a little bump to it with the twins. Everything showed faster and the risks were greater. I couldn't wait to feel them move around, but I was nervous. Sixty percent of all twins came prematurely. The risks were all amplified. Bane seemed to be handling all the information well, but I knew he worried.

I loved him more every day and I wanted my family more

than I'd wanted anything.

Twins. It was going to be crazy caring for two babies. With Bane by my side, I knew we could handle it. Bane laid beside me, peacefully sleeping with his hand on my stomach. It's how we slept every night. He'd told me he wanted to make sure our babies knew he was there and would never leave.

Beside the bed, his cell phone vibrated. Without missing a beat, Bane grabbed the phone, cleared his throat and spoke. "Hello. Yes. Are you sure? That's good news. Thanks, Alex. I will." I wasn't sure how he could go from fast asleep to wide awake in a nanosecond. He looked toward me after he hung up and answered my silent query. "Sarge and Eric's bodies have been identified. Looks like a deal gone bad. We're in the clear. Alex is assembling a team to take care of all the connections and see if there were any other leaks."

Relief coursed through me. I'd been trying to push it to the side with all the worry the twins brought and live in my happy bubble. I was married and in love. Stress wasn't good and I tried to pretend the underlying fear wasn't there. But now that the door had been opened, I had to ask, "Will it ever be safe for us?"

Propping up on his elbow, Bane popped his neck. "Angel, I'm not going to let anything happen to you. I will protect our family."

"I know. I trust you ... implicitly."

"But ..."

I took a deep breath as I thought about all we had been through. "But what if there are still some loose ends out there? What if Eric did tell someone else? What if Sarge had a back-up plan? I'm trying not to stress about it, Bane. But—"

He silenced me with a kiss. "Don't get stressed. It's not good for you. I have a solution, but was going to wait and discuss it with you after the pregnancy."

"What is it?"

Bane sat up and the sheet pooled at his waist, showcasing his muscular torso. Scrubbing his scalp, he watched me closely as he said, "Disappearing. Completely beginning a new life. Never contacting anyone again that we currently know. It's the safest way I know, but it means leaving everything."

It was hard to believe it would be that simple. "How would we do it?"

"Stage our deaths. Then disappear. Start over somewhere normal. Create false identities."

It was no different than what we originally planned when I was going without Bane. The decision had been easy with all that was on the line. "That's what I want to do."

"Okay, we'll go after the babies are born."

I could tell he wasn't sure if I was certain. The pregnancy did make me a little more emotional, but I knew this was the right decision. "Why not now when I'm still early in the pregnancy? When the babies are born it will make it so much harder."

"Maren, this isn't a decision to be made lightly. We—"

I put my fingers to his lips. "I know. Bane, I was willing to do it without you. I was prepared to leave Frankie." Closing my eyes for a second, I pushed the sadness away from losing my brother. "We need to do this. I don't want to look over my shoulder for the rest of my life and wonder if it's okay for the kids to play in the yard in case there's someone waiting to take them."

Rolling me under him, Bane looked me in the eyes. "Are you sure?"

"Yes. I know you'll pick a safe place for us and the pregnancy."

Bane's dick was hard against my thigh. I squirmed. Positioning himself at my entrance, he pushed in. "We'll make all the decisions together. It's you and me, my angel and wife."

I arched into the friction. "Yes. Forever."

CHAPTER 29

BANE

"THANKS, HAMPTON."

"Anytime. I'll be in touch." I hung up the phone. I was going to miss my friend as we set the plans in motion. He was the only one I trusted to help me and vice versa.

Looking at the morning paper while I sipped my coffee, I prepared for my next call using a secure line. I had connections with more people than I realized. Maren spent the last few years buried in work and helping Frankie. She'd merely survived. There were no friends Maren wanted to see one last time. It shocked me how little she was tied to this world. I'd checked on her previous jobs and no one had even reported her missing. They let her stop showing up.

Fucking pathetic.

The water ran in the bathroom while Maren hummed to

herself. We were nearly set to put our plan in action. When, where and how had all been finalized. All we needed now were a few little details tied up and Maren and I would be gone.

If Alex still watched us, he'd see that we were now down to a team of two for the security detail. After tomorrow we'd be down to one. Before New Year's Eve, the last one would be dismissed. With their findings and eliminating the ties, it would seem out of place for me to keep so many men around.

Tomorrow I'd let him know about our plans for New Year's. We were *planning* a trip to New York. Last time we'd spoke, Alex asked for me to keep him updated on my position. It was a normal request, but Maren was right. We'd never truly be safe as long as I remained Bane.

I took a deep breath; this was going to be the hardest phone call yet. The phone rang on the secure line.

"Wales."

"Wales. Bane."

"Bane. I hoped it was you. I got the message that it was okay to take the security threat level down. Thank you for handling the situation. Alli asked me yesterday if you were coming to town any time soon. We're in Tampa currently with the team."

The local newspaper had a shot of Damien and Alli arriving at the hotel with their two children. They were here for two more days before they headed home for Christmas. "I wanted to know if we could get together. There's someone I want you to meet. I'm in Brandon near you guys."

He paused. "Are congratulations in order?"

"They are. I'm married and expecting twins." The pride in my voice was evident.

"Congratulations, Bane. There isn't a man I know more

deserving. How about you guys come to the hotel at six tomorrow? We'll dine in. The kids will want to see you." It meant a lot that Damien knew I'd found happiness. We'd been through a lot together as we solved who killed his sister.

This was bittersweet as I prepared to see those who I considered my closest family for the last time. "Sounds good. We'll see you then."

"This is good-bye isn't it, Bane?"

For a second I remained silent. "It is. I have a past and I need to protect my family."

He let out a breath. "I won't ask any questions. But know if there's anything you ever need, I'm here."

"Thank you. I appreciate it."

We hung up. Maren came out of the bedroom wearing a snug T-shirt. Her protruding belly brought warmth to me every time I saw it. Though the good-byes were hard, I couldn't regret the sacrifice. I was getting everything I'd ever dreamed of with a woman I never imagined having.

The evening winded down as we sat in the living room of the Penthouse suite. Kendall and Ryder, Allison and Damien's children, walked into the room each holding a gift. Kendall was an exact replica of her mother with blonde hair and blue-green eyes. Ryder looked like Damien with his black hair and blue eyes. I wondered what our children would look like. I hoped like Maren.

Kendall, in her little four-year-old voice, said, "Uncle Bane, we got you and Maren a gift."

My heart tore at their words. Damien insisted it would be

good for his kids to see us one last time. They often asked about me. I hoped that was the case. Lying to them felt wrong, but they deserved closure. Ryder, at two, could barely hold the gift in his two hands as he waddled my way. Kendall skipped to Maren.

I cursed Black Division for putting me in this position.

Kendall laid the gift on her lap. "Mommy said to give this to you. Can you come over again? I want to play princess."

Maren fell for my adopted family. A few tears formed in her eyes. "I love playing princesses. My brother used to play that with me when I was little."

There was no escaping Maren's non-answer. Allison mashed her lips together as Damien held her hand. "Open it. I love presents."

Ryder made it to me as he tossed the present on my lap. "Bane! Bane! Bane!" I picked up the little man. "Want to help me?"

Both kids excitedly said, "Yes!"

Paper tore and was tossed on the ground. Within each box was a silver rattle with diamond handles. I read the inscription aloud. "Family lives in the heart regardless of how far apart."

Maren stood and engulfed Allison in a hug. Kendall spoke. "Why is Maren sad, Uncle Bane?"

I patted her head as I stood. "Because you guys mean a lot to us. It was a special gift."

Damien stood and patted me on the back. "You're a good man. I hope one day we can see each other again."

"I hope so."

Sacrifice was something I knew well. Hopefully one day I'd be able to have all those I cared about back in my life. Hope and faith were what I needed to hold on to.

Two days before New Year's Eve, we drove to the airplane hangar. Maren remained quiet beside me. She and Allison hit it off. If we'd been able to stay, I knew they would have been good friends. The night with the Wales had been bittersweet. They were the only family I'd known besides the Black Division.

"Any regrets, angel?" I hoped to hell she didn't have any. She was my true north that kept me steady. We'd be able to face anything together.

Squeezing my hand, her eyes looked to mine. "Never. I will never regret a single moment that brought us together."

That was all I needed to hear. Maren was like the air I needed to breathe to survive. Our first stop to have the babies would be Switzerland. They were medically equipped to handle the delivery along with any complications we may have. The country was filled with expats. It would be easy to blend in. All of the paperwork had been completed.

Everything was set. Hampton decided a fresh start for him and Felecia was best, too. It had been a hard decision with their multiple friends, family, and his business.

We agreed not tell each other where we were going. It was safer that way for now. We'd established one way to communicate with each other in case of an emergency. The only way to warn each other if we'd been found out.

Maybe one day we'd bump into each other again. Only time would tell.

The plan was simple. We were all going away for a few days. Hampton and I could fly. We were renting out a small plane and flying up to New York City for New Year's Eve to see the ball drop. We'd all arrive at the airport along with the bodies Hampton procured to put in the plane. The private hangar would provide the privacy needed for the swap.

Any cameras watching would see three people in Hampton's car and two in mine. Hampton's car had him as a driver with Felicia and a male cadaver in the backseat. Three more cadavers were in the trunk. Hampton mentioned during one of our scheduled check-ins that Felicia was freaked out with the situation, but it had to be done. Maren and Felicia had been through hell over these last few months. Hopefully, they'd never have to deal with anything from the past again.

When we left, I'd be driving with the same driver's hat Hampton had worn on the way in. Felicia and Maren would be out of sight in the back. While we were headed to our hotel, Hampton would fly the plane north. Somewhere in the mountain ranges, Hampton would parachute out and crash the plane into the side of a mountain. If all went to plan, we'd be pronounced dead by nightfall. The flight logs that had been filed would show we rented the plane. We were rigging the scene to look like someone took us out, sending Black Division away from us for good—or that's what we hoped.

Tensions eased with the Eric and Sarge situation, it would cause confusion and misdirect the team on a different path. Human nature was always your best ally in situations like that. The mind ran on emotion. There would be no reason for us to kill ourselves or leave. My history also helped sell the story. Maren had an established doctor. We were having twins.

A car had been stashed near the crash site. Hampton was to meet us at the Charlotte, North Carolina airport in two days to take our flights. Pulling into the hangar, Hampton was already in there. I got out and Maren followed.

Felicia stood near the edge of the car. When she saw me,

her petite frame approached and gave me a smile. "Bane, I'm so glad we made it."

Being held captive for an extended amount of time did something to a person. I'd been there several times and barely escaped with my life. It was part of being an operative. We were conditioned to withstand it mentally. I knew Felicia had nightmares of being taken again, which had been the ultimate deciding factor for them to pick up and leave.

Hugging me, she pulled back. I could see the stress etched on her face. This whole situation took its toll on all of us, leaving us scarred in more ways than we probably realized. She looked toward Maren. "It seems you found your perfect match also."

Through all the years, Felicia had been the strongest advocate of me finding someone.

Maren held out her hand, "I'm Maren. It's nice to meet you. Bane has spoken very highly of you."

Felicia gave me a playful slap on my chest. "He's a real charmer, but he's like family." A few tears formed in her eyes. "I promised myself I wouldn't cry. We still have a few days together." Looking at Maren's stomach, she asked, "May I?"

"Of course."

Felicia put her hands to her stomach and my heart bloomed. "Babies are such miracles. I'm so happy for you."

It was hard to be overly excited in front of Hampton or Felicia. They tried for years to have children but had never been able to. Life was hard at times. The things that happened to good people were unexplainable.

Maren smiled. "They are."

Clearing his throat, Hampton walked up. "All is set. Here are the new phones for us to keep in touch. Minimum contact is best." He kissed Felicia, then looked at me. "Take care of her."

"With my life."

I'd protect these women with my last breath.

Hampton risked his life for Maren, and I'd be forever indebted to him. Because of him, I had a second chance at everything. Kissing his wife, he whispered something in her ear.

I grabbed the two small bags and loaded the car. The majority of our belongings had been left at the farmhouse to help sell the fact that we were indeed only going away for the weekend. Groceries had been bought within the last two days. Appointments were scheduled for the entire pregnancy a month ago.

Coming back to Maren, her eyes widened and fixated on the plane. Three corpses were visible and sitting in the seats like passengers. The fourth was probably laying in the aisle. Hampton would move it to the pilot's seat before he deployed. They were similar to us in build and hair color. I'd seen everything, but I understood why it was unnerving.

The plane crash would incinerate the remains beyond recognition obliterating any DNA evidence, but there had to be bodies.

I escorted Maren toward the SUV. Until we were miles down the road, Maren and Felicia would ride in the very back under the protection of the pull cover. We'd packed some pillows to help with the comfort. Maren scooted in the back and laid on her side.

Leaning in, I asked, "Are you comfortable?"

"We're fine. I promise."

Felicia followed suit. Closing the hatch, Hampton and I nodded to each other. We knew what we had to do. All necessary flight plans had been made. We were scheduled to take off in five minutes. Getting in the car, I slipped on the driver's hat and coat Hampton had been wearing.

Getting in the car, I called back, "Are you guys okay?"

Both responded, "Yes."

Putting the car in drive, I took off. We were about to vanish from our old lives.

CHAPTER
30

MAREN

Two days later

TIME DREW NEAR as they sipped coffee and me orange juice. Hampton arrived last night. All had gone as planned for once. The plane crash made the news and we'd been identified as the casualties. From the videos, Black Division had been on site.

So far, it appeared everyone bought the story of our murder. From researching, Alex appeared to be taking a team to Mexico. As hoped, they believed there was a stone left unturned. If Black Division found someone else connected to this mess, it was good for all of us to eliminate as many people who knew about what happened.

I held on to my juice as I watched our friends. Knowing this was the last time I would possibly see these people was sobering.

Damien and Allison had been incredible people. There had only been one night with them, but I knew we would have been good friends. Maybe someday I'd have that chance to get to know them better. Maybe.

Bane said they knew we were disappearing, but no idea as to the specifics. It was safer that way. Any contact would put them and us in danger. I was glad they knew we were going to get our happily ever after and Bane was too. They meant more to him than he let on. They were his family.

Prior to Bane, I'd isolated myself from everything and everyone. For the first time, I acutely felt the loss of what we were giving up. To keep our babies safe, we had no choice but to disappear. I knew the score and it was worth the sacrifice. However, it didn't lessen how hard the situation was.

If Sarge or Eric told anyone about Bane ... If someone else got the idea to use Bane because of me or the kids ... If Alex was behind Sarge getting Bane back ... we would be in danger. There were too many what if's that we weren't totally sure about.

Bane and Hampton laughed about some good times they had while Felicia and I watched them. We'd talked a lot as we waited for Hampton to arrive. She'd given me advice about having children she'd learned from her friends through the years. I had no guidance as to what I was doing since my mom died at birth. Bane knew about this. My mom went into distress and her heart gave out. It terrified me that I wouldn't be there for our kids. I knew it made Bane nervous also. It was why he was insistent on us being near a top-rated medical facility.

Taking a last sip of coffee, Bane spoke when he set the mug down. "We had some good times. I'll never forget you guys."

Standing, Hampton sat his mug down too. "We did. Who knows, maybe we'll cross paths again someday in some country. Here's to hoping that fate brings us together under a better circumstance."

Bane nodded. "I hope to hell that's in the cards for us."

Hugging me, Hampton whispered in my ear. "Take care of him. You brought him back to life."

"I will. I promise. He did the same for me."

Tears formed in my eyes as I hugged Felicia. In a sense, she had been a mother-type figure for me. I hoped I had her soft-spoken ways with her strength. She was a survivor with unconditional love for Hampton. Through a small sob, I said, "I know we've just met, but I'll never forget you guys. I'll always consider you family."

She squeezed me. "Forever connected. If it's meant to be, it will happen. I'm a firm believer."

I sniffled at her words.

Wrapping his arms around Felicia, Hampton guided her out of the room. We were leaving twelve hours apart. It had been decided Hampton and Felicia would leave first. Our first stop was the Caribbean before we made it to Switzerland. Closing the door, Bane walked across the room to me and wrapped his arms around me. "I know this is tough."

"It is, but we'll be safe this way. Our babies will be safe. The people we love will be safe. I have to believe we'll see our loved ones again."

Bane gave me a gentle kiss and all the love poured around us. "Are you ready to embrace our new life, angel?"

"I am." Bane led me to the fireplace and pulled out all of our documents that used our real names.

He tossed our driver's licenses into the fire. The flames

consumed our old identities. We would have new names, birthdates ... everything.

The fire consumed our id's as we closed out another chapter of our lives. There was no going back, only forward. As the flames ate away at the plastic, I felt the impact of all that happened—all those we loved.

First glances at Discrete Encounters.

Bane's proposition.

Running.

Hiding.

Being captured.

Frankie dying.

Surviving.

Finding out I was pregnant.

Falling in love.

Saving my family.

It was my story, the life thread that made me who I was—who we were. For all those we were leaving ... I would live life to the fullest and love with my entire heart.

———————

Six months later.

My eyes opened and I saw Bane holding two little blankets, his face beaming. "We've been waiting for you to wake up, angel. I have two hungry little babies."

They put me to sleep since my body rejected the epidural. Miraculously, I'd carried the babies to term. But, my pelvis had been too small and I wasn't able to dilate. We'd made the decision before the babies went into distress to have an elective C-section. Bane had been a nervous wreck about me having too much stress on my body.

Pushing a button, Bane raised me up in the bed and I smiled at the green blankets he held. Somehow he was able to reach the remote in his lap while holding our little ones. A sob escaped me. "Are they okay?"

That had been my biggest fear that something would happen to them.

"Angel, they're perfect." He stood as he gave each of them a kiss on the head. "It's time to meet your mom. She's been patiently waiting."

Desperately, I wanted to hold them. We'd decided not to find out the sex of the babies, but had picked out names ahead of time. He placed the first one in my lap. "Meet your daughter."

"Daughter?"

Bane's eyes glistened as he handed me our little girl. The incision was a little sore, but I didn't care. She was perfect. "Hello, my precious, Hope." The name had been chosen because, even in the darkest of times, there was always *hope*.

Bane helped me move my gown. Hope latched on to my breast. She sucked and my world felt complete having those I loved most here. The other baby Bane held cried as I finished positioning Hope. "Hold on, you're about to meet your mom too." He placed the other bundle of joy in my arms. "Meet your, son."

"We have a son and a daughter." The words sounded odd to my own ears as I met the babies that had been growing inside me. A boy and a girl—the perfect combination for us. We were a family. My heart burst within my chest with love.

"We do, angel. They're perfect."

Placing the baby in my arms, he rooted for me also. Bane

helped. "Hello, Aaryan. I have been waiting so long to meet you both. I love you guys." Aaryan meant strength. Through all the trials and obstacles we faced, we were one, and through our strength we persevered.

I held both babies as Bane stroked my cheek. "Thank you." I looked at him questioning. "Thank you for loving me and giving me a life I never thought I deserved. You are my destiny."

Aaryan and Hope cooed and I squeezed them to me, relishing the feeling. Bane leaned down to kiss me. I spoke against his lips. "I love you with my whole heart."

"I love you too, angel."

Though the world now knew us as Jenney and Vin, we would forever be Maren and Bane. And finally through it all … we'd gotten our happily ever after.

Three Months Later…

I woke up startled and glanced at the clock. It was nearly seven in the morning. The twins should have been awake by now for me to nurse. They'd recently started sleeping through the night, which was a blessing. Who would have thought a complete night of sleep was a luxury? Well, at least six straight after Bane made love to me, or fucked me senseless. My body craved him and I looked forward to our time alone at night. Don't get me wrong, I loved being a mother—every second of it. But, I loved our adult time too. Bane's side of the bed was vacant, which piqued my curiosity. The monitor was turned off.

Pushing the cream duvet aside, I padded down the hallway and glanced in the nursery. We'd decided to stay in Switzerland for a while until it was time to move on. I loved it there and the house we'd bought. The wooden beams that ran through it gave it a cabin in the woods type feel.

The twins' nursery looked out onto the Swiss Alps, which was breathtaking to cast your eyes upon. In the rocking chair, facing the mountains, Bane sat holding our two little babies that I loved with every fiber of my being. My entire reason for existing was in this room.

Bane's voice talked soothingly to the babies. "You guys are being so quiet this morning for your mommy. I know you're hungry, but let's let her sleep as long as we can."

Little arms flailed on each side of Bane as he talked to them. They loved their father. Bane was it for me—the love of my life. And I knew he felt the same for me. With every chance he could, Bane showered me with love and affection, telling me I was his destiny all along.

Bane continued speaking to Aaryan and Hope. "I love your mommy more than anything in this world. The first time I saw your mommy, she took my breath away. It's a good thing she said yes to a date."

Moments like that, I would treasure for the rest of my life. A smile emerged on my face as I thought about our first date. It wasn't something we'd be explaining anytime soon to the kids.

Hope made a sound that I knew was about to turn into a blood-curdling scream. They were nearly forty-five minutes past their breakfast time. I tip-toed farther into the room.

"Okay, my sweet babies, let's go get Mommy. I know you guys are hungry."

Bane stood and turned my way. A sexy grin directed at

me created that butterfly-like feeling in the pit of my stomach. Hope and Aaryan made excited baby noises now that breakfast had arrive. They were starving. "There's Mommy." He kissed both of their heads and then spoke to me. "We wanted to let you sleep."

I gave the kids each a kiss on the cheek and then lingered my lips on Bane's. "You're amazing. Thank you. I love you."

"I love you too, angel."

Sitting quickly, Bane handed the children to me who latched on. He knelt in front of me and watched his children. The quiet suckling noise filled the air. "Are you happy?"

Without hesitation, I responded, "More than I ever dreamed I could be. Are you?" I looked into Bane's eyes and saw true happiness emanating from them.

"Yes. This, right here, is my dream come true."

As we treasured another morning together, I thought about all the two of us had been through.

Meeting at Discrete Encounters.

Running from the Black Division.

Falling in love.

Becoming pregnant.

Committing ourselves to each other.

Finding our happily ever after.

Bane had emerged, from the depths of the fiery darkness that had nearly consumed him, and embraced the light... with me. I had found the strength to claim my life ... with him.

We were the real deal—for better or worse, our love would last forever.

Enjoy an excerpt from

TRUST ME

Entire Series Available Now
Meet Damien and Allison Wales from BANE

CHAPTER
1

I'm rushing around my apartment, trying to do some last-minute packing before my trip, when my phone rings. It's my best friend, Sam. We've been best friends since we were in diapers, and our parents had been friends since they were in school. Neither of us has any siblings, so Sam and I have basically been sisters all these years.

We live in Waleska, Georgia. It has that wonderful Mayberry aura about it. I think the population sign says around six-hundred people reside here. Sam and I will both be seniors this fall at Reinhardt University. My true love is photography, but I've always been scared that I wouldn't succeed at it.

Holding the phone between my ear and shoulder, I answer, "Hey, Sam. Are you on your way?"

"Yes. Are you sure you want to do this? Alone? For a week? I'm just not sure if that's the best idea."

Since my parents died, Sam's been my rock. She's afraid I'm using this trip to withdraw from life again.

I zip up my bag. With as much sincerity in my voice as possible, I respond, "I need to do this. I have to do this. It's long overdue. It's been planned since spring break. I know you don't want me to go off the radar for an entire week, but it will be fine."

"I know. It's just that I worry about you. If I didn't have my presentation this week for the sorority, I'd insist on going with you. Just promise me that you will call if it gets to be too much for you to handle. I'm here for you. I know you're strong, but this is going to be a tough week."

Smiling to myself, I can picture her animatedly talking with one of her hands while she's driving. "I know, and I appreciate it. You just have to trust me on this. Everything will be okay."

"Okay, Allison. I don't like it, but I support you."

"You're the best. I don't know what I would do without you."

"You'll never have to find out. I'll be there in five, girl."

And that's why she will be my best friend for life. "Okay, honk when you pull up, and I'll be right down."

I dash over to the kitchen island to make sure all my camera gear is safe and secure in my bag. I breathe out a calming sigh as I prepare myself for this journey. Over this last year since my parents' accident, my small two-bedroom apartment has been my sanctuary. Just like at my parents' place, it has that cozy-home feeling that makes me want to curl underneath a blanket while drinking hot chocolate.

Before I can think too much about the past, I go through my mental checklist again to ensure I have everything for my weeklong hiatus from the real world. Nothing but room service, sandy beaches, pools, and sleep are in my near future.

A honk sounds from outside, and I dart down the stairs. A beautiful May day welcomes me as I walk out of my building to Sam's black Toyota Camry.

Sam is one of those people who just instantly attracts friends. Her personality makes anyone she meets want to adopt her and take her everywhere they go. She is a sports fan through and through, which is the exact opposite of me. She's that person who screams at the TV, encouraging the players or telling them how to play. She's naturally gorgeous with green eyes, a curvy figure, and long nearly black hair that has a natural sheen to it. Sam is currently single, and it is not for the lack of trying from the opposite sex. She just doesn't do relationships.

"Hey, Sam. Got a hot date after you drop me off at the airport?"

She's wearing cutoffs and a cute little green halter top that sets off her emerald eyes surrounded by smoky makeup, and her hair is flowing freely around her face.

"Um, yeah, Carmen asked me to lunch. Since I'm going to be in Atlanta, I figured, why the hell not?" Her voice goes a tad tense.

"Whoa. You mean Greg's sister, Carmen? That Carmen? Doesn't Greg play football for the University of Georgia now?"

Sam and Greg had been secretly hot and heavy at the beginning of her senior year in high school, but it abruptly ended after New Year's Eve of the same year. Sam gave some stupid excuse and refused to talk about it to anyone. She just kept saying it was time to move on. After several attempts, I stopped asking for the full story, knowing she would tell me when she was ready.

I've never been the type of person to force information out of someone. Sam has to be ready to tell me, regardless of what it is, and she just isn't there yet.

My Carmen inquiry has earned me one of those don't-go-there looks. Giving her a moment to calm down, I focus on watching the cars pass by on our way to the Atlanta Airport.

"Yes, she wants to catch up. And, no, there's no chance that Greg and I will end up together. There's nothing between us anymore. Please drop it."

Whatever happened between them hurt Sam deeply. The tone in her voice tells me I might receive bodily harm if I continue down this road.

"Okay. I'm just surprised is all." *It's definitely time for a subject change.* "How's living in the house with the girls going? I haven't heard about the latest fiasco."

Sam and a few other juniors are trying to start the first sorority at our college. I think she's crazy for taking this on, but Sam loves a challenge.

"Allison, I swear that if I wasn't so involved with this project, I just don't know if I would keep forging ahead. I hope we were never this incorrigible to live with when we were back home. We have fifteen girls living in a house right off campus, and sharing the space seems to be a foreign concept. Last night, we discussed labeling food in the refrigerator and the amount of time each person should be allotted in the bathroom. I mean, come on, give me a break. Can't we just be a little more grown-up? Why did I ever think it would be a good idea to move out of your cozy apartment?"

The fake irritation in her voice says otherwise. Deep down, she loves those girls.

I laugh. "Oh, Sam, you know you love it. Hopefully, your charter gets approved, so you guys can become the first official sorority of the university."

We pull up to the terminal, and Sam puts the car in park.

"Damn straight. It better happen before the end of our senior year." She's recovered from the earlier mention of Greg.

After grabbing my luggage from the back, Sam meets me

at the curb to give me a hug.

"I promise to email you the moment I get checked in at the hotel. Don't worry about me. I'll be fine," I reassure her.

"You better."

I can tell she's still not pleased with the idea. She worries about me too much.

As I am heading inside the airport, Sam yells, "Hey, Allison!"

I turn back to face her.

"Don't forget to find some cute-ass guy while you are there."

I smile wryly and shake my head at her as she winks and blows a kiss. I watch as she hops into her car and drives away.

I board the plane, and I'm ready to go. Excitement is beyond me. A change of scenery is just what I need, and I am practically bouncing in my chair in anticipation of heading to the beautiful beaches of Miami, Florida. It's just a state away from Georgia, but it feels like I am traveling across the ocean to a secluded place where I can sit and process all my thoughts.

As I hear the flight attendant go over safety instructions in the blandest voice possible, I lay my head back and think about how my life has changed so drastically in just a year's time. In three days, it will be a year since I received the worst news of my entire life.

Sam and I just finished our sophomore year of college.

There was an art show in town, and Sam had talked me into showcasing some of my photographs that I had taken through the years. My parents had bought my first camera for me at the age of six, and from that day forward, photography became my passion. I'd devoured any book about photography I could get my hands on, so I could learn about all aspects of it. I'd even won a few contests during my high school years. At the end of the show, a writer from a local magazine approached me to tell me he was impressed with my natural talent.

Heading home to our town of Homerville, I say to Sam for the hundredth time, "Can you believe it? They actually liked my photographs."

"Yes, and they want to offer you an internship. I told you." She gives my shoulder a nudge as I drive.

"I know. I know. Tell your parents that I'm sorry I can't stay and chat. I'll come by tomorrow. I'm too excited to tell Mom and Dad my news." I'm bouncing in my seat with excitement.

"Will do. Mama's gonna want to have you guys over to celebrate at some point."

We start screaming in delight as we pull into Sam's driveway. Looking disheveled, her parents, Dean and Chandra, run up to the car. As I roll down the passenger window, I notice the smell of freshly mowed lawns.

With Dean standing solemnly beside her, Chandra says, "Hey, girls. Can you come inside? It's important."

Her tone alone makes me automatically obey her request.

After we walk inside, Sam and I head straight for the couch and take a seat next to one another. Chandra sits on the other side of me. Dean sits in a chair across from me on the other side of the coffee table. Seeing Sam's parents' sad faces, I immediately have that sinking feeling in the pit of my stomach.

A tear slips out of Chandra's eye, and she wipes it away before putting an arm around me. "Allison, there has been a terrible accident, and—"

I know what she is going to say before she has a chance to finish. "No, no, no. Please no. Tell me they are okay. Please." I plead with her as my tears start falling faster and faster.

She grabs me and hugs me against her. "Honey, there was an accident at the four-way intersection in town. The semi couldn't stop, and it hit them."

I just sob and sob and sob.

As Chandra and Sam sit there, hugging me, the only thing I can think about is the terrible fight I had with my mom last week. It was about me not pursuing my dreams of photography.

Life is a bitch at times.

Later, I was told my parents had never had a chance in the little car they were driving, so they hadn't known what hit them. Every day, I pray that was the case.

If it wasn't for Sam's family, I don't know what I would have done. They helped me get through everything—the funeral, the will, and the never-ending paperwork. A lot of it seems like a dream. I couldn't be sure how much I truly functioned, but I went through the motions. Sam was there for me every step of the way. No one could ever have a truer friend.

Decisions regarding the farm had to be made quickly. Animals needed tending, fields needed plowing, and crops needed planting. Selling the farm was the second hardest thing I had ever done. The first had been burying both my parents on the same day.

Within two weeks, it felt like my whole life was completely ripped from me. My heart had been savagely torn out, and each passing week, the hole in my chest kept growing and growing. The pain never ceased.

I became a recluse. I stopped seeing all my friends, and I spent all my energy just getting through the day. Eventually, my friends stopped calling me, and as horrible as it seemed, I was relieved. Sam never gave up on me though. She kept after me and kept after me and kept after me. If it wasn't for Sam's persistence, I don't know where I would be now. This last Christmas, I slowly started to go out to social events. I mainly went to give Sam her social time since she refused to leave me by myself.

My hermit status was one of the main reasons she objected so much to this solo trip, but what she didn't know was that I had knowingly picked a time when she couldn't come.

I open my eyes when the plane wheels squeak as we land. This moment feels right, and I know I have done the perfect thing by coming here alone. I was so persistent with Sam about going on this trip because something kept telling me that I had to go find myself.

I'm hoping to clear out all the old cobwebs from the past year. My fear of not letting anyone in because I'm absolutely terrified of losing someone again will hopefully be a thing of the past. Even though I'm frightened, I pray that I have the courage to put myself out there again.

CHAPTER
2

My taxi pulls up to the hotel in the early evening. *Oh, I am in heaven.* Walking up the long blue welcoming carpet into the hotel, I am greeted by shades of golds and blues. Along the perimeter, the floor has an intricate gold swirl design outlined with blue. Tropical plants are strategically placed to further give that paradise feel. The hotel is fairly empty for a Saturday.

The woman at the front desk with a double French twist updo is impeccably dressed in her light blue suit accented in gold. "Hello, and welcome to the Miami Beach Resort. How may I help you?" she asks in her perfected business manner.

"I'm checking in. The reservation is under Allison Scott." I hand her my credit card. I'm ready to see my room and relax.

"Thank you. We have your reservation for four nights, five days in an oceanfront room. You are in room 717. Here's your room key. Elevators are down the hall and on the right. Do you need any help with your bags?" Her smile is small as she waits for my response.

As I take the room key off the counter, I respond, "No, thank you."

"Please enjoy your stay with us and let us know if you need anything else."

After grabbing my suitcase, I head anxiously to my room.

The sound of the hotel key card opening the door is music to my ears. Taking a deep breath, I cross over the threshold. As the door closes, I take a cleansing sigh of relief and look around with a smile. The royal blue curtain valances remind me of the ocean, the yellow walls make me feel warm, and the taupe furniture and bedding provide me with a peaceful ambience. Immediately, the tension begins to ease out of me while I'm surrounded in this sea of tranquil colors.

Approaching the balcony, I cast my eyes out to the aqua sea. *Breakfast out here tomorrow and each morning after will be a must.*

Remembering my promise to Sam, I grab my phone and head out to a chair on the balcony to email her. *If I text her, we will never stop going back and forth.*

From: Allison Scott
To: Sam Matthews
Subject: All in One Piece

Hey, there! I made it here all in one piece! See? There was nothing to worry about, my friend. Have a great time this week. Good luck with your presentations. I will call on my way back.

Miss you lots!

Oh, I can't wait to tell you about this guy I met. Just following your departing orders.

xoxo

I giggle as I turn off my phone. She's going to kill me for that last line when she finds out I was screwing with her. She's constantly trying to set me up with some of her guy friends. Brad, in particular, has been the most tenacious in asking. He probably just feels sorry for me since I never go out. However, he does nothing for me. He never has.

I want that inexplicable connection I've read about—the feeling that consumes my heart, searing the love in forever. Anything less just seems like a waste since I would be giving a piece of myself to someone forever.

I decide to call it a night, and I settle into my room. The crashing waves against the beach lull me into a peaceful deep sleep.

Squinting from the early morning light coming through my balcony doors, I throw off the covers, ready to embark on my day.

As I sit on the balcony, letting the sun penetrate my pores, I think about one of the last meaningful conversations my mom and I had when I was at home during spring break of my sophomore year. That was the last time I saw my parents before their accident.

In our small farmhouse kitchen, my mom and I are making breakfast before my dad comes in from his early morning chores. The smell of eggs and bacon cooking on the stove fill the house. I look at my mom, wearing a blue plaid apron as she walks around the kitchen, and I think about how much I treasure these moments because it's when we truly talk.

"Mom, do you think it's weird that I haven't really started dating yet? I keep thinking there's something wrong with me."

She opens the oven and checks on the biscuits. "Sweetie,

nothing is wrong with you. You're like me. I never dated any-one prior to your dad."

"How will I know when I've found the one?" I come up beside her as I get glasses out of the cabinet.

She pulls the food off the stove, and then she turns to me, giving me her full attention. She does this when she wants to tell me something important. "How do you know when the peaches from the tree out back are ready to be eaten?"

My brows scrunch together. What in the world do peach-es have to do with anything? *"Um...the color, smell, feel...and the stem gets a little loose, making it easy to pull it from the tree. I don't know. I just know when it's right."*

"Same thing will happen when you meet the right one. Your instincts will take over, and you'll know. Just follow your heart, sweetie. It'll never lead you astray. You just haven't found the one yet. Be patient." She gives me a hug just as my dad walks in from outside.

Those morning chats are now so precious to me.

After finishing breakfast, I go to change into an ivory one-piece swimsuit with a matching sarong wrap trimmed in black. Looking in the mirror, I critique my appearance. I am average-looking with blue-green eyes, slightly tanned skin, and dirty-blonde hair that reaches the middle of my back. At five foot six inches, I'm neither tall nor short, and from my days on the farm, I suppose I am toned. I put my hair up into a French twist, grab my things, and then head downstairs for some pre-lunch sun-soaking.

The large rectangular pool is surrounded by blue-and-white mesh lounge chairs with matching umbrellas. I walk over to some empty lounge chairs sitting next to a few palm trees in the corner, and I settle in. I crack open my latest mystery novel, and I begin to get lost in the book. Every once in a while, I get a whiff of someone's suntan oil, giving off that perfect beach aroma. The warmth from the sun causes my eyes to close slowly.

Screech.

I stir.

Screech.

Metal being dragged across the concrete is making an awful racket, like nails scratching on a chalkboard. I look over to see who in the world is creating that noise, and I see a guy pulling over a chair, making himself at home right next to me. *Damn, I wish he had picked one of the other many chairs available.* I notice he has a nice toned body. Sam would push me to talk to him, but it's the same as always. Something is just lacking.

He lifts up his sunglasses, and I keep mine in place.

"I hope I didn't wake you," he says.

"I was just dozing in and out." Immediately, I pick up my book as I try to send the not-interested vibe, but he doesn't get the message.

"Can I get you a drink from the bar?" He steeples his fingers under his chin as he looks me over.

Cocky bastard. Indifferently, I respond, "No, thanks."

"Are you here on business or pleasure?"

This guy is not taking the hint. I hate to be bitchy, but I just want to be left alone. "Please don't take this the wrong way, but I came down here for some alone time." Being blunt isn't normally my style.

He sighs, getting the message, and heads to the water.

Good.

After I go for a dip in the pool and have a quick bite to eat, the area is exploding with people. I head toward my room to take a relaxing bubble bath. As I near the bar area, I see a waiter wiping off a vacated table.

"Excuse me. What time does the sun set here?"

He straightens up. "Right before eight, ma'am. If you're thinking about catching it, I suggest coming down around seven thirty. Make sure to bring your camera if you have one."

"Thank you. Have a good day." I start to get excited about using my camera. Taking pictures is one of the only things that still soothes me and gives me peace.

"You, too, ma'am," he says as he finishes cleaning the table.

I continue my way up to my room. As soon as I enter, I head to the bathroom to start my bath water. The hotel room comes with a complimentary bottle of chamomile-scented bubble bath. The smell relaxes me, and I add a generous amount to the steaming hot water. Anxious to get into the tub, I strip and ease myself in. Turning off the water, I decide to close my eyes for a bit.

Lying there among the foaming bubbles, I randomly pop them with my fingers while listening to the consoling voice of Michael Bublé. I think about what my next steps might be. *What would Mom and Dad think of what I've become in the last year?* Sometimes, I feel like I don't even recognize myself.

If I were to ask my mom for advice on this, I could hear her saying, *Advice is what we ask when we already know the answer but wish we didn't.*

It's so true. They would be sad to see how I have quit living life to the fullest and have resorted to just existing. I do want to start living again, but I am so afraid of what will happen after the loss I have suffered.

As I climb out of the tub, I ponder about how I'll start reclaiming my life. I've let the pain of my parent's death consume me, and if I'm not careful, it'll continue to devour me until nothing is left.

I decide to take a quick nap before the sunset, so I open the balcony doors and rest as the distant sounds of seagulls and the ocean play me a lullaby.

A few hours later, I emerge from my room, wearing a light blue T-shirt and comfortable black yoga pants, with my camera in hand and my bag on my shoulder. During the elevator ride down, I rummage through my bag for a hair tie, and after finding one, I throw my hair up into a haphazard messy ponytail to keep the hair out of my face while I'm taking pictures on the beach.

Once in the lobby, I head outside to the beach, and a clean, salty scent greets me and wraps around me. After removing my flip-flops, I squish the sand in between my toes. The scenery brings happy memories, and I welcome them as I remember when my family used to head to the beach for long weekend getaways. It's good to think about the memories and not feel like I am being swallowed up by the sadness that normally accompanies the thought of my parents.

Making my way down the shoreline, I enjoy the peaceful feeling of having no expectations. It's just the crashing waves, my camera, and me. In the distance, I see some dolphins tormenting a seagull. They seem to be playing a keep-away game. I prepare my camera and adjust the settings. It's a professional digital camera with a wide-angle zoom lens that my parents had bought as my birthday present after I finished my first year of college.

I begin taking shots from different angles as I try to capture contrasting lights from the sky. There's something magical about taking an image that will help me remember all the smells, feelings, and thoughts I had in that exact moment of time. It's like freezing a piece of history that can never happen in the same way again.

As I start walking, I think back to my apartment, which is covered with pictures I've taken, memories I have made, and moments I will cherish.

"Ow!" *Oh my gosh!* I got so captivated in the moment that I almost ran someone over in the process. My eyes automatically shut from the impact. I decide not to open them as I take stock of how hard this guy's body feels. *Crap, my shoulder hurts from hitting him.*

"Shit." The voice is deep, raw, and powerful.

Now is when I have to face this total stranger and admit that I made a total idiot of myself because I was distracted. *Um, yeah, I totally rock.* He did not sound pleased either. *Well, who would be when some crazy person rams into you out of the blue?* It's time to face that inevitable moment when I wish I could just fast forward, so I don't physically have to live through it.

"I'm so sorry. I was gazing out at the ocean, and I didn't see you." When I look up into the eyes of the stranger, I am immediately frozen into place from the deep blue eyes gazing back at me. They are the purest blue pair of eyes I have ever seen. *Thank goodness I got that last sentence out.* Right now, my brain has completely stopped working, and I am not even sure I can process anything of sound mind.

Mr. Blue Eyes has black hair flopping in that sexy way.

My fingers want to run through it as I pull his mouth down to mine. His lips look to be firm yet soft. His angular jaw is something I could spend hours—

Holy shit! I shake my head to stop my train of thought as I turn ten shades of red. *Did he just ask me something?* "Um, sorry, what did you say again?" *Oh, kill me now.*

"I said, do you always go to such extremes to get attention from guys you're interested in talking to?" His eyes are dancing with amusement.

Just then, I realize that he hasn't let go of my upper shoulders from when he reached out to grab me. My skin is on fire at the spots where he's touching me. I'm confused by my reaction, and it causes me to completely miss what he said...again. "What?"

"Are you seriously asking me to repeat myself for a third time?" He's says jokingly.

Oh, that smile. Would it be weird to start fanning myself? "Um, no...I mean, um..."

Damn him. He is now smirking as I remember his previous question. He's caused my brain to run on a ten-second delay. It's time for a little payback as I play along. "Actually, I was vying for that hot guy's attention over there. By irritating a brute like you, I was hoping that I could play the damsel-in-distress card. Then, he would come to my rescue, and voila, you would be out of the picture, and I would be with someone who deserves my time."

He gives me a once-over, and the heat in his eyes feels as if he is devouring me.

"I think that guy would actually need to be paying attention to your damsel-in-distress act to be able to rescue you."

On a cellular level, my body reacts to the sound of his voice. We are still standing close, and my body is not listening to my mind telling it to take a step back. It doesn't want this feeling to end.

I must remain outwardly unaffected. "Oh, he is, trust me. He's just playing it cool. He's waiting for the best moment to make the biggest impression, so he can ensure never-ending gratitude."

"Have dinner with me," he says, his voice serious and seductive.

All I can do is blink at the sudden change in conversation. It makes me feel like I'm on a rocking boat, and I'm trying to keep it from swaying too much. For whatever reason, I am drawn to him like I have never been drawn to anyone in my life.

"What?" I want to facepalm myself for saying that again to him.

He's on the verge of chuckling. *Gah!* He's so infuriating and intriguing at the same time.

"I think you like the sound of my voice. Is that why you keep asking me to repeat myself?"

"Um…no?" I just want to die. *Seriously, why did I respond with a question?* My cheeks begin to heat again as I get a full megawatt smile, but then he looks confused.

"No, you won't have dinner with me? Or, no, you don't like the sound of my voice?"

My brain is on overload, and honestly, at this point, I am not even sure what my *no* meant. I don't want this moment to end, but he's a complete stranger. *Didn't I learn about stranger-danger in school?*

He interrupts my thoughts. "Hey, listen, a perfectly crowded restaurant is right over there on the beach. Please join me for dinner, and if you want to leave at any time, you can. Plus, I think you owe me after trying to use me," he says as he winks at me.

Oh geez. My heart starts to beat faster. I don't think I could say no even if I tried. My body is obviously refusing to obey my mind. I can picture it now. After saying no, he would start to walk off, only to have me hanging on, not letting him go. *There's only so much humiliation a person can take in a day.* "Okay, sure."

He lets go of my shoulders and rests his hand on the small of my back. That strange feeling is pulsing at the place where he is now touching me, causing an unfamiliar deep ache to grow within me. *I have got to get a grip.* His effect on me is crazy.

He leads me to a restaurant called The Beach Hut. The place has a thatched roof and is open on all sides. When we arrive at our wooden wicker table, the arm pulling out my chair is toned and defined. Every attribute about him is mouthwatering. My mental swooning has to stay in check before I lose all control. He takes a seat in front of me.

The sun has begun to set behind us, casting magnificent orange and purple rays across the sky. Seagulls are flying circles over the ocean as they try to bring in one last snack for the day. A slight breeze blows from the north, and the smell of mesquite coming from the kitchen fills the air. It's perfect. A waiter delivers two water glasses.

"So, what should I call the beautiful damsel in distress?"

He takes a sip of water as he watches my every move, making me feel self-conscious.

Beautiful. Did he call me beautiful?

The waiter comes and takes our order. I pick out the first thing on the menu, not even processing what I requested, as this stranger in front of me continues to fry my circuits.

"Alli," I finally answer him. *Alli? What the hell? I never go by Alli. Why did I use the nickname I have fought against my entire life?*

I am completely taken off guard. I am drawn to this guy, like a bug is to one of those zapper things. I cross my fingers, hoping that whatever this is doesn't end up shocking the hell out of me.

I should go. No, I should stay. Wait...calm down. I feel like my mind is going in never-ending circles because of this guy. *This is crazy. I am crazy.*

When he reaches out and touches my hand, my eyes shoot up to his. There's an undeniable connection between us.

"Don't go. It's just dinner," he says softly.

I look down at our hands and then back into his eyes, and for some unexplained reason, my nerves instantly settle. "Okay."

He lets out a small breath as he releases my hand, and I immediately miss his touch.

He continues on his quest for information. "What's your last name?" He looks at me expectantly.

I get the feeling this guy is used to getting what he wants and when he wants it. *What could he possibly see in me?*

Before I have a chance to answer, our dinner and beers are delivered. It looks like I ordered a burger and fries.

Thinking back to the question I was just asked, I try to answer sincerely. "Can we just have dinner and only exchange first names for now? I need to get to know you a little bit more before I give my last name." It sounds stupid and naive, but if this guy is a creepy stalker and my intuition has completely evaded me, I'll feel a tad safer.

"Okay, Alli. I'm not trying to make you nervous. I'm Damien." He sits back in his chair and lifts one of his eyebrows as if he is trying to make a decision.

His white linen shirt paired with khaki shorts are doing wonders for him. His clothing hangs perfectly on his body, accentuating all the right parts. He has quite a calculating temperament.

I want to crawl over to him, straddle his legs, and kiss him. *Crap.* My mind is being a total traitor right now, causing my libido to make a surprise appearance this evening. *What is wrong with me?*

"So, what happens when I want to see you after tonight?" he asks.

"After tonight?"

What started as an accident has now turned into a potential second date. When he laughs at me again, I realize that he's caught on to when I'm flustered since I just keep repeating what he says. *Damn it.* Luckily, he gives me a minute to redeem myself.

"I guess we can set up something to meet again," I say.

"Whatever works for you, Alli. How many dates do you think it will take until you feel comfortable enough to tell me your full name?"

Part of me wants to be honest and say now, but keeping my last name a secret seems to keep a barrier between us. I don't want to get engulfed in the tidal wave I'm sure Damien can create. Plus, giving him my last name now would put me in the insane category since I just said we should stay on a first-name basis.

Hell, I have no idea how to respond. It's Sunday, and I consider the fact that I'm leaving on Wednesday. "How about three dates?" The likelihood that he'll still be interested by that time is slim, and if he is crazy, I can just disappear back to Georgia.

"Does tonight count as date one?" He takes a sip of his

beer as he waits for my response.

"Sure."

He nods as if he is solidifying something in his head. "I'm looking forward to the third date."

When he takes a bite of his sandwich, I watch in awe as his strongly defined chin moves as he chews.

"So, besides trying to get my attention for a dinner date, what were you doing out on the beach this evening?"

I just shake my head and raise my eyebrow. Finally, I respond, "A waiter told me about the sunsets. I love photography, so I came down, hoping to freeze a moment from this trip to remember it always. What were you doing down there before I practically ran you over?"

"Just enjoying an evening stroll on the beach while unwinding from a busy day. Are you a photographer for a living?"

That makes sense. He seems like the business type. "No, I just finished my junior year in college. Photography is really just a hobby at this point." I shrug as I take another bite. My mind wanders to the interview I have scheduled shortly after my return. It's with the same magazine that was interested in me prior to my parents' death.

"Well, I would like to spend some time together tomorrow. Would you be opposed to riding in a car with me?"

We have finished our meals, and we're both sitting back in our seats, sipping on our drinks.

I check my creepy meter, and I'm still not getting anything. "I know this is going to sound a little crazy and a lot naive, but you're a normal guy, right? I mean, not some—"

He cuts me off before I have a chance to continue. He looks at me seriously and honestly as he speaks, "Alli, what do you need to feel safe? I just want to get to know you. If at any time you feel uncomfortable, I swear we'll leave, and I'll take you wherever you want to go. Just give me a chance."

His words strike me hard as he lays it all out there. I know I shouldn't, but I really do feel safe with this stranger.

"What do you have in mind?" I ask.

"I thought lunch and the beach would be good. How does eleven sound? I can pick you up here if it's not too far for you or just let me know where I can meet you."

The intimate way his blue eyes are penetrating me makes me feel as if he can see deep inside me.

"Here at eleven will work. Is there something I should wear or bring?"

The waiter comes and delivers the bill.

"Dress casual and bring a swimsuit. I'll take care of everything else. It will be about a thirty-minute drive if that's okay with you." He pulls out some cash and pays for our dinner and drinks.

I'm momentarily distracted as I watch him put his wallet back in his pants, and then I realize I've taken longer than necessary to respond. "Sounds great. Thank you for dinner. However, I should be the one buying since I rudely ran you over."

As he stands, he grabs my bag off the floor and then reaches for my hand, and I oblige.

"Alli, it's been my pleasure." He looks like he is about to ask me something else, but he seems to change his mind at the last second.

We leave the restaurant and walk toward the beach. He moves his hand to the small of my back as we pass a couple coming from the opposite direction. Those tingles return. Our time is drawing to an end, and it saddens me.

"I'll meet you here at eleven tomorrow morning. Here's your bag. Thank you for taking a chance on me."

I take my bag from him and look up into his blue eyes. I am once again captivated, and I want to lean in to feel those lips, but I quickly pull back. It's still too soon to kiss him. "I'll see you then."

From the way he is looking at me, I can tell he knows that I find him attractive. *The bastard.*

As I begin to walk off, I decide to give a bold exit line. "Oh, and Damien?" I wait for a few seconds until I know I have his undying attention. "I'm glad fate had me run into you tonight." I give him a wink before I turn and sashay down the beach without looking back.

Even if I make a fool of myself here, no one back home has to know. Reveling in the feeling of being on cloud nine, I decide I'm ready to live.

Enjoy an excerpt from

DISSIPATE

Available Now

ONE

THE RAIN PELTED my face, making my tears obsolete on the dreariest day of my life. I watched the wooden coffin being lowered into the ground with long leather straps. My world had changed in a matter of moments.

Part of me wished I could go back to those precious seconds before my mom had revealed the truth about my name. What I thought had been real was actually a lie.

A lie.

The coffin touched down on the soaked earth. Three men, known as Watchers in our private society, were to the right of the burial hole. They pulled the leather straps from underneath the coffin, causing a sound that had me gritting my teeth.

These were the last moments before my mom would be buried for all eternity. Forever is a long time. It has no end and no beginning.

The Watchers, men over eighteen years of age who had taken an oath of commitment to The Light, stepped away from the grave. Most of the time, they were nineteen before they officially took the title due to the extreme training and discipline of the teachings. Essentially, they watched over our way of life, keeping it pure and simple, ensuring all of our laws were followed. The outside world was filled with sin and was doomed. Sometimes, I felt the position was used as a way to keep females uninformed. Questioning thoughts were not appropriate according to the teachings.

The rain continued as the men put their hands behind their backs and looked toward the Keeper, the leader of our community.

We never spoke of the outside world. There were things we needed from it to survive, but we peacefully coexisted. All of my life, I stayed within the walls of our community called The Society. At the back of my mind, I always wondered what life was like beyond the borders.

Stoically, I stood at the head of the burial hole next to the Keeper. An eerie chill ran down my spine being so close to him. Normally, I tried to avoid his presence at all costs.

Lightning struck and I had to fight not to flinch. We patiently waited until the Keeper deemed it time to speak. The Keeper made all the laws and saw to it that visions he received from The Light became realty. I never understood what The Light was, but to question it was blasphemy. Basically, we were to blindly follow. Something never seemed right with that thought process, but that was life.

The rest of the community, known as Charges, stood behind the Watchers as their eyes casted on the casket.

Thunder rolled through the area as the rain came down harder. My bonnet pressed against my face as I spared a glance at the Keeper. He had on his black tall hat. His shock-white hair peeped out underneath the brim. Every time I took in his wrinkled, papery white face, I shivered. Something had always seemed off about him. My mind was numb as I tried to process the loss.

He cleared his throat. "My fellow family. It is a sad day when we lose one of our Charges. We've learned through our teachings that as life gives it must also take. Yesterday, it took our Anita and we will forever bear the loss. It is a burden we share that serves as a uniting purpose. Anita has left a piece of her light in her daughter, Sarah, which we are grateful for. Are there any doubters of The Light in our presence?"

Sarah.

That apparently wasn't my real name. It was Kenzie Brooks. At least that's what my mom had told me right before she died. *Did the Keeper know the truth?* Glancing up, I looked around at my fellow Charges and the Watchers, all dressed in black and white. *Does anyone else know who I am?* My mind was numb with everything I tried to process.

Everyone in unison replied, "No Keeper. We are a unified group."

The Keeper knelt and picked up a handful of mud, then threw the glob on my mom's coffin. "May we always be a unified group, in life and death."

The Keeper's somber words had me wanting to fall and weep. That action would be frowned upon so I stood strong. Per the teachings, extreme emotions led to the sin that had condemned the outside world. I was supposed to accept my mom's death as something The Light wanted and be grateful she had been chosen to go home. In reality, grateful was the farthest emotion I felt. Selfishly, all I wanted was my mom back.

We stood there and I watched the mud splotch begin to dissipate through the droplets of rain that landed on the coffin, disappearing into nothingness. I wished I could fade away versus dealing with the new revelations my mom had shared with me.

The Keeper put his hands on my shoulder and I inwardly cringed while remaining outwardly unaffected. "We shall proceed to the community hall to eat. Today shall be a meal with no talking as we reflect on The Light that burns within us. Sarah shall be allowed her evening of mourning and tomorrow we shall help her cleanse her home."

No one responded as it wasn't a question, but essentially a command. To waste time and energy on frivolous things was frowned upon.

Mourning time was limited in The Society. After lunch, everyone would be expected to return to life as normal, except me. The teachings said that to focus on death too long was to fuse in a disease that would eat away at the whole of our community. Having now experienced true heartache, the rule made no sense to me. All I wanted to do was fall to the ground and weep for days.

Turning, the Keeper stepped away. The Watchers followed. Not a Charge moved from their spot until the last Watcher had passed by me. It was a sign of respect. My best friend, Matthew, walked by me and his fingers grazed mine. Feeling his kindness and sympathy had my lips trembling for a mere moment. Matthew was nineteen and had recently been named a Watcher. Since his induction ceremony, our time together had been limited. I missed him.

I turned and followed the slow procession. The dirt paths were muddy and my laced-up boots splashed mud on the hem of my soaked, black dress. The old white, wooden community hall doors creaked open as we entered in. None of the Watchers or the Keeper wiped their feet and tracked mud along the wooden floor.

It was evident the Charges did all of the cleaning as they passed over the threshold. The Charges tried to wipe as much mud off our shoes as possible in the two seconds our feet touched the rug to lessen the cleaning time. To delay and keep people from entering was inconsiderate.

No one said a word as we took our seats and the Keeper stood at the front of the room. The Watchers sat at the long wooden table behind him. All of the Charges sat in rows perpendicular to the Watchers.

Matthew took a position toward the end of the table facing the room. For a brief second, our gazes locked before he looked at the plate being placed in front of him. Those crystal-blue eyes framed with blond hair were filled with compassion. Watchers were always served first. Charges were required to get their own plates unless it was a meal of reflection.

The Keeper removed his hat. "Let's use this time to reflect on the legacy that Anita left. Use it to brighten our own lights. Let the food give us the energy we need to continue our mission of living the right way. Outside these walls of our community, sin has filled the people and damned them for all eternity. I am thankful we were chosen by The Light."

We chimed in as a unified group. "To the light that Anita left behind."

Is Anita my mom's real name? My mom hadn't said last night as she told me my true name before she died. *Kenzie Brooks.* The name seemed fitting but foreign at the same time.

I am not Sarah. I am Kenzie. I liked the name Kenzie.

The boiled potatoes and stewed beef were barely palatable as I forced myself to eat. The quiet clanking of utensils against the metal plates filled the silence. At least it had quit raining.

As soon as it was acceptable for me to leave, I would head back home and find the letter my mom had told me about last night on her deathbed.

There hadn't been time last night. During the last hours of a Charge, before they pass, the community gathered at your home to show support. I had only been allowed to be alone with Mom for a few brief minutes. Then she had left me. *Forever.*

From that point forward, there had been someone with me the entire time, and I hadn't been able to look for the letter that was supposed to contain a better explanation. Tonight, I would be alone to mourn my mom and would find it then.

The Keeper stood and displayed his palms to everyone. "You are excused to leave as you finish. Please resume your normal duties and focus on your inner light in preparation for one day when you are called home. No one is to disturb Sarah."

There were nods, but again no one replied. Taking this as my queue to leave, I swallowed the last of the potato and forced it farther down with water. Normally, I would be in the kitchen cleaning but was thankful for being excused from my tasks of the day.

Making my way to the counter, my eyes found Matthew who was still eating. I could tell he wanted to talk to me. Hopefully, we would be able to carve out some time together soon.

Sometimes, when we finished early with our assignments,

we would sneak into the woods to be together. Holding hands, we would sit and talk for as long as time would allow. My body loved and craved the small amount of contact.

If anyone, other than my mom, had found out Matthew and I spent time alone together, we would have been punished. As long as holding hands was all we did, mom thought it was good for me to have a friend like Matthew. There were times my lips tingled, wanting to know what it would be like to kiss him, but I always refrained. The only time I'd seen someone kiss was the joining of two persons into one. It was something I wanted to experience.

Mom frequently broke the rules of The Society when it was only her and I, but had warned me of the severe punishments if anyone found out what she and I did when we weren't being watched. Those infractions mainly consisted of continuing my education past the level of enlightenment. At that point, girls were no longer allowed to attend school. I had never told a soul of my private lessons.

As I approached the counter, I nodded to Greta, a fellow Charge and my mom's best friend. She cleaned with me on most days. Taking the plate from my hands, Greta gave me a sad look that lasted only long enough for me to see it. Her dark-brown hair was put into a bun that was required for all women to wear. Again, my lips trembled.

With my head down, I passed by everyone that I had known as family for as long as I could remember. The Society totaled one hundred and eight, no *one hundred and seven* people now.

Keeping my head down, I continued to walk toward the door that would lead to my freedom for the evening. My heart felt as if a weight pressed on it, threatening to collapse at any moment. I needed to get home.

As I walked down the steps, I turned left to head toward our, I mean, *my* home. It was less than a five-minute walk this way. Before I rounded the building, voices sounded from the side, and I pressed myself against the wall when I heard my name. It was the Keeper and his son, John, who was also a Watcher.

The Keepers raspy voice caused an involuntary shudder. "John, tomorrow evening Sarah will become your wife. You will ensure she continues on the mission of The Light and bear a child with her as soon as possible. She is the only one of age that can be taken as of now. Even though she was brought here at a young age, I do not believe she remembers her past life. We must be sure that she stays on the path and teaches my grandchildren the proper ways of The Society."

My throat was dry as my reality further altered. *Marriage. Child.* He expected me to marry John—tomorrow. My skin crawled with the thought of being married to John and having his kid. He was a widower in his forties. His wife, who'd never been able to have children, passed away four months ago to the same mysterious illness Mom had died from. The herbalists were still unable to find any cure to the illness that plagued our people from time to time. The Keeper said it was The Light's way of bringing people home when it was time.

I wanted to be with Matthew. He would bring me comfort.

"Father, was it in a vision?" John sounded hopeful and my stomach threatened to expel the unwanted lunch I had eaten.

The voice of the Keeper grew impatient as I pressed myself against the building, hoping to remain unseen. "John, I am getting old and I need my son to have a successor. The new Keeper must have offspring. The Light allows me to do what I deem fit in order to keep our way of life regardless if it comes in a vision or not. You know this. Do not question me." He paused for a second before continuing, his voice more controlled. "I will wed you to Sarah and she will be able to give you children. She is nineteen and is the perfect age for childbearing. Be at the church tomorrow evening at eight. I shall have Greta tell Sarah of this development tomorrow and say it was a vision. Sarah has probably already headed back for her night of grieving. No one is to bother her. Go back into the hall. Tell no one we have spoken."

Thunder roared through the sky which caused me to nearly yelp in surprise. I turned and ran the opposite way to my house and would loop back around in the woods. My mind raced as everything blurred. I tried to go through everything I had found out.

I was not Sarah.

I had a past life prior to The Society.

The Keeper wanted me wed to his son in order to bear children.

This was against everything we had been taught about The Light. Regardless if I had believed in The Light or not, any beliefs I did have were vanishing and I felt like I was lost on every level of life imaginable.

Panic wanted me to curl into a ball to protect myself, but self-preservation drove me to keep going. For now, I would push it all down. First, I needed to find the letter my mom talked about. Then, I would try to figure out the mess my life had become.

My legs ran faster and faster as I made it to the tree line. Turning back, I made sure no one had seen me. There were no windows in the community hall. *I need to get home. Home.* The word seemed strange to me now. As I raced to my house, I remembered the glob of mud on my mom's coffin as it disappeared into nothing.

I wanted to disappear into nothing.

TWO

I STOPPED INSIDE the tree line that opened up to my back-yard. To the left was a vacant lot with tall grass. The Millers' home was to the right. They would have duties to complete after the meal and should still be at the community hall. As I was about to walk into the backyard, a hand came down on mine and I nearly came out of my skin.

"Shh, it's only me."

The familiar voice had me heaving a sigh of relief. "Mat-thew, you scared me."

He grabbed my hand in the familiar gesture we were ac-customed to when we were alone. The concern in his face was evident. "I was worried about you. Before I have to go see The Keeper, I had to see you. I'm sorry about your mom."

The loving lilt in his voice brought a new wave of sad-ness. I missed my mom. Uncharacteristically, I leaned against his chest. My actions surprised him, and me, as it took a few seconds before warm arms came around me. We'd never been this close, but I needed the comfort more than I knew. It felt safe and I didn't care that I was breaking some of the funda-mental rules.

I nearly sobbed into his chest. "Matthew, I've missed you."

Matthew relaxed as he got used to the contact. "I've missed you, too. I hate that we haven't been able to talk lately."

Not ready to lose the connection, but knowing we had to separate before someone caught us, I took a step back. The compulsion to tell him everything, as I looked into his blue eyes, was strong. Opening my mouth to speak, I closed it for a second. By telling him, I might be putting him at risk. Confusion on how to best proceed laid heavy in my gut.

"What's wrong, Sarah? You look like you have something on your mind." Matthew's eyes darted back and forth, watching me.

Sarah. How would I even explain my name was Kenzie when I didn't know the answer myself? I swallowed the truth. "I feel lost, but I'll get through it."

"I know tomorrow is the cleansing day, but can we meet in the woods before it all starts? I have something I want to talk to you about." Matthew looked nervous as he waited for my answer.

Another twig snapped and we both took another step back, further separating us and the anxiety of potentially being caught heightened. "I'll find a way to meet in our spot before breakfast."

"I have to go, Sarah. Sweet dreams until tomorrow."

"Sweet dreams until tomorrow." The phrase was something special between us. We always said to each other when we said good-bye.

Another crack in the branches had our nerves on edge. We were definitely on borrowed time.

He mouthed, *I have to go.*

I nodded. As my best friend walked away, I leaned against the tree trunk. *What did he have to talk to me about?*

Maybe he wanted to go to the Light to see about marriage now that I was alone. I wasn't sure how I felt about marriage right now.

After ten minutes passed, only the forest sounds surrounded me. I casually moseyed out into the backyard. Mom and I had a garden out back. As long as anyone didn't see me coming out of the trees, they would assume I was making sure all was okay before heading in for the night. My eyes casted down slightly as they darted back and forth, making sure I was still alone. The fabric of my apron provided a good distraction for my fingers and nervous energy.

I let out a small breath of relief as I made it to the chicken wire that surrounded our garden. The heat of the August sun had nearly withered it gone. Mom and I had been trying to keep it watered, but we were to be sparing with the use of water. The rain today was already causing it to perk back to life. The garden was about ten feet long and had four rows. All families were expected to grow food and contribute to the common wealth of our community.

For my normal nightly routine, I walked the perimeter of the chicken wire to make sure the fence was intact. Working in the garden was a pastime Mom and I both enjoyed.

A lone tear fell down my face as I remembered the quiet laughs we had in here. To outright express an enormous amount of emotion was to waste the burning light within us. All things were to be done in moderation. I had to constantly remind myself of that.

Had those moments in the garden been a glimpse of my mom before this place? Is that why she broke so many rules like continuing to educate me in secret?

The rain drizzled. I turned to head into the house I had known as home for as long as I could remember. The black door was in pristine order, like all other doors in The Society. Every house was white with black doors. The Keeper had said the houses were to be white to keep our community pure from the color that threatened to taint us like the rest of the world. The black represented the sin that tried to get in and ruin our way of life. *Lies. All of it had been lies.*

I stepped inside and closed the door, removing my bonnet and hanging it on the hanger, thankful that no one would be by tonight. Looking at myself in the mirror, which every house in The Society had to ensure one was presentable before going outside, I looked haggard. My green eyes were dulled and hollowed.

All I wanted to do was throw the mirror and shatter it like my heart felt.

I pushed my damp, light-red hair off my face and leaned against the door, turning away from the haunting reflection that stared back at me. My eyes closed shut for a moment as I centered myself and took a deep breath.

If I chose to look at the letter my mom left, my life would be altered more than it currently was. If I didn't, I would be wed to John tomorrow and treated as nothing more than a baby maker. When the time was right, I had hoped The Light would grant Matthew and me permission to marry. He was the only person who got me—or *the me* that I had let him see so far. But if that was what Matthew wanted to talk about tomorrow, was it the right time?

My head throbbed. The one thing I wanted, I couldn't have—to crawl in bed with my mom while I asked her endless questions about what I should do. It was against the Keeper's command to waste time thinking on anything that wasn't productive. All thoughts were to be used for betterment of The Society. That was hard for me as I constantly desired to learn more.

I thought back on the last minutes with my mom.

Candles were lit on every surface, letting The Light know my mom neared the end. It was a haunting site. The Keeper's raspy voice broke the silence. "Anita, your light has shown bright and will live on in Sarah. You will continue to burn bright in the light hereafter."

My mom closed her eyes in acknowledgment. Speech had stopped hours ago as it exhausted her.

A week ago, she started not feeling well. We tried all of the herbal remedies, but she never got better. It was a mysterious disease that took one to two people every year from our group. The sickness started as an extreme headache and quickly turned to excessive vomiting.

Now, not seven days later, she lay in her bed dying and my world was falling apart.

The Keeper laid his hand on top of Mom's and looked at me. His steel-colored beady eyes made me feel queasy. "Sarah, we shall give you a few minutes alone with your mom as time is coming. We shall all be downstairs." A tear seeped from my mom's eye. She appeared as scared as I felt. How was I going to survive here without her? As soon as we were left alone, I lunged toward my mom's bed as I allowed the fear of the situation to take root in my mind.

"Mom, please don't leave me. I can't bear to think of a world that you're not in. You're my everything," I sobbed.

My mom's hand shook as it came to my face. Her fingernails had become dry, cracked and discolored. The herbalist said it was from lack of nutrition since my mom couldn't keep anything down. I leaned into the touch before she had to drop her hand while I tried to memorize what it felt like to be near her—warm and loving.

She softly spoke, "Sarah, I should have told you sooner, but we haven't been alone since I got sick. The truth is in an envelope in the bottom of the locked chest in the attic. The key is hidden underneath your nightstand. There's not much time."

I became desperate. "Mom, please don't go." A sob erupted. "Please. Please."

Her eyes closed. "Shh...sweetheart. I thought I had more time to prepare. You're not going to understand what I'm about to say, but it's the truth. Your real name is Kenzie Brooks. If you want a choice and a say in your life, read the letter. Your inquisitive mind belongs in the world."

My heart raced frantically. Kenzie Brooks. I'm Sarah. The world. Choice. Life. Those words were jumbled in my head as my mom's breathing became more labored. My breathing increased while panic took over. "Mom, please. I don't know what you're saying. I don't understand."

We spoke in hushed whispers. "Kenzie, I love you. You are the light in my world. I'm so sorry for the choices I made, but know that I have loved you with my entire heart. Never doubt that."

Mom stopped and took a few breaths. These were moments I was supposed to treasure, not be told secrets that would change my life more than it was. I wanted to argue with her, but she didn't have much time. Her hand got colder. These were the last moments I would ever have with my mom. I wasn't prepared to be left alone. I wasn't strong enough to survive without her.

She continued, her voice growing weaker. "Regardless of what you think of my decision, know that I loved you. I tried to do what was best for you."

Closing her eyes for a moment, they fluttered open as I spoke, "I love you, Mom. I will love you regardless of what the *letter says. Know that. Always know that I'll never stop loving you."*

"You're so strong, my sweet Kenzie." Mom's eyes fully closed. A few more breaths followed, then she exhaled her last breath.

She was gone. Forever.

The room seemed dimmer without her in it. I crawled up in bed with Mom and sobbed as I held onto her. My body racked with uncontrolled sadness as I lost the only thing I cared about in this world.

She was gone. I was alone. Those two words echoed in my head—gone and alone.

I pushed off the door and decided I was ready to read the letter. Taking off the muddy boots, my footsteps carried me through the kitchen.

Everything in our two-bedroom home was simplistic and white. No decorations hung on the walls.

I raced to the top of the stairs as I jumped over the fourth step, avoiding the squeak. At the top, I turned right trying to avoid eye contact with my mom's bedroom door. She had been alive in there twenty-four hours ago. My heart lurched as it imagined her behind it, waiting for me to come talk to her like I did every night.

The thud of my heart pulsed in my ears, creating a humming sound that felt like it disconnected me from the outside world. Looking around my simplistic room everything seemed emptier with my mom gone. I jogged to my twin bed, along the far wall and perched on the edge as I eyed the spindle nightstand. My stomach churned with unease as I wondered what the letter said.

I took off the lamp and sat it on the floor. Staring at the nightstand, I knew once I turned it over there was no going back, no pretending that my mom had been mistaken in what she had told me. This would become my reality and I was going to have to make a choice. A slight tremor started in my fingers.

The grained wood felt ridged as I ran my fingers over it. Taking a deep breath, I flipped over the nightstand. It didn't weigh much, but it felt like it was one of the most significant steps I had taken in my life. On the underside, I saw the key affixed to the table that unlocked the trunk. Picking it up, I looked at the old iron ornate key.

I retraced my steps back out to the landing. Between Mom's and my room were the steps that came down from the attic. I was tall but was still barely able to reach the string that pulled the ladder from the ceiling. A small creak sounded as the steps unfolded. As soon as they hit the floor, I scurried up the ladder.

Curiosity and fear of the unknown were driving me. The attic had a faint smell from the heat of the day.

In the far right corner sat the chest. Apprehensively, I walked toward it. My mom had told me a story about Alice in Wonderland. I felt like Alice going down a black hole. As I crouched in front of the chest, a crow came and perched on the ledge of the tiny octagonal window.

Caw.

Caw.

Caw.

The sound startled me like the bird was trying to tell on me as I fell back on my rear. The bird pecked twice at the window before flying off.

My erratic breathing quickened as my shaking hands put the key in the lock and turned it. The attic always gave me nightmares with the looming shadows that seemed to come out of nowhere.

Getting up on my knees, I opened the chest as it creaked in protest. On top was the quilt my mom had made for my wedding day. My hands traced over the stitching, memorizing the pattern. I took it out and put it aside. Underneath were more blankets and the dress I was to wear at my wedding. Each mom who had a daughter made a dress and quilt when they turned sixteen. They were not to see them until the day of the wedding where they were given over to a Watcher in holy matrimony. Males were not allowed to marry until they became Watchers.

In theory, a couple approached the Keeper to ask The Light if they had permission to marry. Scoffing, I wondered what had been truly visions or was everything a manipulation.

There was a black backpack I had never seen before at the bottom of the cedar lined trunk. I picked it up and sat cross legged on the floor. In the front zipper, there was an envelope with my name on it.

My sweet Kenzie

It was my mom's handwriting. I caressed the words with love as the sun lowered in the sky. The last of the light shone through as I opened the envelope and a small key fell out. I read.

My dearest Kenzie (Sarah),
If you are reading this, it means I am no longer with you.

I'm sorry I left you alone and that you're possibly confused right now. Time is limited as I can't get caught writing this letter before someone comes to check on me. I'm too weak now to make it to the doctor in the outside world for the proper medication, whatever it may be.

Sarah, your real name is Kenzie Samantha Brooks. My real name is Jessica Brooks. Your father's name was David Brooks. We came to The Society when you were almost three, after your father had died in a motorcycle accident. My world was lost. I had no family, no way to support us, no hope left for survival. One day, we were at a park in a nearby town. The Keeper approached me and called himself Jacob. I'm sure I looked lost and lonely.

I don't have time to explain how we came to The Society, but there's another letter at the address listed at the end this note that explains everything.

When we came here, I told the Keeper your real name was Maggie. I'm not sure why I lied, but it was a good decision. At The Society we were isolated, had a home, no bills, and were able to be together. You and I were left alone and it was the closest thing to feeling complete I could imagine.

As years passed, I began to see that those who completely succumbed to the ways of The Society were lifeless and hollow. They lacked that spark. I feared that would happen to you. The moment you appeared lost or a vision came for you to be married, we were going to leave. There was no way I would ever ask you to marry someone that you didn't love as much as I loved your dad. I know you think you and Matthew are supposed to be together because of what The Keeper said. All I ask is that you search your heart, Kenzie. Make sure it's not because it's expected for you to marry him.

Kenzie, you have a gift for life, and a beautiful inquisitive mind. Don't let that flame become an ember and die out. Don't let it be snuffed and the vibrant Kenzie I have always known become smoke within the wind dissipating into nothing.

My only regret is that I didn't get you out of here before I died.

Kenzie, I only gave about twenty-five percent of what I had to The Society. Everything else, I put in a safety deposit box along with more things from your father and me. The choice is yours Kenzie. The key in the envelope goes to the safety deposit box at the bank address listed below. Your birth certificate is at the bottom of this backpack and will be enough to get you into the security box. I was able to sneak the money and the certificate in when we initially came here. It's been underneath the boards of one of the steps.

When you get to Arkansas, go to the bank, then find a library. They're an amazing wealth of knowledge and will be able to get yourself more up to speed of current events. Your inquisitive mind will help you adapt quickly.

Check out colleges, I think you would enjoy it with your enthusiasm for knowledge. If you decide to give college a try, tell them you were homeschooled and need a placement test. Being a teacher, hopefully I prepared you enough. The one thing you'll be lacking in is technology since our lessons never included it.

Whether you choose to stay or run, burn this letter. They can never know you found it and know the truth. This letter will make you an outcast forever, eliminating your freedoms. You know too much about The Society for them to let you go. Do you remember Rebecca Donovan, our neighbor from ten years ago? After her husband died, she wanted to leave and experience the outside world. She met with the Keeper to let him know. Only I knew about her talk with him. After the meet-

ing, Rebecca died within a week.

I always wondered if that truly was a coincidence.

If you choose to leave. Make sure you lock this chest, put the key in my dresser and take the backpack with you. Put the house together just as it would be. Leave a note that says you cannot live here without me and have to join me in the light. They need to think you're gone, Kenzie. They won't want you out there, knowing about The Society.

As soon as you get in the woods, change into the jeans and T-shirt that are in this backpack. They will probably be a little big, but they will work until you can get more. The nearest bus station is a three-hour walk to the northwest. Use the stars like they taught you in class. Get rid of your clothes as soon as you can.

Leave no trace. Tell no one.

Get a bus ticket to Fayetteville, Arkansas where the bank is using the money in the backpack. After that, go on an adventure. I have no connections in Arkansas so you should be safe there if you decide to stay.

The choice is yours. Live your life.

Don't stay out of fear or the need to be near our home. Kenzie, I'll be with you wherever you go. The world is a big beautiful place despite what you've been taught. Embrace it.

The things I showed you in secret and asked you to never tell anyone—dancing, painting, birthday parties, and stories— are from the outside world. If you decide to leave, you're going to be frightened, but you're strong enough, sweetheart.

I know you have more questions than I've given you answers to. You may never get all the answers you seek and I'm sorry for that. If I had the time to write everything out, I would have. But, I know you'll adapt and be fine.

Remember, do what your heart tells you, not your mind.

I hope you know, even though my actions don't necessarily make sense, that I love you with my entire heart. You and your father were my everything. Live your life Kenzie. Make your choices.

Be Free.
I love you forever and always.
Mom

First National Bank
Box # 158
College Avenue
Fayetteville, Arkansas

As I finished reading, my breaths were coming in and out nearly ragged as I tried to process everything quickly. There wasn't much time to decide.

The sun was almost gone and the routine of burning the candle at my bedroom window came to the forefront of my mind. We were to light a candle that burned anywhere for two to ten hours every night until the flame died out. It signified that our time here on Earth was limited and to always focus on the flame burning as you never knew when it could vanish. I raced down the ladder, abandoning my letter on the floor. I made it to the drawer and calmly put the candle in the window and lit it solemnly like I did every night. One of the Watchers would walk down the street, making sure everyone had their candles out. I stood there like I always did and watched the flame dance for a couple of minutes, imagining two figures dancing. One evening, as the last of the sun's rays came through the attic window, mom showed me how to dance in the attic. I treasured those memories.

I took a step back and drew the window sheer down a safe

distance from the flame. Turning away, I walked toward my bed. If someone was watching, they'd assume I was exhausted, which I was, and turning in from my day of grieving.

My mom is gone.

Every time I thought about it, my heart shattered a million times more. Now, I had the weight of the truth bearing down on me. I still wasn't sure if I fully comprehended the consequence of what my decision would entail. The unknown scared me. I was running out of time to decide.

Did I stay or go?

Did I choose to be free or confined?

Did I leave the only place I knew as home?

THANK YOU

FOR ALL THE messages and e-mails regarding Bane … thank you! Without them, this story would not have been written. I always tell my family I have the best readers in the world. Thank you for all the love and support you show. It's immensely appreciated.

To everyone who was part of the process, thank you for all that you did to make this possible. Mad love for each and every one of you guys.

To my editor, Nichole, thanks for putting up with all my many questions and making the story shine. I can't wait to work with you on our next project.

To my Betas—April, Brandy, Kelly, Maren, Nikola, and Anna, thank you for all your honest feedback. It means the world to me.

To the Korner, thank you for always putting a smile on my face. You guys are amazing and I'm lucky to have you guys in my life.